NEVER A HOSTAGE

BOOKS BY JAN THOMPSON

Romantic Suspense/Thrillers

Protector Sweethearts (6 Books)

JanThompson.com/protector

Defender Sweethearts (6 Books)

JanThompson.com/defender

Binary Hackers (4 Books)

JanThompson.com/binary

City/Coastal/Beach Romance

Seaside Chapel (7 Books)

JanThompson.com/seaside

Savannah Sweethearts (12 Books)

JanThompson.com/savannah

Vacation Sweethearts (8 Books)

JanThompson.com/vacation

JanThompson.com/books

NEVER A HOSTAGE

DEFENDER SWEETHEARTS
BOOK 2

JAN THOMPSON

GEORGIA PRESS

Never a Hostage (Defender Sweethearts Book 2)

Author Website: JanThompson.com
Book News: JanThompson.com/newsletter

Published by Georgia Press LLC

eBook Cover Design: Lynnette Bonner
Paperback Cover Design: Lynnette Bonner and Rocking Book Covers

eBook ISBN: 978-1-944188-92-4
Paperback ISBN: 978-1-944188-93-1

To my Lord and Savior, Jesus Christ, who died on the cross to save me from my sins and rose again from the grave to give me eternal life in heaven.

For God so loved the world that He gave His only begotten Son, that whoever believes in Him should not perish but have everlasting life.
—John 3:16

ABOUT DEFENDER SWEETHEARTS

CHRISTIAN ROMANTIC SUSPENSE NOVELS

Defender Sweethearts is a sister series to the Protector Sweethearts Christian romantic suspense collection. While the heroes in Protector Sweethearts search for lost treasures and lost people, the Defender Sweethearts novels focus on protecting the helpless and hopeless.

- Book 1: *Never a Traitor*
- Book 2: *Never a Hostage*
- Book 3: *Never a Fugitive*
- Book 4: *Always a Maverick*
- Book 5: *Always a Champion*
- Book 6: *Always a Guardian*

For more information about Defender Sweethearts:
JanThompson.com/defender

ABOUT NEVER A HOSTAGE

DEFENDER SWEETHEARTS BOOK 2

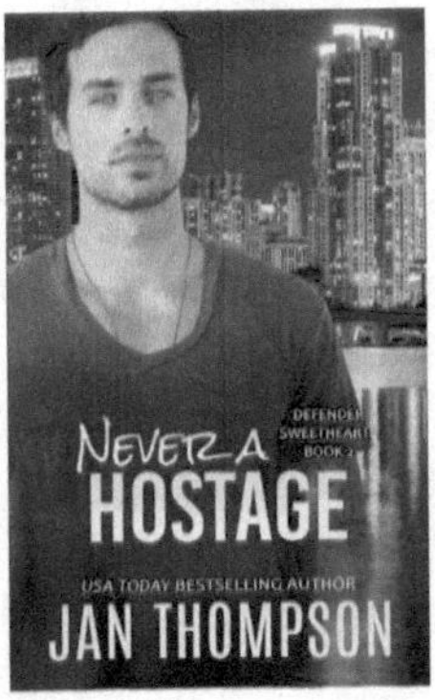

Three people in a web of lies.
Two private investigators seeking truth.
One hostage plan gone wrong.

Private Investigator Pilar Santiago takes us to Miami, right into a hostage crisis. Cade Sumter is dispatched to rescue her.

Going undercover in a hotel...

When a former senator's estranged wife hires Pilar to spy on her husband at a hotel in Miami, Pilar just assumes it's another routine job. At most taking two days of work, all she has to do is record the meeting that the former senator will be in and then leave. Collecting five hundred thousand dollars has never been easier.

Giving up is never an option...

The meeting never takes place. However, criminals have entered the hotel and taken former senator Felix Braun-Dean and his mistress hostage. Or have they? Caught in the middle, Pilar is unable to leave the building. She decides that she might as well make the most of it and starts to observe and collect data.

Getting into a swamp of trouble...

Disguised as a line cook, Private Investigator Cade Sumter manages to get inside the hotel. He's there to swing down the vine, swoop up Pilar—with whom he's fallen in love a year ago when they were teammates in an overseas project—and take her home safely to her family...

Not!

A tropical storm hits Miami, and the captors leave but not before they take Pilar, Cade, and a handful of other hostages to a private swamp where nobody would find them.

How do Pilar and Cade get out alive?

Never a Hostage is Book 2 in *USA Today* bestselling author Jan Thompson's Defender Sweethearts Christian romantic suspense collection, a sister series to Protector Sweethearts. While the heroes in Protector Sweethearts search for lost treasures and lost people, the Defender Sweethearts novels focus on protecting the helpless and hopeless. The main characters in Defender Sweethearts come from the supporting cast in Protector Sweethearts.

Never a Hostage (Defender Sweethearts Book 2)
JanThompson.com/hostage

Defender Sweethearts
JanThompson.com/defender

For Book News from Jan Thompson:
JanThompson.com/newsletter

NEVER A HOSTAGE

CHAPTER ONE

Former Senator Felix Braun-Dean became angrier by the minute as he went into a tirade in the presidential suite in the art deco Callahan Hotel. Every three or four seconds, Braun-Dean would yell and cuss. That seemed to be the extent of his linguistic capability.

As a Christian, Pilar Santiago didn't want to hear any of it, but she was on her hands and knees cleaning up someone's vomit near the door under a large mirror that showed enough for her to witness an event that she was probably not supposed to see. She was starting to sweat through the borrowed polyester housekeeping uniform she had on.

If she listened enough, would they try to kill her next?

But first, all this cursing coming from one person —and wasn't he only a hostage in this entire fiasco?— was too much for her ears to bear.

Counter it with the Word of God.

Yes, the Word of God could counter the F-word fireworks.

However, the only verse that came to Pilar's mind was James 4:8.

Draw near to God and He will draw near to you. Cleanse your hands, you sinners; and purify your hearts, you double-minded.

Braun-Dean started to throw things at his goons, and they had to take it in silence. Ashtrays, half a hamburger with the lunch plate it was on, and whatever else the otherwise-respected millionaire could put his hands on.

"You, what's your name?" he yelled.

Pilar realized Braun-Dean was talking to her when the mirror showed his angry face approaching her from behind. She stopped wiping the mirror, where there were once lipstick marks.

"Maria, sir." She was really nervous and her voice showed. She didn't want to give him her last name—her fake last name.

"Maria, Maria, quite contrary..." His voice had a lilt to it and Pilar wanted to throw up.

He waved his arm about, his old Vietnam era tattoos showing on his wrist, the spiderweb creeping out on both sides of his gold-and-diamond Rolex.

"Clean up this mess before I get back from the casino," he snapped.

His entourage followed him out, leaving Pilar alone in the penthouse with the mess on the thick carpet.

Someone moaned from the California king-sized bed.

The owner of the lipstick that had been thrown against the mirror over there.

"Ma'am?" Pilar stepped toward the bed.

More moans.

The smell of stale whiskey rose from the bed. Two eyes beneath matted platinum blonde hair opened. The rest of her was hidden under a white comforter.

"Whoopee are you?" She slurred some more words, but they were unintelligible.

Pilar assumed she was asking "who" she was instead of "whoopee."

"Housekeeping, ma'am." Pilar held her breath. "Would you like me to change the bedsheets, ma'am?"

Miss Platinum didn't answer right away. Slowly, pale white hands pushed the comforter away, revealing her half naked body. She grabbed her forehead and moaned. "Where's my pill at?"

Pilar had no idea what she was talking about.

Miss Platinum looked up.

Watery red eyes stared straight at Pilar.

Pilar vaguely recognized her. She'd dyed her hair, but her eyes and nose looked similar to the photographs that FBI Special Agent Ruby Tanaka had shown her. Except she looked worn out. Her skin was pale and her eye makeup smeared on her cheekbones.

Zuriel.

She was most likely the same woman that Roxanne Braun-Dean had called a homewrecker. To be fair, Roxanne and her husband hadn't lived together for several years, though they still owned joint properties in Tennessee, Georgia, and Florida. Real estate properties aside, Roxanne told Pilar that Braun-Dean should share his pot of gold: bitcoin cryptocurrencies amounting to the billions.

Their contested divorce case had cost untold millions of dollars to date. There was no end in sight even with arbitrators trying to make both parties satisfied and then live with the results.

Throughout the ongoing messy divorce proceedings, Zuriel was always by Braun-Dean's side, further making Roxanne outraged. Zuriel was pretty, without wrinkles, half of Roxanne's age, and stood to become the next new Mrs. Felix Braun-Dean, a title that Roxanne had brandished like a crown every chance she had.

Roxanne told Pilar that Braun-Dean was a womanizer and had no loyalty to anyone he slept with. That was her only consolation when it came to her husband's current pinup of the month. Roxanne was confident Zuriel wouldn't last.

In any case, Zuriel was a win-win for Pilar.

Pilar would find a way to get close to Zuriel and then gain her confidence per her assignment with Agent Tanaka. Tanaka wanted Pilar to keep an eye on Zuriel. Whether that was easy to do remained to be seen.

As for Pilar's main job for Roxanne, the former socialite's worry centered on something else: Braun-Dean's wallet. Roxanne wanted all the money she felt was entitled to her. She had raised two daughters for Braun-Dean and hosted lavish parties while Braun-Dean was out there making deals. Now she wanted to know who those associates were. She wanted to use them in her divorce proceedings to extract at least sixty percent of Braun-Dean's hidden assets.

Without a prenup, Roxanne felt that she had failed herself. Her sob story made Pilar feel sorry for her, but it wasn't enough to make Pilar take the job. That was, until Roxanne dangled five hundred thousand dollars in front of her for two days of work.

Looking back, it was the worst decision Pilar had ever made, but at the time, she had no idea it was going to go down like this. So she followed Braun-Dean to this hotel where the former senator was supposed to meet with some of his financial backers. Roxanne wanted photos and videos and names of those people—especially anyone called The Steward.

While Pilar was at it, she could also watch Zuriel.

Easy peasy.

What had begun as a simple spying operation had turned into an unexpected life-and-death situation.

Pilar might not be able to make it out of the hotel alive, let alone report anything back to Roxanne. At this point, Pilar didn't care that the former senator had hidden billions of dollars from his estranged wife. None of it could save her life.

Pilar's associates were investigating the matter, but she wouldn't know the outcome without access to her burner phone, which had been confiscated by whoever was running the show.

Who, actually?

"Where's my pill at?" Zuriel put one leg over the bed and fell right off onto the carpet. "Oh, look. My leg went to sleep."

"Whoa!" Pilar rushed to help her get up.

Zuriel grinned and laughed as she leaned on Pilar.

Pilar put her right back onto the bed. Pilar smelled stale alcohol on Zuriel's breath.

She grabbed Pilar's arm. "Please just one, okay? Just one. Or two. I won't tell."

Pilar didn't know how to reply to her.

"Felix has the bottle. You can get it for me." Zuriel's broken nails dug into Pilar's flesh.

"Owww."

Zuriel released her arm. "Sorry, sorry. I just need my medicine."

"What kind of medicine?"

She named it.

It was an opioid.

Pilar felt sorry and tried to pray for Zuriel but didn't have the words to say to God for this poor addict—or recovering addict.

Zuriel started to cry. "I've already gone to rehab once. It's no fun."

"When was that?" Pilar asked.

She ignored Pilar. "I was fine when I got out."

Ah, so she was having a relapse. What a bad time. Zuriel needed help.

Zuriel dragged herself off the bed again. She rummaged through some suitcases and found a bottle. She popped two pills.

"Change the sheets while I take a bath." As she staggered away, Pilar noticed the black-and-blue bruises all over her back, stretching from her neck to her hips. One exposed arm was also covered with bruises.

Pilar's hands shook. She felt sorry for Zuriel.

The noise of the bathroom door slamming shut slapped Pilar out of her emotions. She turned away and stepped on something on the floor. A fork on the carpet.

Pilar wondered which she should do first—clean up the mess on the floor or change the bedsheets.

Is this something I can pray about?

She decided to clean up the mess first because she didn't want Zuriel to walk all over it. Besides, Pilar had to get on the good side of the bad ex-senator.

She went outside the room to her cart and brought in a dustpan and a broom. She swept up the ice cubes and the hamburger. Then she picked up the pens and notepad—

She pocketed the notepad.

The pen had mayonnaise on it, so she threw it out in the trash can.

She sprayed the carpet with whatever she could find in her cart and wiped it with rags. Thank God the carpet was stain resistant.

Outside the door, a little bit down the hallway, was the supply closet where Pilar found a vacuum cleaner. Working quickly, she vacuumed up the carpet until it looked nice and clean.

She replaced the missing pen and notepad on the table with new ones, and noticed crumpled papers thrown into the trashcan near a floor reading lamp.

Carefully, she tied the trashcan liner and put it outside in her cart for sorting later on. She needed to comb through the trash to see if Braun-Dean had left any information she needed to collect.

After replacing the trashcan liner, Pilar washed her hands in the sink by the bar.

She pulled the bed linen off the bed, averting her eyes from the stains on the white sheets. There was nothing here for her to collect except for a few strands of long hair on a pillowcase. They looked like they belonged to the woman in the bathroom.

Pilar made quick work of replacing the linen. Her two-day training at another hotel helped her make this bed properly. Like a professional. After this, she might have to start making her own bed at home properly instead of just piling everything up in the middle of the bed.

Miss Platinum was still taking her sweet time in the bathroom when Pilar finished making the bed. Out of tune, the woman was belting out songs from the eighties, which made Pilar wonder if she might be older than she looked.

Having finished her work, Pilar knew she had to vacate the premises before she was accused of something.

She was at her cart when the man who had been attacked by his boss came to the room. She wanted to say "Are you okay?" to him but she didn't want to arouse suspicion.

The last thing she needed was to appear curious.

She simply nodded to him.

He didn't nod back. There was pain in his eyes, but there was a bandaid above his left eyebrow. It looked new.

Pilar wanted to ask him questions, but this wasn't the time.

"Are you done?" he asked.

Pilar nodded. "All done, sir."

"Zuriel in the room?"

Ah, so her name was really Zuriel. So Pilar had recognized her correctly. She had different colored hair from the photo that Pilar had been given, but the rest of her features checked out.

"I don't know who, but someone was in there when I cleaned up the room per the senator, and she was in the bathroom when I cleaned up the floor and made the bed."

"Per the senator?" His eyebrows rose.

Uh-oh.

Pilar had forgotten to speak broken English.

"Did I use the word correctly, sir?" Pilar looked concerned. "I saw it on TV and thought I should use more English words."

He laughed. Dimples showed. "You used it right, but he's not a senator anymore. He lost the election and he is now an ex-senator."

"Oh. Sorry." No, she wasn't. She had known that information since her client hired her to be a guest in the Callahan Hotel to photograph and record evidence of Braun-Dean's financial shenanigans to be used against him in the divorce proceedings. Well, that was before his business meeting was canceled and replaced by this hostage crisis. Pilar and her associate hid in the laundry room, and the next thing she knew, she was a housekeeper.

"How did you know he was a senator?" the man asked.

Caught red-handed. "I heard people talk."

"You should stop eavesdropping. Look in the dictionary to see what that means."

Someone called down the hallway. "Benson! Ben!"

The big man shrugged and walked toward the voice. He disappeared around the corner. "Whatcha need?"

So his name was Benson. Pilar was glad he left because she wasn't sure how much longer she could keep up her false accent.

Pilar couldn't wait to get out of there before Braun-Dean returned. She wanted to sort the trash, put the hair sample in a ziplock bag, and find a way to get all these things to the outside world.

The service elevator made a lot of noise going down. Pilar took slow and deep breaths to calm herself down.

"Lord, help me." She wondered if she could stand another day of this.

Where are my backups?

An injured Aidan Ming Wei had escaped the building, promising to send help. He hadn't wanted to leave when the hotel was taken over, but Pilar made him, like a big sister would, to save her younger brother—even though Ming was at least a year older than she was.

She prayed that Ming had made it out safely and gone to the hospital to get his fractured wrist treated.

Pilar felt like she herself was a hostage now.

It had been hours since she shut the laundry room door so that her colleague could escape into the dark night. She'd selected a clean uniform and put it on. Found "Maria Estuardo" on a name tag in the lost-and-found bin. Grabbed a cart, and away she went.

Why hadn't she left with Ming Wei?

Because her instinct told her that something was off. She and Ming had seen Braun-Dean slap a woman in a private dining room. She couldn't even cry or he'd slap her again. She was in bad shape and looked like a prostitute, but Pilar couldn't be sure.

Whoever she was, she didn't look like the same woman in the penthouse suite or the same woman their client had even worried about.

How many women were there in this hotel room who had been abused or prevented from leaving?

Things were getting complicated.

For now, Pilar's main task was to stay alive and gather as much information as possible. She'd only been stuck here since morning, so it wasn't like she was losing hope, but she had to give herself a mission so that she wouldn't lose her cool.

Stay in character.

She repeated it to herself silently as if it would help. However, her time in drama club in college was coming in handy for her job as a private investigator.

She prayed for Ming that he would be safe and be able to find help. If she knew him well enough, he'd call Helen Hu of Hu Knows, Inc., for support. Helen knew a lot of law enforcement people, plus private security people, and the collective group of people, people, people would surely rescue her.

And that poor woman in the penthouse.

And anyone else who might be stuck in this hotel.

Ah, why am I even in this job?

If she had listened to Grandma and married that guy she'd introduced Pilar to, she'd be staying at home, away from all this drama. But no, she never wanted to marry just any guy.

The only person she might consider dating would be Cade Sumter, whom she'd met in Dubai when she was working with Ming. After their life-and-death experience on that project, Cade returned home to the States to work for Helen Hu.

Yeah, she could date Cade. He was cute and single and two years older than Pilar. And he had a good-paying job. Grandma would totally approve.

Pilar determined that if she got out of this mess, she'd try to be brave enough to ask Cade to dinner. Would he accept the invitation? Something to look forward to, anyway.

If she made it out of this hotel alive.

Pilar pushed her cart slowly down the hallway toward the elevators, praying and planning and trying not to panic, when she heard a loud noise.

A gunshot.

Definitely a gunshot.

The noise seemed to have come from the kitchen around the corner.

Should she keep going where she was heading, or should she go to the kitchen to see what was going on?

For a split second, Pilar blanked out and froze in place, her fingers gripping the cart handle bar tightly.

Until someone pulled her down to the floor as a second gunshot rang out.

CHAPTER TWO

Pilar Santiago's housekeeping uniform smelled like fresh laundry and her hair like gardenia from his mother's garden in Oregon. Cade had never been this close to her in any circumstance, especially not in such a shootout at the kitchen corral.

Cade kept his eyes open as he and Pilar pressed down on the carpet, side by side. Pilar was looking the other way, so he couldn't tell if she might be frightened—

No. She wouldn't be.

This brave lady had saved his life in Dubai the year before, and nearly lost hers. They had both recovered side by side at the hospital before flying home to the United States.

At the hospital, Cade decided that he would follow Pilar to the ends of the earth. He made a career-changing decision to apply for a job at Hu Knows, Inc., so that he could continue to work with

Pilar in some capacity—even though Pilar was only an associate of Hu Knows, and ran her own company out of Miami.

Crouched in the hallway outside the kitchen, Pilar turned her head. Her eyes widened.

"Cade?" she whispered.

"Monty," Cade said, pointing to himself. Then he pointed to Pilar. He kept his voice low. "And your name?"

"Maria." She pointed to her name tag. "Maria Estuardo."

How interesting.

Maria Estuardo in Spanish could be Mary Stuart in English. That had been the name of a certain Scottish queen who had been executed in long-ago England. Might that be Pilar's end while in disguise?

Not if I can help it.

"Monty and Maria." Cade smiled a little. He was happy to see Pilar alive. Since six o'clock this morning, Cade had been busy in the kitchen, without an opportunity to look for her.

And now their paths crossed outside the kitchen, which was down the hallway from the laundry room.

Pilar didn't seem to be physically injured. She had the perfect cover as a hotel housekeeper. Job security and all that.

She looked tired though, and Cade wondered how much sleep she'd had—if at all—last night. He decided that when this was all over, he'd make it a point to check in on her to make sure she had enough rest and ate well every day.

Wait a minute. What?

They laid there in silence, looking at each other.

The shooting had subsided, but Cade didn't want to get up.

A voice broke into their stares. "Get up, you two!"

Cade felt the business end of a barrel pressed against the back of his head.

When he looked up, he didn't recognize the gunman. Well, to be sure, he had just arrived at the hostage hotel at six o'clock this morning, so he'd only met a few people.

"The chef said you made the hamburgers for lunch." The gunman gestured with his weapon, which looked like a classic Beretta 92FS.

Cade nodded, trying to remain calm. "Maybe point that away from me if you want dinner."

The gunman laughed and put his Beretta away. "What did you put in it? Extra onions? Mr. Braun-Dean wants you to make him two sliders."

"Now?" Many things shot through Cade's head. If they called their hostage by name oh-so-politely, he wondered if Braun-Dean was really a hostage. What if this entire hostage situation was staged?

"Yes, now." His voice was stern.

Cade helped Pilar to her feet, keeping his eye on the gunman's Beretta, stuffed into his tight belt.

"Maria, third floor needs extra help. A mess there." He raised an eyebrow at Pilar. "But first, clean up the kitchen."

"Yes, sir." Pilar's hands shook as she reached for the cart.

Just as Ming had briefed Cade and Helen, Pilar was undercover as a hotel housekeeper. He'd have to find a chance to catch up with her, but for now, they both needed to stay alive. These same people had broken Ming's wrist, and they might do worse to Pilar and Cade.

It was obvious to Cade that the hostage takers brandished their weapons about, even as the building was surrounded by the Miami Police Special Threat Response Unit that comprised both the Special Weapons and Tactics Team as well as their Crisis Negotiations Team. Those Miami SWAT and CNT officers were probably eager to get the hostages out, but for whatever reason, there were delays.

Now that Cade was inside the building without the ability to communicate with Helen and Ming, he had no idea what was going on or what the Miami PD and FBI had found out.

This was Day 2, and nothing had progressed because there was a high value hostage on the third floor, Josephine Callahan. She was not only the owner of the hotel, but she was also a billionaire venture capitalist. Her family, full of wealth and influence, wanted to meet the demands of the captors, and those criminals were biding their time.

Cade walked Pilar to the kitchen, right into a crime scene. On the floor, the chef de cuisine was sprawled next to the sous chef, both lying in pools of blood the color of spaghetti sauce. Neither one of them was moving.

Pilar's knees went weak at the sight. Cade held her up with one arm. He kept his stronger arm free in case he had to protect them both from the gunman.

"Ted, what did you do?" A second gunman appeared at the door.

Cade made a mental note of the name. Ted was

the gunman who might have killed the two chefs while Cade was taking a bathroom break.

That break had saved his life. Maybe it had saved two lives. The kitchen worker whose job he'd taken over this morning had been tasked to prepare sandwiches and help chop vegetables or whatever needed. He didn't have to cook.

However, late this morning, the chef de cuisine had a mental breakdown due to the stress of being held hostage and the sous chef accidentally cut her hand while slicing tomatoes, so Cade ended up making the hamburgers that Braun-Dean had ordered for lunch.

All those years of grilling hamburgers had paid off.

Once again, Cade was reminded that Romans 8:28 was true. God had indeed worked out everything for his good. Years of eating homemade hamburgers for dinner and a fortunate bathroom break.

> *And we know that all things work together for good to those who love God, to those who are the called according to His purpose.*

Would that verse be true again this afternoon? Cade glanced at Pilar. She looked like she was about to throw up.

"How about I clean the kitchen?" Cade asked Ted.

Ted stared at Pilar. "Maria, Maria. You look terrible. Like all the blood has drained from your face."

"Blood?" Pilar grabbed her stomach and ran out

of the kitchen, but didn't make it out before she threw up.

"You okay?" Cade patted her shoulders and back.

"Ted, maybe you should have taken the chefs out of the kitchen first," the second gunman said.

"Shut up, genius!"

"Now the kitchen is contaminated." Genius looked around. "We have to feed nineteen people."

Nineteen? Cade recalled that there were only eleven people in the entire building. The rest of the hotel guests had been released.

How could there be nineteen now? How did eight new people enter the building with Miami Police outside? All the doors were shut except the back door—the same one he'd entered this morning, pretending to be a grocery delivery man.

When Cade had entered the hotel, everyone was still asleep except for the line cook. Cade swapped clothes with him, and the line cook pushed the empty cart out of the hotel to his freedom.

That exchange had told Cade that something was off with this hostage situation. It seemed poorly planned. No one was clearly in charge. They didn't know—or care—that one of the kitchen staff had left the building and was replaced by Cade.

Something was not only off, but it seemed that this entire event was a...

Ruse?

Then again, Cade was confident there was an order among the captors. For example, Miami Police could not send an undercover officer because the last one, embedded among the hostages, had been murdered brutally in front of Mrs. Callahan, and the photo relayed back to them. If they sent another undercover officer, the hostages would be shot in the head one by one.

Even so, Helen Hu had insisted on a worker swap. The Callahan Hotel was able to provide the Miami Police with a list of kitchen workers, and Cade volunteered to be the sacrificial lamb.

So far, he'd survived the morning.

"I'm going to ask Mr. Pop what we should do." Genius walked out of the kitchen before Ted could answer.

Mr. Pop? Cade wondered if he was the leader of the gang or if it was just a nickname for someone.

"Clean up!" Ted ordered Pilar before he stalked off.

Cade wanted to say something to Pilar, to catch her up on what happened outside after Ming left and before Cade showed up.

Pilar didn't look like she wanted to talk right now. Without a word, she handed Cade a pair of gloves and she put on a pair herself. The gloves fit too tightly on Cade's hands and might rip soon.

Pilar then put on a mask. She handed Cade a mask as well. "The smell is awful."

Cade nodded. The mask fit over his mouth and nose.

"I don't know how to begin." Pilar's voice cracked. She avoided looking at the two deceased chefs on the floor.

"I think we move the bodies out of the way first." Cade couldn't believe he said that aloud.

And Pilar threw up again.

CHAPTER THREE

Have mercy on me, Lord!

Sure enough, God did. Pilar was filled with warmth and thankfulness at what happened next.

Before Pilar and Cade could begin the distressing work of cleaning up the kitchen floor after a brutal double homicide, four able-bodied men walked in, led by Ted.

Ted yelled at Pilar and Cade to get out of the kitchen. Then he yelled at the four men to haul the two chefs into the walk-in freezer.

"No!" Cade blurted. "No, please. We need the meat and produce in the freezer to prepare daily meals. You don't want Senator Braun-Dean to pitch a hissy fit when he finds out that you've just stuffed two dead bodies into the same freezer."

Ted literally pointed a gun at Cade.

Pilar froze. She stared at Cade, wondering how the latter was going to handle it.

Cade didn't move.

Then Ted chuckled. "You'd be right, my man. You just protected me. I owe you one."

My man?

Under normal circumstances, Pilar could see that Ted would be a nice guy, making new friends all the time. He just told Cade that he owed him.

However, from what Pilar could tell in the last twenty-four hours, Ted was a powder keg.

Then again, he definitely wasn't in charge.

Pilar put two and two together and figured that someone with authority had ordered Ted back to the kitchen. He'd murdered the chefs, so now he had to clean up the mess he had created.

All of that made Pilar believe that the person in charge of the hostage situation was still hidden from her. Who could it be?

She recalled what she had seen on the fourth floor right after lunch time. It seemed to her that Braun-Dean was in charge. But why would he take himself hostage? Surrounded by law enforcement on both ends of the building, it made no sense if there was no way out.

Unless Braun-Dean was considering suicide by cop...

Probably not. His estranged wife had told Pilar that Braun-Dean was a proud man, and killing himself to escape something was beneath him. He didn't want people to laugh at his obituary and call him a coward.

Then who would hold Braun-Dean hostage and why?

Pilar couldn't make heads or tails of the situation

because she was missing some information. If she could talk to Cade privately, they would need to exchange news.

Three days ago when Pilar had been a guest in the hotel, she was heavily disguised. When guests on the third and fourth floors were taken hostage a day ago, and everyone else was kicked out of the hotel, Pilar remained behind, switched gears, and made herself one of the last two remaining housekeepers.

"Maria!" Ted's voice chainsawed down the hallway.

It was then that Pilar realized she'd been pushing her cart away from the kitchen entrance. She scolded herself silently for not being more aware.

"Hey you! Maria!" Ted sounded angry now.

Pilar took a deep breath and turned her head. "Yes, sir?"

He waved his walkie-talkie at her. "Cleanup on the third floor. Bring lots of rags."

"What?" Pilar's imagination threatened to spiral out of control.

She told herself it was probably nothing. "Did someone throw up?"

Ted didn't laugh. "Now!"

Wasn't the other housekeeper, Alma, already upstairs on the third floor? Perhaps Alma needed extra help. Last night, she was scared to death and couldn't finish cleaning the bathrooms.

Pilar glanced at the kitchen door, hoping that she could see one last glimpse of Cade.

No one else showed up. Ted walked away, walkie-talkie in hand.

You know, who uses walkie-talkies anymore?

One more thing that didn't add up. Pilar told herself not to over-analyze anything. She had to take everything in stride and focus on staying alive.

She had to accept that this entire hostage situation was bizarre. To begin with, why hadn't the Miami SWAT rescued them yet?

She picked up some rags from the utility room. She wasn't sure what she could be cleaning up, so she picked up a box of plastic covers for her shoes. Just in case she had to step over liquid on the floor.

A crackle of thunder startled Pilar as she pushed her cart toward the service elevator. She hadn't been paying attention to the weather report in the last three days, but it was still October, and hurricane season in Florida wasn't over yet.

Might there be a hurricane or a tropical storm coming?

Most of the time, Floridian hurricanes would hit the west coast first. Every now and then, the storm blew across the state and deluged Miami. Otherwise, she could expect only tropical storms. They'd survive it.

Were their rescuers waiting for the weather to change?

Pilar had no idea, and no way to ask anyone outside any questions, with her burner phone gone.

The service elevator took her to the third floor, where she could hear people crying and sobbing. Some men yelled. Pilar could have told them that they should pray instead and save their breath.

Help would come in due time.

But would it?

One could always hope.

The hallway lights flickered in the thunderstorm. Pilar could hear heavy rain through the window at the end of the hallway. Rain covered the hurricane-grade glass, and she couldn't see through it. She knew that the other side of it was the back parking lot, and she could probably see police vehicles if she looked outside of it.

Surely the captors knew that too.

The crying grew louder as Pilar pushed her cart slowly toward a conference room, where the hostages were held. She last counted about thirteen of them.

For whatever reason, this old hotel hadn't been operating at full capacity. One could say that the snowbirds hadn't returned to Florida from the northern states where they usually spent their summer months. They would usually not return until after the last of the hurricanes was over. Maybe November.

Meanwhile, the Callahan Hotel continued to operate at a loss. Josephine Callahan hadn't sold the hotel due to nostalgia. Her Cuban parents had met and fallen in love in this very hotel back in the fifties.

Some years later, the hotel had been in disrepair when Mrs. Callahan returned to Miami as a self-made millionaire. She didn't have to spend too much money on the hotel but she managed to save it from demolition.

The restoration had taken over five years and put the businesswoman into debt. Her husband left her for a socialite, and Mrs. Callahan never remarried. She now lived in a suite on the third floor.

Pilar parked her cart in front of the conference

room where two guards stopped her. The conference room door was closed.

"Mr. Ted sent me up here to clean up." Pilar was nervous. Unintentionally so.

She wasn't sure what she was supposed to clean up, but flashes of scenes from the kitchen downstairs made her shudder.

One guard nodded to the other.

Pilar thought that meant one had seniority over the other.

The second guard opened the door.

Pilar hesitated before she pushed her cart in—and was assaulted by a horrible smell of sweat and blood.

Blood?

There, on the floor, right in front of her cart was a woman sprawled out on the floor. She was badly beaten and covered with blood and bruises.

"Alma!" Pilar screamed and dropped on her knees beside her fellow housekeeper. "Oh Alma, what happened?"

"She fought the guards," a woman said. "They beat her up."

Pilar looked up. It was Josephine Callahan. She had a cut on her face, and her silver hair was all disheveled. Her dress was a mess, and one sleeve was torn right off. Her ankles were tied up, but her arms were free. She was eating a piece of bread.

Alma raised a bloody hand.

Pilar grabbed it without hesitation. "Alma, I'm here."

Alma tried to speak. It sounded Spanish.

"Shhhh. Help is coming," Pilar whispered back in Spanish.

Truth be told, she had no idea if help was coming at all.

"Please tell my children that I love them," Alma said in Spanish.

"You tell them yourself." Pilar wanted to cry.

"I'm not going to make it out. I'm going to die."

Pilar braved herself. "Then let me ask you. If you die now, will you go to heaven?"

Alma nodded.

"Why?"

"Because I believe in Jesus Christ who saved me from my sins." Tears rolled down Alma's face. "I love You, Jesus. Take me now."

Please, not yet.

Pilar tried to hug Alma, but was afraid to because Alma was moaning in pain. Pilar wondered if she had broken bones. Her one working hand gripped Pilar tightly. The other arm was dangling by her side.

Pilar took her pulse. It was fairly strong.

She turned toward the door. It was still closed, but one of the guards had entered and stood inside the door. He had a baton in his hand. It looked like a baseball bat, smeared with something red. Perhaps that had been the weapon that had inflicted pain on Alma.

"Please, Mr. Guard." Pilar switched back to English. "She needs to go to the hospital."

He tried to avoid eye contact with her.

Pilar stared at him from a distance. She didn't try to approach him, not with the baton in front of him.

"No one leaves this building unless Mr. Pop says okay." He smirked.

"Then please ask Mr. Pop."

He laughed. "That's not possible."

"Mr. Pop is on the fourth floor, right? I will go ask him."

"You know Mr. Pop?"

Pilar had no idea. "I don't know."

"Then who do you ask?"

"Mr. Ted. He knows."

"Ted?" More laughter.

"Help my friend, please." Pilar pointed to Alma. "You see she is dying."

No, she probably wouldn't die. Alma looked like she had been beaten up badly, but Pilar prayed that she'd live. She would if they took her to the hospital.

"Have mercy on my friend." Pilar was on her knees, begging.

The guard got on his walkie-talkie.

Pilar tried to listen but Alma was moaning again, so she was distracted. However, she heard two words: "Ted" and "okay."

"My ribs are broken," Alma hissed in Spanish.

How would Alma know unless she had experienced it before or known someone who had broken ribs?

"Also my right arm."

Pilar nodded. She looked up at the hostages. "Any doctor in the room?"

No one replied.

"No doctor?"

The guard stepped toward Pilar. She sat back, not knowing what he was up to.

"Ted says if you can carry her to the door, she can go," he said.

Pilar was thinking of the elevator.

"Use the stairs."

"You want me to carry Alma down three flights of stairs?" Pilar asked.

"What he said."

Pilar lifted weights at the gym once a week, but Alma was heavier than she could carry. Could she drag her down the stairs?

"Can I use a cart?" Pilar asked.

"You're asking too much. If you can't carry your friend down the stairs, she stays here and dies."

"I'm not strong enough to carry her."

"No one can help you."

Pilar asked Alma if she could stand up. Alma nodded and then screamed when she tried to move.

Pilar touched her legs and Alma let out new screams. It seemed to Pilar that at least one of Alma's legs might be broken.

What to do?

The thunderstorm outside increased in intensity.

Pilar closed her eyes and prayed. "Lord, please help me get Alma to the hospital."

A crazy loud thunder startled Pilar but she kept her eyes tightly closed. "Please, Lord. Please."

Then she opened her eyes, but it was all dark.

CHAPTER FOUR

Cade wasn't sure whether to thank God for the backup generators that brought electricity back to the hotel or to thank Him for the tropical storm that could potentially bring an end to the hostage crisis.

Well, both then.

As soon as he decided that, 1 Thessalonians 5:18 came to his mind.

In everything give thanks...

Everything, including the oxygen that he breathed—although he wasn't looking forward to getting back to the kitchen. Going for the more intangible, he gave thanks to God for his soul, emotions, abilities, capabilities, and oh, his desires also.

He was sure now, more than ever, that if they ever got out of here, he wouldn't keep his feelings about

Pilar to himself. It was time to confess and let the chips fall where they may.

For now, Cade was glad that he and Pilar were alive. He prayed for a swift end to the operation before the captors found out who they were: private investigators in real life. Their zero association with the Miami Police or the FBI in their present predicament might help extend their lives, but only temporarily.

While Ted's men cleaned up the bloodied kitchen floor—a task that they seemed to have done before at least once, from the looks of it—Cade had other things he was assigned to do. The guards on the third floor wanted snacks and drinks.

In the dry pantry, Cade found a couple of bags of unopened sweet potato chips, as well as some all-natural ginger ale. No alcohol allowed on duty, Ted had said.

How ironic that the snacks he'd deliver to the third floor seemed healthy, considering the unsureness of their survivability.

He saw Pilar's housekeeping cart first. At first, Cade thought that Pilar was probably cleaning a room nearby.

Then he heard her beg the guards about something. She was speaking a mix of English and Spanish. Even though her accent was clearly a put-on, her words were heartfelt and she was crying. Cade heard the door slam and then he couldn't hear anything but muffled words.

He rushed toward Pilar's voice and the shut door. He drew a deep breath so that he didn't look panicked.

He handed the tray to the guard at the door. "Here's your snack. It's for two people. Should I bring more?"

He was indirectly asking if there was more than one guard. He could overpower one, but not two with weapons.

"He's inside."

Cade heard noises, like someone beating something. "What's going on?"

"Discipline." The guard took the tray and placed it on the floor. He ripped open the bag of chips. "What's this garbage?"

"Sweet potato chips. Good for you. Loaded with vitamin A."

"It has no taste." The guard chewed it.

"Should I bring some salt for you to sprinkle on them?"

"No need. I'm hungry."

Cade tried to think of reasons not to leave until he saw Pilar with his own eyes. He pointed to her cart. "Where is the housekeeper?"

The guard pointed to the door. "Inside."

"Cleaning?"

"Trying to save somebody's life."

"Oh? I know CPR. I can help."

"Nah. She's near death."

"Why? Who made the call?" Cade blurted.

The guard eyed him. "What is it to you?"

"Uh, I'm sorry. I get concerned about human life."

"Worry about yourself." He drank the ginger ale. "You got beer downstairs?"

"Mr. Ted said no alcohol. Sorry."

"Mr. Ted?" The guard laughed. "He was one of us."

"Now he's heartless and cold?" Cade tried to lead him somewhere.

"Something like that."

The door opened and another guard came out. His knuckles were bloodied. He was sweating bullets, but that could be due to the long-sleeved jacket he wore. Totally the wrong outfit to wear in a warm Florida October.

Before Guard Two closed the door, Cade was able to see a woman on the floor and Pilar holding her up. Pilar was crying.

"What happened to you?" Guard One asked.

Guard Two brushed it off. "Gotta wash my hands."

After he left, Cade remained. Stared at the door and thought of the quick scene he had witnessed.

"Someone hurt inside?" Cade asked. "Do we have a doctor in the building?"

"A doctor? A caretaker is more like it." Guard One laughed.

"Maybe we should let the dying go. No need for a third death in the hotel today."

Guard One studied him. "Bad luck, you mean?"

Cade shrugged. He didn't believe in luck, but he wanted to keep the conversation going. "Just dump the dying outside the door and the local police waiting outside will take care of her, you know?"

"Now why would we do that?"

"It shows compassion. Might reduce your sentencing."

"We're not going to get caught." He sounded confident.

"I don't want to get caught either."

"You? What did you do?" Guard One finished one bag of chips and started on the other.

"Bar fight. Two years." Cade made it up. Firstly, he was a faithful Christian who never drank at a bar nor had he fought in one. As for the years, the statement was misleading at best. He had no idea what the two years were for. Random numbers.

"That bad, huh?" Guard One sounded sympathetic.

"So, I'm here helping you because I'm cooking for you. That makes me an accomplice. Today I witnessed two dead chefs in the kitchen. Now another hostage might die."

"Maria in there asked for us to let her friend go." Guard Two came back. "But I told her if she could carry Alma down three flights of stairs, we could let her go."

"Alma? Is that the poor woman's name?" Cade asked casually.

"Maria can't carry her." Guard One snickered. "Why did you even give her such a task?"

"I'll carry her for Maria," Cade volunteered.

"You? What for?"

"In exchange, I will give you an extra hamburger each at dinner," Cade said.

"You carry the dead woman downstairs and you make us extra hamburgers?"

Cade nodded.

"Are you stupid or what?"

"Is that a bad bargain?" Cade asked.

The guards laughed.

Guard One shook his head. "Let him carry her down the stairs."

"But..." Guard Two seemed to be one who had more thinking power, but he had no authority.

"You follow them. Point a gun to Maria's head or something. Make sure there's nothing fishy."

"How about we open a window and drop Alma down? Wouldn't that take less time?" Guard Two asked.

"Yes, but take this as your test," Guard One said. "See if you can come back alive with Monty here."

Oh, so Guard Two was in training.

Cade wondered if he could take them out. Perhaps he could if Pilar helped. Pilar wasn't a weakling. Even though she had never been in the military or police, she had trained in mixed martial arts. Cade pitied anyone kicked by her.

"Open the door," Guard One ordered the other guard.

Guard Two complied.

Cade walked into the smell of fight.

Pilar looked up at him, her eyes searching.

"He's going to carry Alma downstairs for you." Guard One didn't step any closer to Pilar or Alma on the floor.

"I'll go too," Pilar said.

"No. You stay here and clean up this mess."

"Yes, sir." Pilar didn't look at Cade. Didn't want to give away their business relationship.

Alma had passed out. Her breath was shallow.

Cade worried about her dying between the third

and first floors. Why couldn't they take the elevator? What kind of a perverse game was this?

He debated how to carry Alma. Princess or fireman carry? Which would reduce any further damage to the poor woman? Perhaps it would depend on where the injuries were most concentrated.

Cade turned to Pilar. Before he could speak, she answered, as though she'd read his mind.

"She seemed to have cowered down when beaten," Pilar said softly. "Most of Alma's injuries are on her back and extremities. And head. She has blows to her head."

"The blood?"

"Knife wounds. Stabbed in the back."

Cowards!

"One broken arm and one broken leg."

"Fireman carry, it is." Cade picked up Alma gently and put her over his shoulders.

He left without saying any more to Pilar. Her eyes were red, and her lips moved, as though she was praying silently. Or maybe she was simply traumatized. Either way, Cade wanted to return to her as quickly as possible.

He didn't know where the stairways were, but Guard Two did.

"When we get downstairs, how do we let Alma out of the door without them shooting at us?" Cade asked.

His question achieved two purposes. Firstly, he wanted to gain Guard Two's trust. By saying "we" and "us," he was identifying with the guard. He was on their side, so to speak.

In reality, he was far away from that. He wanted

to take Pilar and run for their lives. Take her to Miami Beach and have a conversation at a tiki hut on the beach. Tell her how much he'd fallen in love with her and how he wished he could work in Miami with her and never let her out of his sight every day.

Well, to get to that point, Cade had to survive this trip. Outside, SWAT might be ready to grab Guard Two. What if they mistook Cade? Would his life be in danger?

He prayed that Ming and Helen had sufficiently connected to the Miami Police. When Cade had first arrived in Miami, Helen told him that there was a mole somewhere—whether at the local or federal level —leaking police activities to the captors. That was the only reason two police officers had been gunned down as soon as they infiltrated the building.

Secondly...

Secondly? Cade couldn't remember the second reason he had to create a rapport between himself and Guard Two. Must be something to do with Alma, but the purpose escaped his mind now.

Alma was light on his shoulder, but the stairwell was all metal. Cade prayed that he wouldn't fall headlong. He had to hurry up because he didn't want Alma to die on his shoulder. However, he wasn't familiar with these stairs and they looked old and worn down.

"Don't you want to walk in front of me to show the way?" Cade asked Guard Two.

"You think I'm stupid?" Guard Two waved his baton where Cade could see it.

What good was a baton when a hailstorm of bullets rained on them?

They reached the bottom of the stairs. All was quiet.

Cade heard a click behind him. That was when he knew that a baton wasn't all that Guard Two carried.

"Put her down as close as you can to the door." Guard Two pressed the barrel to Cade's head.

Cade put Alma down on her back. She wasn't conscious.

"Now we go back upstairs." Guard Two waved what looked like a Ruger Super Redhawk. The barrel itself was over seven inches long.

No wonder he had worn his long-sleeved jacket. Cade wondered what else Guard Two hid in that jacket.

Cade decided not to ask him if he had the pistol to protect himself from the other guards, or if it was a standard issue by this group of captors.

Speaking of captors, Cade also wanted to know who they were exactly.

But first, a conversation.

"Are we going to leave her here on the floor just like that?" Cade pointed to Alma.

Guard Two nodded, ushering Cade toward the elevator. The hallway was empty, and they were the only two people there.

"How would the outside people know she's in here?" Cade told himself that if he didn't use trigger words like SWAT or police, Guard Two might let his guard down.

"They'll find out soon enough." Guard Two pressed the number three button on the elevator panel. The door closed, and up they went.

"Soon enough?" Cade asked.

"Tonight... Ah, you ask too many questions."

Tonight?

Something was going down tonight.

Cade had to keep him talking.

"I asked because I want to live, find a girl, get married, have kids. I don't want to die too soon." It was the truth.

Guard Two laughed. "You're idealistic."

Oh, a big word. "You're not?"

"Married and divorced in one year. She gave me the cutest princess on earth...but..." His face suddenly turned from a quick smile to outrage. He railed at his ex with a roar of expletives. "She snitched, and I went to prison. She remarried and had more kids. Can you believe her good fortune?"

Cade put his palms up. "Maybe put away your pistol first?" *You know, before you get too angry.*

Guard Two seemed to realize then that he was still brandishing his Ruger. He put it away in the inside pocket of his jacket.

"If she got away, she's not for you." It was all Cade could think to say. What did he know? He was a single man all his life until now.

"You're right." Guard Two leaned against a wall. "Are you a praying man, Monty?"

Cade almost forgot that he was a cook named Monty. "Yes, sir. I am."

"Then pray that we all get out of here alive and can move on with our lives. You can get married. I can see my daughter."

"What's her name?" Cade asked calmly.

"Anastasia. We named her after her mother." His

eyes looked far away. He sighed. "Two years old. I've only seen her three times since I got out."

Now that he was involved in a hostage situation, he might go right back in behind bars. Cade didn't have the heart to tell him, considering he had a Ruger bodyguard with him.

In a way, Cade felt sorry for Guard Two.

"You know, I never did catch your name," Cade said.

"But I know yours. Monty. How did your parents name you that?"

See, there? One lie after another.

One of the reasons Cade didn't join any of the clandestine agencies after he left the Coast Guard was that he worried he'd have to lie. However, when he worked in Dubai as a bodyguard, he saw a lot of things he couldn't speak about. Lying by omission was also a type of lying.

Now he had to make a connection with Guard Two so that he could find a way to save Pilar and himself from certain death. Which meant he had to lie to Guard Two about his name.

"Actually, it stands for Montana, where I was born." It was true that he'd picked the fake name based on where he was born so that if anyone asked, he'd have enough morsels of truth in his statements to pass a lie detector.

He had been born in Montana, but his parents didn't live there. They had been traveling in an RV across North America, when his mom went into labor in Billings.

And no, they hadn't named him Monty. They named him Cade, after his maternal grandfather.

He had pulled the name Monty out of thin air to create the cover persona of a line cook.

"What about you?" Cade volleyed the ball across the net.

"Max."

"Whoa. That's a powerful name." He meant it.

"It's short for Maximus—not Maxwell, as some people think."

"Or Maximilian?"

"According to Mama, that crossed her mind, but she was going for maximum effect, and Maximus was the closest to it." His shoulders sagged. "Mama wanted me to go to college, but I dropped out in middle school."

"You could always get your GED and then go to college. Your mom would be proud."

Max nodded. "Yeah. I gotta stay clean."

"Maximum power man, you can do it."

"That's how you stay alive, sweet talker?"

Cade clamped up.

CHAPTER FIVE

It turned out that Cade was now the only cook in the kitchen. Pilar found out soon enough that, to his credit, he asked for an assistant and suggested "Maria the housekeeper." Some sort of conversation must have ensued from that because Ted himself came to the housekeeping department to ask for Pilar personally.

Pilar was in the laundry room putting bloodied rags into the commercial washing machine, when Ted walked in, startling her. He laughed at her nervousness.

"Seen too much today?" Ted asked.

Pilar nodded. Tears in her eyes appeared without being summoned.

"It's going to be okay." Ted's voice was gentle.

Pilar feared what he might do next. She froze in place, still holding a bundle of towels in her hands. She wasn't about to ask, "May I help you?"

"Monty needs a helper in the kitchen," Ted said.

Pilar looked around. She was the only person there. "Alma is injured."

"You go help him cook dinner tonight."

"Me?" She shoved the last towels into the washer.

"Yes. You. From now on, you will help Monty to prepare every meal."

"Does this mean I don't have to clean toilets anymore?"

Ted laughed. "No. It means you now have two jobs."

"Oh."

Pilar looked for detergent and Clorox. Her hands started to shake because she didn't know where they were, and Ted might ask if she was a real housekeeper.

She opened and closed cabinets. Her eyes started to blur.

"Pods are in that cabinet." He pointed to Pilar's left.

She opened the cabinet door, and sure enough, the detergent was there.

"You didn't know." Ted's voice steeled.

Pilar blinked. "Because Alma always does the laundry. I never do anything."

"She spoiled you." Ted snarled.

Something had hit a nerve.

Pilar started the washing machine. She was worried that Ted was still in the room with her only because she wondered if he carried a weapon with him. Even without one, he was muscular and had twice her body mass. He could take her down, and she had nothing to help her rise up.

"M-May I look at my schedule?" Pilar pointed to her cart.

"What schedule?"

Slowly, Pilar walked toward her cart. That put a distance between captor and captive. She picked up a printed sheet of paper and made a show of pointing here and there.

"I haven't finished cleaning the third floor. I came downstairs to wash the dirty linens and to get more rags. We're running out of rags because..."

"Because it's carpet." Ted came closer to her. "If they had installed marble floors, you could clean the mess right up."

Oh.

Pilar didn't know how to continue the conversation from that angle. Originally she wanted to say that they had run out of rags because the captors didn't respect human life, but that might cause Ted to prove her point.

"Finish cleaning the third floor, and then go to the kitchen to help Monty make dinner."

"Yes, sir." Pilar reminded herself that she was Maria and Cade was Monty. She feared that his real name might accidentally slip out of her mouth.

Ted walked past her, seemingly satisfied that he had scared her at all.

When Pilar was alone again, her heart started calming down. She took a few deep breaths and told herself she could do this.

So help me, God.

After Pilar finished cleaning the hotel rooms occupied by the hostages, she put her cart away and went to the kitchen to join Cade.

She wasn't sure if there were cameras and recorders in the kitchen, but she wasn't taking any chances. Still, she had to find a way to communicate with Cade.

Cade was wearing a denim chef coat with two rows of buttons down the double-breasted front. It reminded Pilar of a pea coat. A bandana wrapped around his head instead of a chef's hat. He looked...

Veritably handsome.

Pilar cleared her throat.

Focus on the assignment, why don't you?

But Pilar's eyes were not cooperating with her business mind. They went to his jeans and then shoes —hiking shoes, like hers. Perhaps Cade had the same mindset of a quick getaway. Back in Dubai, both of them had only worn boots at the resort where they'd been the protective detail of the socialite scorned. That way, if they had to make a dash for it, they were not running in sandals.

This time in Miami, Pilar expected an easier job than Dubai. Then again, this job seemed different. Yes, Roxanne Braun-Dean had hired her to do a task. She was being paid by the hour. However, all that went out the window when they were all held hostage, right?

Oblivious to her jumbled thoughts, Cade was busy frying ground meat—a lot of it—in a big stainless steel frying pan on the stove. There was another frying pan with a lighter color meat in it. He used the same ladle to stir fry both pans.

"Is this pork and is that beef?" Pilar pointed to the two pans.

"You got it. There wasn't enough beef for dinner. You okay with pork and beef mixed together?"

What difference did Pilar's own preference make at this point? Food was food. On normal days, she actually preferred beef tacos without other types of meat mixed in. But she could eat pork too. It didn't matter.

"What are we cooking?"

"Well, it began with Mr. Braun-Dean asking for hamburgers for dinner," Cade said. "I was going to cook hamburgers just for him. Everyone else would get beef-and-pork tacos. Then he changed his mind and wanted tacos too. He wanted to eat what the rest of the hostages were eating."

See? Something was wrong with that.

Pilar was mulling over it when Cade spoke again.

"There's another coat in the pantry." Cade pointed to another end of the kitchen.

In the pantry, Pilar saw some steak knives in a box. She wondered if those belonged to the dead chef. They could come in handy as weapons, but not against handguns.

She counted at least two dozen knives, and there were more. Had to be more for a hotel this size. Could she use those knives?

Pilar wasn't confident of her own knife-throwing skills, even though she'd learned how to from Ming's wife, Sabine. Every time Pilar visited the Wei family on Tybee Island, she and Sabine would go to the River Run Indoor Range in nearby Savannah, where Sabine taught her some *bo shuriken* throwing strategies. After a while, Pilar could throw those steel spikes accurately.

Could she potentially transfer that knowledge to these steak knives. Maybe? Maybe not? She wasn't sure.

Pilar didn't want to hurt anybody. She wanted to take the high road. However, if push came to shove, if she had to defend her life, then what choice would she have?

Regardless, Pilar was glad to know where she might find some sharp knives.

"Maria!" Cade's voice echoed into the pantry.

"Coming!" She quickly put on an apron she'd found, shoved two sharp steak knives into her front pockets, and returned to Cade's side.

She kept her head down, away from the cameras, and stared at the frying pan. The ground meat was mixed with chopped onions.

"I didn't know that hostages could order what they want for dinner," Pilar whispered.

"They took my phone or else I'd look up standard meals for hostages."

"You're joking at a time like this?"

"For levity?"

"Shut up and cook." Pilar didn't regret a word she said. The longer they stayed holed up as hostages, the lower their chances of survival might be.

Cade didn't get angry with her. He might remember that she had rarely lost her cool, not even when they had setbacks in their project in Dubai. In her part-time job as a mixed martial arts fighter, she was not only calm under pressure in the octagon, but also outside the cage in real life. That spilled into her day job as a private investigator.

But...

Right now she wanted to run to the gym and hit the punching bag. It was her go-to stress relief. Sometimes Cade had gone with her. Also in Dubai.

Hmm. They had done a lot of things together. Pilar glanced at Cade to see if he was upset that she'd told him to shut up. She wouldn't have said it to him if they barely knew each other. Did he know that? She'd said it to her brother more often than she'd said it to Cade, for example.

"It's going to be okay." Cade smiled a little.

That smile. He knew just what she needed, didn't he?

Then he gave her a hug. She wanted to pull back but he leaned toward her ear. "Knives versus bullets, you know?"

She stiffened up. If Cade had noticed that she'd try to smuggle two steak knives out of the pantry, the captors would too—especially on camera.

Pilar closed her eyes, then blinked. She wasn't a person who'd cry at the drop of a hat, but emotions might be a good ruse.

She let the tears flow. Made a show of it for the camera.

Cade looked like he didn't know how to respond. Pilar leaned into his shoulder and turned her face toward his ear. "Are they watching?"

Cade patted her back. Whispered in her ear. "Four cameras."

His breath was warm, and as crazy as it sounded, Pilar thought she might be falling for him—right in the middle of this hostage crisis. What in the world was happening to her?

She stepped back. "I'll put them back."

"Suspect that they already saw everything. Take off the apron here."

Pilar did slowly, and wrapped the apron around the steak knives.

She understood what Cade was trying to tell her. Carrying the knives around would be an act of defiance. It would do her no good and might get her killed.

They'd be better off overpowering the captors and taking their firearms. Could Cade and Pilar do it together as a team?

She watched Cade turn down the heat on the stove and cover the ground meat with a lid. "How about you heat up tacos in the oven? I have to make one more batch of meat."

"Show me how to use the oven."

"Seriously?" Cade led her to the commercial oven. "You still don't know how to cook?"

"I've always known how to make sandwiches. That's enough." Pilar shrugged. "I'll marry a man who can cook."

The corner of Cade's lips smiled again. "I volunteer."

Pilar ignored him. "How many tacos are we making?"

"We need to feed nineteen people altogether." Cade warmed up the oven. "Three tacos per person on the top floor, and one each on the third floor. All guests get two tacos each."

Guests?

Cade seemed to be conveying information more than just for dinner. From what he said, Pilar calculated that there were three hostages and four captors on the fourth floor, five hostages and two captors on the third floor, two guards who moved among floors, plus Cade and herself.

The two guards who moved around were Ted and one other guy.

So who was the nineteenth person? Pilar didn't dare to ask.

She prayed that Alma was in good hands. Pilar wanted to ask Cade about Alma. How could she ask without arousing suspicions if anyone was listening in?

Then again, she had established Alma as a friend. The captors couldn't suspect anything.

"Did my friend Alma get to the hospital?" Pilar asked quietly.

"Yes." He didn't elaborate.

"You didn't leave her downstairs to die, did you?" Pilar tried not to panic.

Cade shook his head. "Max told me that Ted made arrangements for Miami Police to open the door and drag her out. If they were to step any further into the hotel, then the captors would start throwing hostages out of the window."

That told Pilar that there were cameras everywhere, including at the foot of the stairs, where the captors could see if the Miami Police complied with their agreement.

Perhaps their next step was to identify the captors.

Pilar tried not to dismiss the idea that Braun-Dean had staged the hostage situation himself. His wife said he was capable of anything. That, Pilar took with a grain of salt because the couple was estranged and headed for divorce. Anything that could be used against the other party would be par for the course.

"Any cheese allergies?" Pilar asked.

"Two people."

"Let me guess. They're on the fourth floor."

Cade didn't smile. "Like I said..."

"Got it." Pilar cut him off.

Secrets on the fourth floor.

Pilar had cleaned that floor at least once a day. She had seen a lot, but wasn't sure how they all connected. She wished she could exchange notes with Cade.

On the fourth floor were some interesting characters.

There was the former senator Felix Braun-Dean, who didn't act like a hostage. In fact, he had tantrums every day. He liked to throw food and his mistress across the room, though not necessarily at the same time. The mistress was bruised all over but never on her face or arms. Pilar suspected she might also be drugged.

Then there were the guards who worked for someone who hadn't shown himself—or herself. Ted seemed to be in charge of several of them, but he took orders from someone above.

If she could compare notes with Cade...

"So here's how you heat up the corn tortillas." Cade waited for Pilar to say something.

"What?"

"Earth to Pi—Maria. Earth to Maria. It's taco night. It should be easy unless you make it hard for yourself."

"You want me to heat up the tortillas the way I've

been taught?" Pilar didn't want to bring up her taco card, but she did grow up in Miami eating all sorts of tacos from fish to beef to vegetarian.

"Whatever you want. Just have a bazillion taco shells ready in like twenty minutes."

"Yikes."

Cade chuckled.

Pilar glared at him. "How could you find humor at such a time as this?"

Cade raised an eyebrow. "You mean when we're all going to die?"

Pilar couldn't read him. Not only did he seem to be in character as a cook, but he also didn't look like he was going to freak out and foam at the mouth. In fact, he was calm and...

Thinking?

Oh, she prayed that Cade's mind was really thinking of an escape plan. Pilar had to get out of here. She had a grandmother to go to, and a younger brother to put through college. Right now, Oscar was taking care of Grandma in between taking classes at a local college. They would both be fine in case something happened to her because she had made plans for them in the event of her death.

But Pilar didn't want to die just yet.

Cade scraped the last pieces of ground beef off the frying pan into a giant mixing bowl.

"Why don't you make some beef tacos and some pork tacos instead of mixing them together?" Pilar asked.

"Mr. Braun-Dean said to mix them together."

"Is he a chef?"

"He's the customer."

"Or the captive," Pilar whispered under her breath.

"I actually heard that."

"And?"

He stirred the ground pork in the pan. Leaned toward Pilar. "Talk later."

Pilar made a show of pointing to the giant mixing bowl where Cade had dumped all the meat. "Is that enough for nineteen people?"

"I'm cooking one more batch. I think it will be enough because we'll also have lettuce, tomatoes, salsa, cheese, and whatever else we can find in the refrigerator. Maybe sour cream and guac."

Pilar nodded. "I better get to work. Where are the cookie sheets?"

"I don't know. Look in the pantry."

Sure enough, they were there, stacked up on the top shelf of a steel rack. She found a step ladder and carefully brought them down. All the time, her eyes were darting here and there, looking for any kitchen tools that could be small enough for her to smuggle out of the kitchen and use later as a potential weapon.

There was none.

She looked again.

Nope. None.

Maybe her mind was tired and unimaginative this afternoon. It had been an ordeal for her, and they were not out of the dark woods yet.

While the multi-rack commercial oven warmed up, Pilar lined several baking sheets with taco shells at an empty work table. She faced the stove, and watched Cade busying himself at the stove. His back was toward her, but she felt a sense of comfort that Cade was in the same room with her.

It wasn't just his presence that made her feel less alone, but it was the backing behind him. Cade worked for Helen Hu. The fact that he was here meant that Ming had contacted Hu Knows, Inc., and its powerhouse of connections—including the digital assets at Binary Systems, Inc., that had often worked together with Hu Knows to crack cases that law enforcement couldn't. Sometimes gray areas were best left to citizens.

Was this a gray area? It seemed to be a simple hostage situation, no?

But...

There were simply too many unanswered questions.

CHAPTER SIX

Cade had barely finished cleaning up the kitchen when the lights went out. He wasn't sure how long it was out since he didn't have his phone with him and the oven and microwave clocks were electricity-dependent.

He stayed put in the darkness, listening to the thunderstorm. He had known that a tropical storm was coming. He wondered what the captors would do in the event of a deluge. This area of Miami was prone to flooding.

The standoff with the police outside seemed to be happening in slow motion, which baffled Cade. He still hoped that all this would be over soon, everyone escaping safely, and then he could invite Pilar to dinner. He imagined cooking her favorite dishes—whatever they might be—and giving her flowers. He wondered what kind of flowers she might like.

The lights came on, and Cade felt bad that he had wasted the time daydreaming about Pilar, who might not even be interested in him. He should've used the time to pray to God for delivery instead. Had he placed Pilar over God on his priority scale? Heaven forbid.

He took off his chef coat and put it in the hamper. He was alone in the kitchen, but someone should be here to escort him to his room any minute now. He walked to the door but was unable to open it.

They had locked him in the kitchen.

He pounded on the door. "Anyone out there? Anyone?"

Nobody answered.

Not one to sit around and mope, Cade tried to think of happier thoughts to counterbalance the predicament he was in.

His happier thoughts immediately landed on Pilar. Was she okay? Where would they put her for the night? With the rest of the female hostages? Alone in a separate room?

The more he thought of Pilar's situation, the worse his imagination got. Before he knew it, he started to fear that the captors—all men!—might violate Pilar. Just the thought of such a possibility made Cade angry.

He balled up his fist and pounded on a nearby steel table. "They better not!"

But if they did, what would he do?

He closed his eyes, paced the floor, pounded the table, and paced some more.

Then he stopped right there in his tracks. Looked up at the ceiling.

"God, You can protect Pilar. Please don't let

anything bad happen to her." He wiped an eye and then the other.

Whoa. When was the last time I ever cried?

Here he was, tearing up for a woman he had only known for one year, and not even a full year at that. He wanted to smile when he recalled their moments in Dubai.

Apple.

The word came to his mind.

What?

Apple.

Cade straightened up. It was Pilar's favorite fruit. He rushed to the refrigerator. No apples. Only tangerines. He grabbed a few and stuffed them in his pockets.

Then he realized what his mind was doing. Even as he wrestled the dark situation they were in, Cade's mind was looking for silver linings. If he made it out of this hotel alive, it would be because Pilar was on his mind. All-things-Pilar felt bright and sunshiny to him. He could see her smile in his mind. Her can-do attitude, her levelheaded problem-solving ability.

Tremendous thunder shook the kitchen, and Cade dropped to the floor. It felt like an earthquake. As far as he knew, Miami had never been the epicenter of earthquakes. However, its proximity to Cuba, which was near tectonic plates, meant that Miami sometimes felt the effects of earthquakes in the Caribbean.

Yeah, Cade was filled with trivia like that, but Pilar liked his random knowledge, and it made for good continuing conversations with her.

So, was this an earthquake or just the roars of a

tropical storm? He leaned toward the tropical storm because Helen and Ming had discussed that prior to Cade's entry into the hotel.

He couldn't see the outside from this kitchen on the ground floor because he was walled in, but he could certainly hear more thunder.

Thunder that only God could make.

Ah, yes.

Cade bowed his head, feeling ashamed.

Lord, forgive me for being agitated. For not praying. For panicking. For being afraid. For not looking to You first. I worry about Pilar...

Cade shook his head and laughed. "Lord, thank You for reminding me that Pilar can take care of herself. She's an MMA fighter, albeit part time. She can shoot any weapon. She can also throw knives. What am I worried about?"

Cade was confident Pilar would survive this.

And so he must too.

Before he could conclude his prayer, the door flung open. Max came in, accompanied by a gunman he hadn't seen before. When Cade looked again, Max wasn't carrying a baton himself.

Oh, so they had upgraded from batons to guns.

"Put your wrists out in front of you," Max ordered.

This wasn't the time to ask why or chit-chat about their blooming friendship. Cade complied without a word.

Max slapped handcuffs on his wrists.

"What's going on?" Cade felt that he had a right to ask.

"We're going for a walk." Max smirked.

That told Cade that Max was distancing himself for whatever reason. Perhaps he didn't want to have any emotional attachment to the hostages, just in case he had to kill them. Cade couldn't be sure, but that was what he thought.

The other gunman pushed Cade forward. "Let's go!"

Handcuffed like the other hostages, Cade waded through rising water in the hot and musty tunnel underneath the hotel. The tunnel was crude, and black mold was everywhere.

Cade covered his nose with his shirt collar, but it kept falling off his face. Duct tape over his mouth prevented him from biting into the cloth. All he could do was take shallow breaths and pray that he didn't catch any respiratory problems after this was over—if he survived this walk of death.

The water continued to rise and it was up to his ankles now. Every now and then, a rat floated by, but only when the guards' flashlights shone onto the water. The other times, they walked in the dark.

Cade heard gushing water and occasional squeaks of sewer rats, whose end might be miserable if the flood water filled this tunnel.

He counted five women hostages walking beside him. One of them was Josephine Callahan, whom he recognized but who didn't know him. Where were the male hostages?

All of them were able to walk on their own volition. Perhaps the captors had left the infirmed behind.

The guards kept pushing the people forward, but the hostages walked slowly because their shoes came off in the water. Some had lost their shoes completely and were walking barefoot. Whatever their problems were, they were slowed down.

The water rose quickly. Cade wanted to hurry everyone else along. He tried to get the guards' attention but they ignored him. They hit several of the women with their batons to get them moving faster. It backfired because one woman tripped and fell into the dirty water.

The tunnel was narrow and the ceiling was low. Cade had to bend his head and shoulder every now and then just to clear the passage. So did the two guards herding the hostages.

Cade squinted as he tried to look past his group to the first group ahead. If his guess was right, Pilar was with that group that would include former senator Felix Braun-Dean and his girlfriend.

He could make out moving figures, but only when flashlights shone on them. Even then, he could only see the backs of their heads. Many wore long sleeves, except for Pilar in her housekeeping uniform. October was normally warm in Florida, so Cade didn't understand why the captors were wearing long sleeves.

Cade chided himself for not being observant in this project. He couldn't remember the color of Pilar's blouse. Well, to be fair, she had worn a beige uniform when they'd met outside the kitchen. In the hail of gunfire, Cade was more concerned about safety than fashion.

But that piece of information could have come in handy now as he tried to spot Pilar in the group ahead.

The flowing water made it harder for them to walk.

"Move fast and get out of the tunnel or move slowly and be eaten by rats," Max the guard said.

People started screaming through their duct tape.

The guards laughed. Shook their heads.

"Women," Max said.

So is your mother.

Cade had no opportunity to voice it aloud.

They came to a stop eventually. All flashlights were on a rusty ladder going up that didn't seem like it could hold this much foot traffic.

A captor from the first group climbed the rusted ladder. He disappeared above the tunnel ceiling.

Sounds of metal being pounded ensued. Then creaks and grating noises.

"Come up!" he finally said.

Felix Braun-Dean went up first. He was at least three hundred pounds. Nobody climbed on the ladder while he was on it.

Cade found it interesting that Braun-Dean didn't have any handcuffs on. Wasn't he a hostage? Did they miss a detail in their stage play?

Then Braun-Dean's girlfriend climbed up. She was wearing tight fitting pants and a pair of five-inch red pumps. Perhaps she had taken them off when she walked through the flood waters, and then put them back on once they reached the ladder. Her wrists were not cuffed.

Following her, a woman with her hair tied up in a

bun on top of her head. She turned briefly towards the tunnel.

Pilar.

Cade wanted to believe that she had turned her face toward the flashlights to let him know that she was safe. Either that or she wanted to see if all the hostages were there. With the lights in her face, Cade wasn't sure how much Pilar could see beyond the guards holding the flashlights.

Her wrists were handcuffed, but she managed the climb. She was still wearing her beige housekeeping uniform, which was quite loose around her.

After three more guards climbed up, it was the second group's turn.

A guard waved to Cade to go up first. Perhaps he was being nice, but Cade suspected that the reason might be one of power. Cade was the only male hostage in the group. The two guards probably thought that they could more easily subdue the women than an able-bodied male who looked like he was athletic and fit.

Well, they didn't know that Cade had been more fit a year ago when he had exercised more. The last few months, he'd been confined to paperwork at Hu Knows, Inc., writing reports for the other private investigators who didn't want to use artificial intelligence to write their reports for them. So they'd dictate to Cade, and he'd write them out in what he hoped wasn't purple prose.

His major in college was Criminal Justice, not English. Sure, he could write reports and essays, but his primary goal had been to be an investigative reporter for a local television station.

After college, he couldn't find the job he wanted. He ended up working as a personal assistant to an expatriate in Dubai. The expatriate hired Ming Wei to investigate why someone wanted to hurt her. Ming Wei was in the middle of the assignment when he had a family issue and had to fly home to the States to deal with it. Ming handed over the project to a fellow private investigator, and Pilar was her name.

Cade wasn't sure when he had started to become really attracted to Pilar. Truly, she had been on his mind since the first day they had met in Dubai. His interest grew once he learned that she was single.

However, she seemed to be married to her job. The more she told Cade about her job, the more intrigued Cade was—about the life of a private investigator.

When Pilar finished the Dubai project and handed the criminals to the local authorities, she came home to Miami. Cade missed her so much that he quit his job and decided to try his hand at being a private investigator. Eventually, he hoped to work with Pilar, but for now, he had to find a firm that could pay him a salary so that he could pay for food and lodging.

Ming Wei's firm was too small to hire him, and Pilar worked alone. Ming recommended Cade to Helen Hu, and he passed the interview. With his Criminal Justice degree, he didn't have to have three years of investigative work experience. Therefore, he was able to go straight to his training courses, complete them, and earn his Georgia PI license.

The reciprocity agreement between Georgia and Florida allowed Cade to work in both states.

What he really wanted to do was work with Pilar every day, but he wasn't sure if Pilar felt the same way. He would be willing to move to Miami and work with her, but until he could establish himself, he wasn't ready to venture out on his own.

Perhaps he and Pilar could form a partnership. That way, Pilar didn't have to work alone.

Then again, Pilar might like to work alone. She was called in whenever Ming Wei needed an extra hand. She'd told Cade about a project she did for Ming in Key Largo that involved a woman who left the witness protection program and found herself in grave danger. Sometimes Pilar had to work in Georgia or other states in which her PI license would be accepted, but most of the time she hung around her hometown of Miami.

This time, though, it was the other way around. Pilar got the job first, and then she called Ming for backup. The details were sketchy when Helen Hu had briefed Cade on their flight from Savannah to Miami. Ming had all the details but he was injured and was in surgery to repair his hand by the time Cade and Helen arrived. That guy seemed to get hurt a lot. Helen said that his brother-in-law should retire, but Ming was a stubborn one.

At the top of the ladder, the manhole opened up to a garage floor, where a van waited. From the wet tire marks on the floor, Cade suspected that another van had left, perhaps with Pilar inside.

The garage door was closed, and it was hot inside. Cade guessed that the temperature was in the mid-eighties.

Cade heard heavy rain and thunder. Sometimes

very loud thunder. Cade had never lived in Florida nor had he visited much, but he had heard all those news reports about hurricanes. He wondered if a hurricane was on its way. Back in Georgia, the thunderstorms were heavy too, but not this severe.

Helen hadn't said anything about the weather before she approved his ingress into the hotel. Cade had been a last resort. When undercover police officers were killed by the captors, they had to send someone who didn't work for law enforcement, and who might be able to handle firearms and fight off the captors if needed. Cade volunteered because of Pilar. He signed every non-disclosure agreement and waiver that they put in front of him.

Whatever it took, he wanted to get inside the hotel and rescue Pilar.

He wouldn't call her his princess, and neither was she a damsel in distress. In fact, he would call her his queen, though she was two years younger than he was.

A guard directed Cade to the van, telling him where to sit. They put him in the back, away from the driver. He wasn't sure why, but wouldn't he be able to escape from the back of the van more easily than the front?

Nonetheless, he knew that he wasn't going to run away—not until he had Pilar with him.

The van wasn't running, and the air-conditioner was off. Cade sweated inside the van. He wiped sweat off his face with his handcuffed hands.

As he waited for the rest of the hostages to show up, he closed his eyes to pray. He recalled learning to pray from Pilar. She prayed frequently. It warmed his heart that they prayed to the same God.

He wondered what Pilar's prayer would be. He looked forward to praying with her. That way, he didn't have to guess what she prayed, although it seemed obvious that she'd pray for safety and protection from harm.

That reminded him of 2 Samuel 22:3, which Pilar had shared with him back in Dubai. He'd committed it to memory, and now prayed the verse back to Almighty God.

And he said:
"The Lord is my rock and my fortress and my deliverer;
The God of my strength, in whom I will trust;
My shield and the horn of my salvation,
My stronghold and my refuge;
My Savior, You save me from violence."

CHAPTER SEVEN

Alligators were not on Pilar's mind when she accepted the job to spy on Roxanne Braun-Dean's husband and his mistress in that hotel in Miami. She had expected a ho-hum day. Unfortunately, one day of work had turned into three days of captivity.

Now, in the midst of a midnight tropical storm, she and the other hostages had been moved from a modern, busy, crowded city to a cypress swamp somewhere in Florida. Pilar guessed that there would not be a gas station for miles and miles all around this place.

The van ride was rough, and Felix Braun-Dean complained endlessly in the middle seat between two guards. In front of them were Ted in the passenger seat and the driver, whom Pilar didn't recognize.

Now handcuffed, Pilar was in the bucket seat behind Braun-Dean. Zuriel, the drugged-up woman, was sleeping next to her. Her head slid down onto Pilar's upper arm, and Pilar didn't try to push her away. Maybe if they were friendly, Pilar could find a way to distinguish between the real captors and the real hostages.

In a way, Zuriel had reached out to Pilar first. Back at the Callahan Hotel, when they were gathering to climb down the hole in the floor to the underground tunnel, Zuriel had recognized Pilar who had been cleaning the fourth floor at least twice a day.

Pilar didn't think Zuriel knew who she was because most of the time the latter seemed to be in a drug-induced state. Slurring her speech, unable to walk properly, staying in bed most of the day.

With her handcuffed hands, Zuriel pointed to Pilar. "I want her."

She turned to Braun-Dean. "Pretty please? I need an assistant."

Braun-Dean, also now in handcuffs, chuckled. "An assistant? Can you afford one?"

Zuriel leaned against Braun-Dean, and didn't say another word, except to complain when they were slushing through the floodwater in the tunnel beneath the hotel.

However, Zuriel had gotten her way because the captors singled out Pilar to walk with Zuriel.

She remembered glancing back a few times in the dark tunnel, waiting for flashlights to show her where Cade might be in the separated groups. Unfortunately, the rest of the hostages moved slowly and she lost sight of Cade.

A bump on the road jolted Pilar from her memories. The van continued to drive through the torrential downpour.

Pilar tried to look beyond the windshield to see where they were going, but the raindrops were so thick and the night so dark that she couldn't even see the windshield wipers.

Nobody talked in the van, so she couldn't tell friend from foe. So far, they were all foes. She didn't know where Zuriel stood, but she stuck to Braun-Dean.

The big question was: who were the real hostages and who were the real captors?

If Cade were here...

No.

Correct your thinking, Pilar.

So what if Cade wasn't here? The most important thing was to acknowledge that God was here. Holy God Himself—the master of the universe, the creator of all humankind, the author of her faith, the beginning and the end—was here.

> *"I am the Alpha and the Omega, the Beginning and the End," says the Lord, "who is and who was and who is to come, the Almighty."*

Revelation 1:8 admonished Pilar to remember who she worshiped. She worshiped God.

Therefore, she had to run to God in times of trouble, not to Cade.

Who was Cade anyway? The man was also in the same predicament as Pilar.

She prayed that Cade would be okay, just as a flash of lightning lit the cloudy skies. A crash of thunder didn't stir Zuriel from her sleep.

Still leaning against Pilar's arm, Zuriel whimpered a little.

Pilar felt sorry for her. She prayed for Zuriel, for God's perfect will to prevail, for Him to protect them and get them to safety, for...

Pilar dozed off.

When she awoke again, she was being yanked out of the van into rainy darkness and a strong smell of decay and decomposition. A flash of light revealed that they were standing on packed earth, surrounded by green water and...

Cypress trees.

They were in a swamp.

If only this were a vacation, Pilar could have snapped many photos to send to Mom back home. Pilar had always wanted to visit the Okefenokee Swamp at the border of Florida and Georgia. However, she doubted that this was that. In fact, it was more likely to be a private swamp, which existed in Florida.

A private swamp.

Where they might all be murdered without anyone knowing.

The captors pushed them ahead, yelling at them in the thunderstorm. It was hard to hear their words, but their batons spoke volumes.

Zuriel clung to Pilar like a baby sister, and Pilar felt sorry for her all over again. She wanted to protect this seemingly helpless woman.

One of the reasons Pilar became a private investigator was to help people. At first, she wanted to join the US Marines, but she didn't pass the fitness test. That spurred her on to lose weight and stay fit. She got into mixed martial arts, and the fights earned her money. She thought she'd be doing that for a long while, but her grandmother pleaded with her to find a safer job. So she joined the police academy.

After a year as a police officer, Pilar felt restless and wanted to travel the world. One of her mentors at the Miami Police retired after fifty years of service and opened a private investigative firm. Pilar wanted to work for him but he had a heart attack and retired before the paint even dried at the office.

Not deterred, Pilar earned her PI license and started her own one-woman business. Most of her first clients were relatives and friends. Grandmother had a big family and a wide sphere of influence in her church community. In fact, in those early days of Pilar's business, Grandma answered the phone for her. Grandma called it "working the switchboard" even though she used the latest iPhone model.

Between the two of them, they had helped many women and families in their local community. Not a millionaire by any stretch, Pilar was never short of food. Sometimes the battered or maligned women paid their fees with food and things they sewed themselves, such as winter coats and shawls or throw pillows. So Pilar was never hungry or cold.

Not in Miami anyway.

Now Pilar felt a chill as the whistling wind whipped up all around her. Her single-layer housekeeping uniform felt inadequate against this tropical storm. Yeah, she was sure it was a tropical storm—which wasn't as bad as a hurricane—instead of a usual thunderstorm.

The group moved in a single file over a boardwalk. Flashlights showed Pilar that they were heading toward some rustic huts perched over and around the swamp. When light shone over the water, Pilar spotted pairs of partially opened eyes seemingly staring back at her.

Each pair of eyes were accompanied by a matching pair of nostrils.

"Do alligators sleep with their eyes open?"

"Look how skinny they are." Ted laughed. "They're waiting for their midnight snacks. Any volunteers? This will end your misery."

At that philosophical moment, Pilar realized that their water escape route would be impossible.

CHAPTER EIGHT

Heavy rain drummed the zinc roof all through the night, and crackles of thunder rocked the hut. Cade could hardly sleep.

Firstly, he was chained to a pole in one corner of the hut where some of the captors took turns to sleep in shifts. He was on a thin sleeping bag which made him feel like he was sleeping directly on the floor planks. In between the rain and thunder, he could hear sloshing underneath the floor, which told him that the hut was directly on top of the water—the swamp where alligators made their homes.

Secondly, the door was locked and the windows were closed, making this wooden hut stuffy. It smelled like a college football locker room. Dirty socks galore. Mom would pass out if she were here.

Mom had raised five sons, and spent most of her life doing laundry if she wasn't cooking for seven hungry people. Retired now, Dad used to coach their high school football team, and at one point, all five boys were in high school and on the football team at the same time.

Cade still remembered the multiple laundry baskets Mom had to deal with all by herself because she didn't trust her sons to clean the clothes enough to meet her standards. Dad would rather go outdoors to mend a fence on their working farm outside Cheyenne, Wyoming, than cook and clean indoors.

Cade didn't know why, but right then, in the middle of the night, he missed Mom. After the kids had grown up, they all left home to far-away places, leaving two empty nesters to themselves.

Cade was the middle child, but he was the last one to leave because he wasn't sure what he wanted to do. The gap year between high school and college only delayed his decision-making process. As a result, Cade ended up finishing college one year later than friends his age. After that, he was the only son who went home to stay with his parents and work in Cheyenne.

It was rare for Cade and his siblings to go home at the same time these days, not even during Christmas. Cade was hoping to go home for Thanksgiving this year, but now he decided that perhaps he shouldn't wait that long to go home.

Cade determined that as soon as he got out of here, he'd ask Helen for some days off to recover, and he'd fly home to see his parents. He'd bring Pilar with him. That way, he could ensure that Pilar was safe and didn't get into trouble while Cade was visiting family.

Pilar?

Yes, Pilar.

In all his life, he hardly dated, and for sure he'd never brought a girl home to see his parents, but if he did, it could only be Pilar.

She was the third reason he couldn't go back to sleep tonight when the thunderstorm pelted the roof and woke him up.

He wondered whether Pilar was housed in the women's quarters or separated from the other hostages. He worried about her being taken advantage of, being an attractive woman. Then again, she was fit and trained, and she could protect herself.

Still, Cade found himself praying for Pilar's safety more than his own. He wanted to be the one to protect her and get her to safety. Then he worried whether he himself would make it out alive. Well, as long as Pilar could go on and have a good life, he'd be satisfied—

Not.

He felt selfish and wanted to enjoy the good life with Pilar.

He wondered how to approach Pilar and tell her that he was interested in getting to know her better outside of work.

Then again, when did Pilar ever not work? She seemed to work around the clock all year long.

It seemed to Cade that the only way he could catch a break with Pilar was to be available such that he could invite her out the first moment she had free time.

Yeah, that was what he needed to do.

Cade yawned, thinking he might go back to sleep, but his eyes remained open. He heard the door creak and wondered who'd walk in. Shadows in the dark, hushed whispers, and then the door shut again. The thunderstorm intensified, so Cade couldn't hear anything else.

Was that a shift change? He hadn't paid attention because the rain that woke him up wasn't in sync with the captors' schedule.

All Cade knew right now was that he should try his best to go back to sleep. Wasn't he plain old worn out from cooking all evening at the Callahan Hotel, walking in the underground tunnel, and being transported to this swamp?

Cade closed his eyes but no more sleep came. He wondered what time it was.

The answer came when the door opened again and light streamed into the hut. At first, he thought it was the gentle morning light, but when he couldn't see the sky, he knew that it was still dark. It was an artificial light.

Cade squinted, his eyes trying to adjust to the light. Soon, he realized that they were lights from lamp posts outside the hut.

He shifted. His body ached all over. Might that be a sign that he was aging? Ever since he'd returned from Dubai, he had upgraded his quality of living by moving to a bigger apartment, buying a new king-sized bed, and using 600-count pima cotton sheets instead of the cheap ones he'd had since he graduated from college.

Spoiled by a comfortable bed he returned to every night, Cade couldn't adjust to the hard plywood floor he'd slept fitfully on. No rustic camping for him!

He heard Max's voice first. If circumstances had been different, they might even be friends.

"Rise and shine!" Max hit Cade's legs with his baton.

Cade thought that Max just wanted to hit him while knowing that he was already awake. However, Max hadn't hit him hard. His calf muscles just burned a little, but his bones were intact.

Max unchained him. Shook his head in the process. "I'd shed a tear, but you and I are on different level playing fields."

"Ain't that the truth." Cade tried to make light of it. "If I don't cook, you have no food. I'd say you need me."

Max made a face as he stepped back to watch Cade get to his feet. Cade's legs wobbled, and he could feel pins and needles up and down his left leg. He held the pole he'd been tied to all night to gain his footing.

"Gimme a minute." He massaged his leg muscles.

"Sure. Take your time. It only means you have less time to cook breakfast. That's all."

"What time is it?"

"About six o'clock."

"When is breakfast?"

"Six o'clock."

Cade pointed to the chains on the floor. "Even if I woke up, there was no way to walk out of here. Even if I could, I don't know where the kitchen is."

"Stop whining." Max led Cade out of the hut.

This wasn't the time to counter Max. Cade let it slide. But the worst thing anyone could say of him was that he whined. His four brothers would never say that to his face when he complained.

On both sides of the boardwalk were railings, but

they seemed flimsy to protect anyone from what lay beneath the surface of the green water. Cade didn't want to step too close to the edge but he knew alligators were in the swamp.

It was still too dark to see. Lamp posts were not all lit. The Floridian sun didn't rise until at least 7:30 a.m. in October.

"Is this a resort of some sort?" Cade fished for information to piece together.

"This is a private swamp."

"Oh?"

"What? You want a tour?" Max laughed.

"Something like that."

"If you want to get out of here alive, you stick close to me and do as you're told."

Stick close to Max?

And here was Cade thinking that if he could get Max on his good side, there was a chance he might be able to find a way out of this place.

Now he found out that Max was playing some psychological tricks on him.

"Why should I stick close to you?" Cade asked.

Max didn't answer.

Ironically, his silence gave Cade the answer he sought. Max was lonely and could use a friend to talk to. Perhaps he found that he could talk to Cade easily.

If that was really the case, then they could help each other. Cade could mine Max for information about this private cypress swamp, especially escape routes, while being the brother that Max wanted. Perhaps Cade could even lead Max to Christ. That would be worth the price of admission to this place.

The smell of the swamp grew thicker as Max led

Cade down the weathered boardwalk outside the hut and around the swamp.

Parts of the boardwalk creaked when the men stepped on it. A couple of pieces of wooden planks were loose.

"Gotta nail those down." Max kicked one of them with his steel-toed boots. The plank came right off. Parts of it were rotten.

"I guess they didn't seal it well enough." Cade hoped his small talk would make Max let down his guard.

"You know those things?"

"I had to do odd jobs when cooking didn't put enough food on the table." Cade followed Max around a corner where more huts were.

All right, they were bigger than huts. They looked like two connected cottages. Cade guessed that the kitchen was somewhere there.

"I know the feeling," Max said. "I only took this job because they paid—"

Splash! Splash!

The noise came from behind a wooden fence that closed off a part of the boardwalk. Cade could hear men shouting, hooping, and hollering.

Splash!

"What's going on?" Cade asked, afraid to speculate.

"You want to see?" Max teased him.

"Am I allowed?"

"I'll open the door and you peek."

Cade didn't want to bring up the fact that Max had said breakfast was late. He wanted to peek behind the fence. Yeah. See what was going on and gather more intel.

When Max opened the wooden gate, nothing could have prepared Cade for the sight of a tub at the edge of the boardwalk with a man's leg sticking out of it. In the water, several frenzied alligators were fighting over what looked like...

Cade had no words. Blood drained from his face.

"Chef One and Chef Two," Max deadpanned.

Cade staggered back.

And prayed to the good Lord for mercy.

CHAPTER NINE

Six women in a sweaty hut made Pilar think of a sauna.

Her hair felt hot and sweaty, and the hair tie that had held her mid-length hair in a bun on top of her head since Miami was starting to loosen up. She had to retie her hair a couple of times. When her hair was down, she felt even hotter in this awful place.

Her polyester housekeeping uniform made it all worse, but she couldn't take it off for obvious reasons. Oh, how she longed for her cooler cotton shirts.

The windows were sealed shut, and a lone light bulb hung above them. Perhaps the perpetual light was meant to mislead. Pilar had no idea what time of day or night this was. If she were to guess, she'd say it was at least past lunch time because her stomach growled.

No one had fed them since they'd arrived at their new prison. They'd been shoved into the hut and locked in with two dirty bottles of water and a small stack of plain corn tortillas to share among six female hostages.

Looking around the hot hut and thinking of their desperate state, Pilar wanted to scream. But there would be no relief. To make noise would mean to draw attention to herself.

Still, their situation was dire. No cell phone to call for help. No weapons to defend themselves. Pilar imagined the boxes of steak knives at the Callahan Hotel. She wondered how far away Miami was from here.

She had observed that the captors were all men. They had left the male hostages behind at the hotel. Only female hostages had been taken to the swamp. Why?

Several women were napping to preserve their strength. Pilar wanted to do so too, but Josephine Callahan wanted to talk. Once the woman got going, she couldn't stop talking. She kept following Pilar around to different parts of the hut, offering to share her ragged blanket with her.

"Thank you, Mrs. Callahan, but it's too warm for a blanket, don't you think?" Pilar had lost her broken English accent that she had tried to put on back at the Callahan hotel, but she didn't care anymore.

"Call me Josephine—or Jo Jo, as my ex-husbands all called me."

Pilar didn't think she was that friendly with her. Pilar had more important things to do, like figuring out why they'd been locked up here for so long.

At first, Pilar had been with Zuriel. However, Zuriel's request for Pilar to be her maid had been denied by someone—either Braun-Dean or the captors. So they threw Pilar into the hut with the other five women hostages.

Seven hostages in all, counting Pilar and Cade.

Why are they keeping us here?

Pilar found a spot by a wall where she could feel a bit of air coming in from the outside. Light came and went through that slit in the wall, and Pilar realized that she was observing day and night.

Now it was day, but she hadn't been a Girl Scout, so she didn't know how to count the minutes or hours. October was still pretty warm in Florida, which meant that Pilar could guess whether it was morning or afternoon just by how hot the wall felt and how warm the incoming air was.

Pilar put her hand in the slit. The air was warm.

Afternoon?

"What are you doing?" Josephine asked.

Pilar almost forgot that she was still being followed.

Maybe Josephine felt safe with Pilar.

Pilar didn't feel safe with her. If Pilar made a mistake, Josephine might realize that she wasn't a housekeeper after all. In the event that Josephine had to save herself, she could use this piece of data to trade for her freedom or favors from the captors.

So Pilar didn't want to talk to anyone at all—especially Josephine. As the owner of the Callahan Hotel back in Miami, Josephine might know who worked there. She'd soon find out that Pilar wasn't an employee. Then what?

"Tell me about yourself," Josephine sat down next to Pilar. "What's your story?"

All this time—hours—that they'd been in the hut, nobody asked Pilar what her name was. Josephine chatted about her ex-husbands, problems with her children, her two cats and five dogs, and whatever else popped into the woman's head.

Pilar let her talk, but she was frankly getting tired of hearing about how rich life could be. Advertising her millionaire status could get Josephine killed, so why even bother?

Pilar wanted to find out if Josephine knew something that she hadn't known, but she didn't feel like engaging in a conversation with her.

Finally, Josephine stepped out of her me-mentality and asked about Pilar.

"What's your last name?" Josephine repeated. "I only know that your first name is Maria because one of the hostage takers called you that back at the hotel."

"Isn't it enough for me to be Maria?" Pilar was genuinely tired. "I'm so tired and I want to go home."

"That's how I feel too, but home is not always a happy place for me." And then Josephine went into a long monologue about feeling like she didn't belong in the millionaire class. She was hoping to snag one of those divorced billionaire men, but it had been to no avail.

Actually, Felix Braun-Dean was a billionaire, thanks to his bitcoin investments plus monkey business with non-governmental organizations funneling money through his estranged wife into his account back when they were a lovey-dovey married couple who partied with the rich and famous.

Would Braun-Dean be a target for Josephine? If so, would Josephine be in trouble with Roxanne?

After all, Roxanne had divorced the senator because he had slept with one too many mistresses.

Now we're talking.

"A divorced billionaire, you said?" Pilar turned toward Josephine. "Tell me more."

"Well, not necessarily divorced. I'll take a widower also."

"Oh?"

Josephine leaned over. She smelled like she hadn't showered in three days. At least Pilar had showered the day before—or whenever they had been at the hotel.

"If you tell me your story, I will tell you how to snag a man." She straightened her spine. "I should know. Been married four times, you know."

"You said five times." Pilar was surprised that she had been listening after all.

"I said one was annulled. I was twenty. Daddy didn't approve." Callahan looked sad. "He was my first love. He was devastated. Me, not so much. Daddy wanted me to marry an upwardly mobile millionaire with potential. My baby didn't make the cut."

"Your baby?"

"His name was..." It seemed that Callahan couldn't say the word aloud.

"You can whisper it."

Callahan shook her head. "We could all be in danger if I say his name."

Now this was getting interesting.

Pilar could play along and see where it went. "If I tell you my story, would you tell me who this first love of yours was?"

"Is. He's still alive."

Pilar nodded, trying to buy time as she cooked up a story for Maria Estuardo. It had to be tragic, like her namesake. It had to be believable. Pilar's imagination wasn't great since she dealt with only facts every day.

"My name is Maria Estuardo," she began. "My parents died when I was young, and my grandmother raised my brother and me."

That backstory was true for Pilar Santiago, not Maria—a stranger whom Pilar had never met, whose housekeeping uniform Pilar had only put on. Since the story was true for her, Pilar felt that she could convey it in a believable manner.

"Oh, I'm so sorry." Callahan reached over to pat Pilar's arm, but Pilar pulled it away.

Callahan retracted her hand. "So sorry. I can't imagine my kids without me. Without their fathers, yeah. Who cares about three philandering fathers in a row, but me... Oh, my kids think the world of me!"

"I'm glad you're around for your kids. Treasure the time because life is short." Pilar meant it.

Callahan waited, but Pilar had nothing more to say.

"That's all?" Callahan asked.

"My life is not as colorful as yours. I work all day and night, and have no time to take voice lessons like you do or fly to South Korea for plastic surgery."

"I'm sorry. Did I come across as self-absorbed?"

"Your word. Not mine."

Callahan leaned over again. She put her hand up to cover her mouth. Some of her acrylic nails were broken off. She looked like she wanted to whisper in Pilar's ear.

Pilar held her breath and leaned slightly.

"Felix was my first love," Callahan whispered.

Felix?

"Braun-Dean?" Pilar whispered back.

Callahan nodded.

The plot had just thickened. Pilar wasn't sure how to respond or what to make of the information that Callahan had just dropped on her lap.

Felix Braun-Dean was Josephine Callahan's first love back when she was twenty years old. They were forty years removed from the puppy love days, but Callahan hadn't forgotten the man.

"The Callahan Hotel?" Pilar couldn't form a proper question.

Callahan scooted over.

Pilar looked around to see who else was listening. One of the women was still sleeping. Probably confused about whether it was night or day. The other three were chatting among themselves at the other end of the hut.

"You mean how did my first love end up staying at my hotel?" Callahan asked.

"Something like that."

"This was the hotel we met in back when we dated. This was how we kept our relationship secret from Daddy." Callahan's eyes looked far away. "After I divorced my second husband, I had enough money from the settlement to buy the hotel and save it from demolition."

"Did you have to restore it?"

"Oh yes. That took another two marriages before I had enough money to complete the restoration. Whew. It was close."

Ah, such was the story of the professional wife.

"Then what happened?" Pilar was intrigued now.

"Then one day, F booked the presidential suite on the fourth floor. I didn't know at first, but he kept coming back year after year. That was when I looked him up and realized who he was."

"Was he..." Pilar wanted to ask whether Braun-Dean was already a senator at that time. But if she asked at all, Callahan might get suspicious. How would a housekeeper know much about the senator? Saying she had seen it on TV would be a stretch because Braun-Dean seemed to have faded into obscurity after his failed attempt at keeping his Senate seat.

"Huh? What did you want to ask?" Callahan waited, hands on top of each other on her lap. She looked like a noble lady.

"Never mind. Please continue."

"As I was saying, he stayed in the presidential suite many times," Callahan continued. "Come to find out, he has vacation homes in Florida, Georgia, and Tennessee, but has chosen to stay at the Callahan Hotel, and only in the presidential suite. If it's not available, he won't come."

"Maybe he knew you were the owner," Pilar suggested. "Could that be why he stayed there?"

Callahan shook her head. "Callahan is my third husband's last name. I don't think F kept up with who I married after we broke up because he hated me forever. I chose money over him, you know."

"Go on."

"Besides, I've lost a lot of weight and had plastic surgery." Callahan made a circle with her fingers around her face. "New nose, higher cheekbones, and ortho-something surgery to reshape my jaw."

Orthognathic surgery? Pilar almost said the word, but it would have given her away. Unless, of course, the real Maria also knew about this surgery. That was for the real Maria to say, not for Pilar.

"When I wash away all this grime, you'll see how pretty I am." Callahan lifted up her chin slightly. "I've been under the knife a few times, so F would probably never be able to recognize me again."

Pilar wanted to ask Callahan if surgery was painful, but she decided to focus on Callahan's relationship with Felix Braun-Dean.

"So you have no contact with him and he doesn't know you're one of the hostages?" Pilar asked.

"It would appear so." Callahan sighed. "I should've stayed at home. I would be in my Jacuzzi at my beach house now, eating caviar. Instead I'm stuck here. No idea if we'll ever be rescued."

"Why do you think Braun-Dean and his girlfriend are separated from us? If we're all hostages..."

"Equal opportunity?" Callahan laughed.

"Something like that."

Callahan stopped laughing, and whispered in Pilar's ear again. This time, her words landed like an anvil.

"Because I think this entire hostage situation is staged."

CHAPTER TEN

After a full day of not seeing Pilar, Cade became worried. He couldn't remember how many times he'd prayed for Pilar to be safe. He was most anxious about her not being violated by the male captors. It made his blood boil thinking about it, even though he and Pilar had agreed to make the kitchen their rendezvous point if anything happened to either of them and they had to flee from danger.

Granted, Cade wasn't sure what would happen after they met at their designated safe space. Ideally they would leave the swamp and go home. Until then, neither he nor Pilar was safe.

He wrestled with fear for Pilar's safety as he tried to pray to God while he was cubing ten pounds of meat that had been previously frozen and thawed out. He didn't want to cook this mystery meat at all, but the captors wanted to feed it to the hostages.

Max had told him that it was freshwater alligator

tail, though Cade tried not to believe him. Maybe Max was lying. Maybe he was telling the truth.

Cade leaned toward the latter because the meat wasn't beef, for sure. It was light-colored like pork, but it was lean and had striated fibers—which would make him think that it could have come from a gator tail with its heavy-duty muscles. When an alligator swiped its powerful tail, it could maim or kill. In the water, this tail propelled the beast.

And now it was food.

Cade wasn't into game meat. He also preferred chicken over pork. Today, however, he wanted tofu for dinner.

Cade wondered if human DNA was in the alligator meat as he fed the cubes of it into a meat grinder. Out came ground gator that could pass off as pork. Would it taste like chicken?

Tonight's dinner for the hostages and most of the captors was meatball spaghetti. Lots of it.

He couldn't imagine Pilar eating the poor things—the poor potentially man-eating alligators. If he could get word to her, he'd tell her to stick to the salad and just starve until they were rescued.

Speaking of which, Cade wondered if the Miami Police figured out where the hostages had been taken. If he could get a message out to Helen, that would also help.

But what message?

Sure, Felix Braun-Dean and his mistress, along with six women, had been held hostage. By whom? Cade had no clear information. All he knew was that Braun-Dean had been treated differently.

Take dinner for example. Ted had sent a message

through Max that Cade was to grill four porterhouse steaks, with mashed potato and green beans on the side. Everyone else was getting gator meatball spaghetti.

What did that tell Cade? Four people were Very Important People. Who?

If Braun-Dean and his mistress were the VIP hostages, that left two more seats at the steak table. They might be the most important top-two captors. If so, Ted was probably one of them. Who was the other?

Cade heard chains rattle. The kitchen door unlocked and opened.

Max entered. Mumbled something.

Cade stopped the meat grinder because it was so noisy he couldn't hear Max.

"I said, when's dinner?" Max said.

"Six o'clock?" Cade wasn't sure when he'd be done. It was already four in the afternoon.

"That's fine. Get the steaks done at five, and then everyone else gets spaghetti at six."

"Yourself included?"

Max nodded. "Yeah. Why?"

That told Cade that Max wasn't the fourth VIP at the steak dinner.

"Curious, is all."

"You know what happened to the curious cat?" Max chuckled.

"Stuff of fables," Cade said. "I'm more worried about not being able to cook for two dozen people alone. Can I get some help to make the meatballs? You know, the housekeeper who helped me cook tacos at the hotel? What was her name again? Maria?"

Max lifted an eyebrow. "You into her?"

"No." He answered too quickly and it was a lie. It just rolled out of his mouth. He was interested in Pilar, but this wasn't the time. They had to get out of here alive first before anything else could happen. "I just need help, that's all. You want to help me?"

Max shook his head. "I'll get you some help. Why her?"

"She can cook." No, she couldn't—but then again, anybody could make spaghetti, yes? But in truth, Cade wanted to keep her close. "We don't have time to test another helper. Let Maria help me tonight. If she fails, we get someone else tomorrow."

"Makes sense. I'll see what I can do." Max looked around. "You got fruit here? I'm hungry."

"Apples in the refrigerator." Cade pointed. "I can cut it up for you, and put a dollop of peanut butter if you want. There's not a lot of it left, but if you eat here in the kitchen, no one would know you just got special treatment."

"You need a favor."

Bring me my girl.

Instead, Cade said, "I need help in the kitchen."

"You got it." Max went to sit down at a kitchen table nearby, waiting for his apple treat.

Cade washed his hands thoroughly at the kitchen sink with its lukewarm water. He used dish soap to try to get the grease off his fingers.

"Skin on or peeled?" Cade asked.

"I like apple skin."

"Yes, sir." Cade tried his best to be polite to Max, even though he was probably not among the highest spots in the hierarchy of hostage takers.

Max straightened up a bit when Cade said "sir" and Cade knew that he got him.

"One apple or two?" Cade was at the refrigerator, staring in.

"One is enough. Dinner is coming."

You better like gator meat.

Cade washed the apple, cored it, cut it up, and plated it. He found an unopened jar of peanut butter from the pantry. Using a butter knife, he slapped a large mound of it to one side of the plate.

Max seemed pleased with the presentation. He was about to dig in when Cade stopped him. He placed a white cloth napkin on Max's lap.

"Enjoy, sir." Cade waited to see if Max needed anything else.

"Go make dinner, Monty."

Monty.

Cade almost forgot that his undercover name was Monty. He made a mental note not to forget again.

In the pantry, Cade busied himself gathering spices to make gator meatballs. He stared at the shelves, picked up breadcrumbs, and then tried to think about the closest recipes he had made that might work with gator meat.

He recalled growing up in Wyoming. His father and brothers were game hunters. Cade, not so much. He preferred to cook with Mom in the kitchen. Between the two of them, they had tested all sorts of recipes for everything from rabbits and squirrels to elk and antelopes, to everything in between, including deer.

Ah, Cade had cooked mule deer meatballs before. He could do that here. He'd never eaten gator meat before, so he couldn't compare, but he decided to adapt a deer meatball recipe. Why not?

Feeling like he was in some sort of cooking competition, Cade found a dry baking tray and collected all the things he needed for a modified un-venison meatball spaghetti. He picked up bread-crumbs, oregano, salt, and black pepper.

Moving on to the walk-in cooler, Cade retrieved a block of parmesan cheese, onions, and garlic. He selected some eggs to be his binding agent.

Then he spotted a slab of bacon. Hmm... Maybe he could use the bacon drippings to make the meat-balls less dry. Then he could eat the bacon for dinner—and share it with Pilar—instead of eating gator himself.

He returned to the pantry to pick up some dry spaghetti pasta. He'd thought he would have to make the spaghetti sauce from scratch, but to his delight, there were large cans of spaghetti sauce on the bottom shelves by a wall that he'd almost missed.

"You like to cook, don't you?" Max ate the last bite of apple. He stood up.

Cade nodded.

"Then I'll leave you to it." Max stretched. "I'll see if I can bring Maria to help you."

"Much appreciated. Will give you extra meat-balls." Cade bowed his head slightly.

"I wonder how gator meat tastes." Max laughed.

"That makes two of us."

"If you fail this dinner, you could become gator grub."

"I'm fully aware of that. Why we need Maria to

help me with dinner. That way, I'm certain not to fail."

Max crinkled his eyebrows.

"At least you'll have company at your last supper." Max laughed out loud and traipsed out of the kitchen, locking the doors behind him.

CHAPTER ELEVEN

The next morning, one cup of coffee, thick and black, with no sugar and no cream warmed Pilar and kept her awake just after sunrise at the cypress swamp. The boardwalk creaked under her shoes as she rolled the room service cart toward Braun-Dean's hut.

On the serving surface of the cart, two domed steel cloches covered hot breakfast for the VIP hostages. Cade had prepared them in the kitchen. It would seem that his summer job at Waffle House had paid off because many years later, his ability to cook might be the reason Cade was still alive.

Pilar's escort was a hairy man who looked like he hadn't shaved in some months. His belly almost protruded from under his too-tight shirt. He wasn't very big otherwise, maybe a couple of inches taller than Pilar. Still, she wasn't sure if she could take him down without getting injured herself.

Normally in the MMA octagon, she battled only

women. Herself by no means a champion, Pilar knew she shouldn't try messing with a man twice her girth—especially if he held a baton in one hand and carried a handgun in his belt holster.

No, sir. I'm not dying today.

When Pilar turned a corner on the boardwalk maze, the cart's wheels creaked. Pilar could have said, "Need oiling." Or some such small talk. However, she decided against it because she was too tired to keep up with her Hispanic accent, trying to speak like Grandma at the market.

Better to say nothing at all, she decided.

Mr. Belly also said nothing, but his stomach rumbled.

"Have you had breakfast?" Pilar asked without thinking.

So much for her plan to talk at a minimum.

Mr. Belly shook his head, looking like a sad puppy.

"Kitchen has eggs and bacon."

"Not for us." More sad puppy eyes.

"What?" Pilar feigned confusion. "They're feeding all of us, so..."

She let her words trail off, fishing for pennies for Mr. Belly's thoughts.

He said nothing.

Pilar reached down into her pocket and pulled out a paper-towel-wrapped biscuit with a couple of slices of bacon inside. She handed it to Mr. Belly.

At first his eyes widened. Then he leaned forward a bit to sniff it.

"Biscuit and bacon," Pilar whispered as she kept pushing the cart.

Mr. Belly's jaw dropped as he grabbed the smuggled food and shoved it into his pocket. He nodded slightly to Pilar. "You're not too bad."

"Trying to survive, you know." Pilar's voice cracked and it wasn't an act.

"I'm sorry."

So help me escape, Mr. Belly.

They came to a stop where two guards stood at the door of a hut. They were the same ones who'd guarded the hostages imprisoned inside the ballroom at the Callahan Hotel. Pilar supposed they got a promotion.

"Hey Tito," one of them said. "You bringing us breakfast?"

"Not for you, Max." Mr. Belly asked them to open the door for Pilar to get inside.

"When do we get our breakfast?"

"I don't know, man."

That was the last thing Pilar heard as the door closed behind her. She was standing at what looked like a foyer, but there was a wall in front of her. On both sides of her were short hallways with guards. One of them motioned for her to go his way.

He was a small man with a pasty complexion. His neck and face were covered with red angry patches that he kept scratching. His waist was so thin that Pilar thought someone should feed this kid.

On second look, she realized he wasn't a kid. He had a bit of gray in his hair, in fact. However, considering his skinny arms and legs, Pilar put him at maybe a hundred and fifty pounds thereabouts.

About her weight, plus or minus the extra cinnamon buns she'd binged on just a few days prior.

She could probably wrestle that handgun out of his spindly hands. If she needed a firearm, this man would be a good candidate to get one from. When he walked, he moved like he was about to lose his balance. Kind of like a stack of long twigs or dried-up branches.

Pilar maneuvered the cart to comply with his instructions. Down the hallway she went until it ended at a door. When the door opened, she could hear laughter interspersed with coughing.

Pilar paused. She didn't want to be in a closed hut with sick people.

"Keep moving!" Mr. Skinny snapped at her.

"Somebody's coughing. Sick?" Pilar asked quietly.

"So?"

"I don't want to catch anything." Pilar couldn't believe she'd said that.

"You want to catch a bullet instead?" Sunken eyes threatened to bore into her head.

"Ah..." Pilar took half a step back. "Let me think..."

"Are you kidding me?" He looked a bit angry, and veins showed on his neck.

Yep, if Grandma saw this man, she'd say he needed to eat more.

Pilar pushed the cart, and the man didn't say another word. However, he had shown that he had a temper, and it was under a loose lid. Even though Pilar could overpower him and take his weapon, she also knew that he could lose his cool. An armed man losing his cool spelled disaster.

Some hut this was. It didn't look massive from the outside, but inside it was a series of interconnected covered hallways that Pilar couldn't keep track of.

Inside the main room, it looked like one of those oversized glamping yurts. A bit rustic, but it had sofas and armchairs, rugs on the floor, and a bar. No beds. That meant the sleeping quarters were probably in another connected hut or behind some wall or something.

In the sitting area, Felix Braun-Dean was sneezing and coughing up stuff. He looked terrible, unlike how he had been when they were back at the Callahan Hotel. If he'd caught a cold, would they end the hostage farce soon? That was, if Josephine Callahan was to be believed.

Pilar looked beyond the apparently sick former senator. She didn't see Zuriel anywhere. Who was the second breakfast plate for?

"Breakfast is here," Mr. Skinny said.

Braun-Dean pointed to a dining table away from the living room.

Good. Pilar was worried she had to get close to a sick man. Didn't want to catch his cold—

She caught herself.

Here she was in a life-and-death situation. How could she worry about a common cold? Well, colds could kill too. If she got sick, it would be harder for her to survive being a hostage. She had left all her meds at home in Miami because she'd thought her spying operations at the Callahan Hotel would be during business hours.

Mr. Skinny escorted Pilar to the dining table, as if to make sure she didn't do anything untoward. *You know, like maybe go berserk?*

Pilar almost laughed at her own joke but clamped up when Mr. Skinny gave her a suspicious look.

Silently, Pilar set the table. It was easy. She picked up two placemats from the lower shelf of her cart, along with two sets of silverware—real ones, not plastic —and arranged two place settings for two diners.

Then she lifted one cloche and placed the large plate of yummy-looking breakfast with sausages, eggs, ham, bacon, and two slices of buttered toast. It seemed overloaded on the protein side.

The other plate contained an omelette with sliced avocado on top, a small cup of cut fruits, and two halves of an English muffin, with a small condiment bowl filled with jam of some sort.

Pilar didn't want to assume, but she guessed that the second plate was Zuriel's—if Braun-Dean was the meat-and-potato sort of guy, even though this morning's breakfast didn't have potatoes.

More stunning was Pilar's realization that Cade could really cook.

For someone who was not a cook at all—or who burned everything she got her hands on in the kitchen —Pilar felt impressed by her friend.

Friend?

Well, business associate then.

But Pilar had come to consider Cade her friend. If they made it home alive, she'd ask him to cook breakfast for her.

She caught herself again.

Would that be appropriate to ask Cade to make breakfast for her?

Hmmm. A question for another day.

Right now, Pilar was salivating over the breakfast in front of her, which she couldn't partake of. The only thing she'd had since she'd woken up was a cup of black coffee. She had given Mr. Belly her bacon biscuit.

Pilar poured coffee into two mugs she had brought with the cart.

Mr. Skinny watched her the entire time. "Mr. Braun-Dean wants lots of cream and sugar in his coffee. Miss Zuriel only wants water."

Pilar nodded. She knew all that. The instructions had been handwritten—scrawled on paper—and given to Cade the night before.

Pilar placed the creamer on the table next to a small bowl of sugar.

She stepped back as Braun-Dean rumbled toward the table. He was favoring one leg. Perhaps his weight was wearing down his knees, but who was Pilar to guess or judge?

She stacked the steel food cover domes on top of the cart and was about to push it away when a lilting voice called her name.

"Maria, good morning!" Zuriel appeared out of nowhere and waltzed toward the dining table. She was wearing a pretty floral blouse and a pair of form-hugging tight pants. She seemed rested.

"Good morning, ma'am." Pilar watched Zuriel as she approached the dining table.

"Come have breakfast, my lovely Zuriel."

"I'm on my way, sweet Felix!" She danced to an imaginary beat, and Braun-Dean clapped.

They seemed to be immersed in their own reality

inside this hut, although Pilar suspected that Braun-Dean was aware of things.

Zuriel sat down, but not on her own seat. She was on Braun-Dean's lap. She kissed his pock-marked forehead and then pouted her lips.

"When are they paying the ransom so that we can go sailing in your new yacht?" Her voice was sweeter than saccharine. "We've only been on it once."

"In time, my lovely Zuriel." Braun-Dean's hands were all over Zuriel. His cough seemed to have taken a break.

He stopped abruptly when his eyes looked up and saw that they were not alone.

"We'll leave you to your breakfast, sir." Mr. Skinny pointed to the cart as a silent order for Pilar to leave them alone.

"Come back when I call ya, Laphonso."

Well, Mr. Skinny had a big name.

Pilar pushed the cart slower than normal, wanting to catch everything the two of them said.

"I'm tired of being holed up here," Zuriel said. "How about we go on a boat tour? See the gators."

When Braun-Dean didn't say anything, Zuriel pressed. "Just around the huts. Not going far."

"If you behave, I might let you." And then the coughing started again.

CHAPTER TWELVE

Zuriel was quite the persuader. Pilar had no idea how she'd done it, but Braun-Dean approved a short tour of the cypress swamp shortly after breakfast.

Not wanting to go "alone," Zuriel asked Braun-Dean to let Pilar accompany her. He did better—or worse—than that. He ordered Laphonso—formerly known as Mr. Skinny—to arrange for the tour and escort them there and back.

An hour was all Braun-Dean had given them. But it would be enough for Pilar to scope out an escape route. It was all she thought about as they walked past the kitchen—which made Pilar think of Cade for a split second.

Behind the kitchen, a rickety dock stood over the light brown water, which was grayish and darker in shady areas. The 9:30 a.m. sun was maybe forty-plus degrees above the horizon, not quite overhead yet.

Above the sloped kitchen roof, it cast a shadow over the dock and a portion of the water.

If Pilar hadn't known that it was the day after the tropical storm had ended, she wouldn't have been able to tell it from the sunny morning and the slight breeze that washed over them, bringing to Pilar's nose an earthy smell of peat mixed with some sort of fishy smell that she couldn't describe.

The air was warm, not too humid yet. Pilar felt a bit warm in her chef's coat, but she didn't feel like taking it off.

The sun continued to rise in the sky, and now shone down on Zuriel. Her colored blonde hair shone with a halo around it. She had paired her tight and stretchy floral blouse with black capri pants and a pair of five-inch heels. She carried a rhinestone-encrusted crossbody purse.

She took selfies against a swamp backdrop, smiled for the camera, and seemed to have forgotten that they were all hostages without freedom.

She jiggled her fingers in the air, letting the sun play on the big rock on her right ring finger. Not on her left ring finger. Looked like she wasn't engaged to Braun-Dean yet.

"Five carats." Zuriel put her hand in front of Laphonso. "You like?"

Laphonso looked at the ring and then at her. "I like."

So there they were, standing at the dock. There was not a single boat in sight.

"How long do we wait?" Zuriel tapped the boards with her heels. "I don't know how long I can stand here in my Blahniks."

"Not long." Laphonso sidled up to Zuriel. He looked nervous, as though meeting the queen. He seemed aware that this wasn't a woman he could mess with. Still, he offered his arm. "You can lean on me."

"No. Don't touch me or Felix will be upset."

Laphonso stepped back. "Sorry, sorry."

"Thank you for taking us on the tour." Zuriel only looked at Laphonso when she talked.

"No problem."

How could they have a normal conversation like that?

Increasingly, Pilar wondered if Josephine Callahan was not only right about this entire hostage situation being staged, but that perhaps no one was meant to be hurt.

Yet that didn't explain why they'd murdered two chefs and beaten Alma to a pulp.

Something didn't add up. And there was no way for Pilar to find out.

She had to bide time and study the enemy—if she could figure out who they were in the first place. It was probably not wise to rule out Roxanne, who had hired her to spy on her estranged husband.

Right now her opposition would be anyone who held them prisoners and wouldn't let them go. Yeah, she'd start from there.

Pilar could hear several Floridian birds but was unable to identify them. If her brother were here, he'd be able to tell the difference between the calls of a heron versus an egret.

Across the water, an ibis landed on a muddy bank near a clump of cypress knees jutting out of the water.

Pilar watched it for a while, and then heard a hawk in the sky.

She looked up but didn't see anything in the sky but puffs of clouds. She turned toward the sun, closed her eyes, and let Vitamin D soak into her face.

She did that because facing the sun also meant she was facing the west windows of the kitchen. She squinted to see if she could spot Cade inside.

Nope.

Disappointed, she wondered what Cade was up to now, whether he was trying to find ways to get them out of this prison.

Pilar heard a boat in the distance. Everyone turned to look as a flat-bottomed jon boat came their way, slowing down as it approached the dock. The boat operator aligned the side of the sixteen-foot boat to the dock and cut off the engine.

He didn't get out of the boat. "You Laphonso?"

Laphonso nodded.

"I'm James. Got a call saying you want a little tour?" He looked like a teenager or at most a man in his early twenties. He was tanned from too much sun, and wore a padded baseball cap over his washed-out plaid shirt.

Laphonso nodded again.

"This is going to cost you extra, but you knew that." James chuckled. "We could've done the tour when I came earlier to deliver groceries. Might have saved me some gas."

"What time was that?" Pilar asked casually.

"Six o'clock. I guess it wouldn't have worked out."

Pilar made a mental note for tomorrow. If he and

Cade could somehow commandeer the boat when James made his next grocery run...

Laphonso led the two women down a couple of steps to a low wooden platform. It had some mud on it from the tropical storm, so Pilar slowed down her steps, not wanting to slip and fall into the gator-infested water.

Speaking of alligators, she glanced at the water. The tannish water was calm. She couldn't see through it.

Zuriel stepped into the boat, stilettos and all. She had great balance on her feet and didn't need Laphonso's help at all.

Laphonso climbed in right after Zuriel and sat down next to her on the center bench, as though to prevent anyone else from taking the seat.

He didn't bother to help Pilar at all. Instead, James did. Up close, he looked like he could be about her younger brother's age. As her shoes landed in the boat, Pilar noticed that the capacity plate said the boat was suitable for three people.

"There are four of us." Pilar pointed to the plate.

"Officially." James asked her to sit down.

Pilar wondered if James the boat operator had any idea what was going on at the swamp resort. Did he know that they were not tourists?

Right now he was the first person who had come from the "outside" world. Would he be willing to help them escape?

Yet she couldn't leave without Cade Sumter.

Pilar chose to sit on a portable seat nearest to James, who sat down at the transom edge, his long hairy legs jutting out of his cargo shorts. His shoes almost touched Pilar's legs a couple of feet away.

"What kind of engine is that?" Pilar pointed.

"This one? Six horse powered Mercury four-stroke outboard motor."

"Impressive. Who owns it?"

"Me."

"They must pay you well."

"Yep. But I have no girlfriend, no family. It's just me. I can afford this. Plus I need it every day to bring goods to the resort for guests like you."

Guests? You have no idea, James.

James navigated the boat away from the dock, cruising at no more than three miles per hour.

Pilar looked back toward the dock, hoping to spot Cade somewhere. He was nowhere to be found.

"Couldn't you just drive a truck with your supplies across the bridge?"

"Maybe, but my bait shop is on this side of the swamp. Easier for me to hop in my boat."

"Makes sense. Does your boat have a name?"

"Destiny. Didn't you see it earlier?"

"No, sorry. I wasn't paying attention." She had only paid attention to the capacity sticker.

"You want to drive it?" James pointed to the tiller. "I'll show you how to navigate."

"Okay. When we get a chance."

Pilar had driven a smaller jon boat than this but it had been a long time ago when she had more time to spend with Dad. He was an avid outdoorsman. He could kill a deer and skin it. As he got older, he didn't like sitting in the deer stand all night, so he decided to spend more time fishing.

Whenever Pilar came home from college, she'd go fishing with Dad in his cherished Roughneck 2070. The only person he'd allow to drive that boat was Pilar.

As soon as this mess was over, Pilar should check in on her parents, who lived in Boca Raton. They were only an hour north of Miami, but Pilar had been anywhere but home in the last six or seven months. On the other hand, Oscar still went fishing with Dad every Saturday whenever he didn't have to study for a test.

"What time is it?" Pilar asked James.

"Almost ten. You hungry?" James dug into his cargo pocket and out came a ziplock bag of crackers. The bag didn't look new.

Pilar didn't want to eat any of the crackers in it. She shook her head. "No, thanks. I'm not hungry. I had coffee this morning."

"It's just saltine crackers." James put the bag back in his zippered pocket.

"How big is this swamp?" Pilar asked. She had spoken loud enough above the somewhat less noisy four-stroke motor noise, but her proximity to James meant she didn't have to shout.

"About a hundred acres, give or take."

At the slow speed they were going, she'd be surprised if they'd cover a quarter of it in an hour.

"Will we see gators?" Zuriel yelled from the center bench.

"Maybe!" James yelled back. He looked out across the water. Pointed at something.

It looked like a log. Pilar stared to see if she could spot some eyes. No eyes.

"Just a log!" Laphonso complained. "The lady wants to see gators. Let's go there."

As though they could order an alligator parade.

"Do you live in this place, James?" Pilar asked casually.

"Not in the resort, no." James looked at her.

He had long eyelashes. He had an old scar on one cheek near his ear. Pilar debated whether to ask him about it. If he were self-conscious about it, the small talk could backfire and he might close up. Otherwise, he would just answer it and move on.

Pilar decided not to risk it.

"But you deliver fresh groceries every morning," Pilar said instead.

"I guess some of it is fresh, whatever Skip brings me." He shrugged. "The rest are in cans."

"So Skip goes shopping for you?"

James chuckled. "He gets to town, yeah. You need anything from town you can't get at the resort?"

Freedom.

"Different kinds of cheese, maybe?" Pilar asked. She was going somewhere with it, but only if James cooperated.

"I like cheese too. What kind of cheese do you have in mind?"

"Oh, any kind. Gourmet." Pilar reminded herself to be careful with her words. She was supposed to be a hotel housekeeper who spoke poor English. Here she was, about to spill the beans on various cheeses.

"Gourmet. You mean like pepper jack?"

That was hardly gourmet to Pilar, but her point was about to be lost. "Does Skip get you pepper jack cheese?"

"I can ask next time. Which cabin are you staying in? Need to deliver the cheese somewhere."

Need to what?

This young man clearly had no idea what was happening at the resort.

"Look! Look!" Zuriel nearly stood up. She was almost leaning to one side of the boat. "Gators!"

"Ma'am, you need to sit down!" James ordered her as the boat rocked a bit.

Pilar grasped the side of the boat. She looked where Zuriel was pointing but saw nothing except for thick bushes and cypress trees with their network of knees jutting out of the water.

Laphonso pulled Zuriel back down to her seat.

"We'll see more in a minute." James steered the boat.

They passed by an anhinga drying itself on a cypress knee, but he dove into the water before the boat could reach it.

On the other side of several cypress trees, the trees cleared a bit and there was a bank that led to a winding footpath disappearing into the forest.

There, at the edge of the water, several alligators were sunning themselves.

They were maybe thirty feet away.

"Get closer!" Zuriel said.

James made a face and ignored her.

"Would they be spooked if we got closer?" Pilar asked.

James didn't answer. "I think we'll just watch them from here."

"Where does that lead to?" Pilar pointed to the

gators, but really she was pointing to the banks and path behind them.

"Half a mile up that path, you will get to Doc Sam's cabin." He turned to Pilar, as if the information might help her later. "He's the only doctor around here. He's retired, but he still practices when we need help."

Pilar made a mental note about the escape route.

"Back when Doc Sam's wife was alive, he cut a path from his house to the bait shop where I work. She used to come often on her 1953 Indian Chief motorcycle, painted a blazing red and yellow, her favorite colors. The bait shop was the only place she could go shopping, trading pelt and smoked meat for quilting fabric and candy for her husband."

Pilar listened.

"She died two years ago, and nature has taken back most of that path, except for a small bicycle path. That's what Doc Sam rides now because it doesn't need gas, you know. Walk along that path and you can get from the cabin to the bait shop. Walk off the path, and you might disturb snakes and their nests."

"Have you ever outrun snakes?" Pilar made it light to keep him talking.

James laughed. "Maybe at night. It's October and it's cold at night. They sleep, you know. Those cold-blooded reptiles."

"So you think you can outrun snakes at night?" Pilar had never seen anyone doing it.

"Never tried."

"I'm thinking that they just need to strike you as you run by them."

"But if I'm five feet or more away from them, I

think I can do it." James sounded confident. "Remember that I have legs and I can sprint. Snakes can only crawl on their bellies, like the Good Lord said."

Pilar would like to dive into the Bible about how God had cursed the serpent, but was now the time? Then again, perhaps if she talked to James about things that didn't seem threatening to Laphonso, she could gain James's trust.

"You mean Genesis 3:14?" Pilar recited the verse.

So the Lord God said to the serpent:
"Because you have done this,
You are cursed more than all cattle,
And more than every beast of the field;
On your belly you shall go,
And you shall eat dust
All the days of your life."

"You sound like Doc Sam," James said. "He's tried to talk to me about the Bible."

A connection.

Pilar was glad she didn't brush off the topic.

"Now that he's widowed, does he live alone or does he have kids?" she asked.

"Their only daughter died of meningitis many years ago." James turned pensive. "He's eighty-four, and wants to die here and be buried next to his wife in his backyard."

"Eighty-four years old and living alone in the woods? He must be a tough guy."

"He is."

Interesting. "Does he get his groceries at the bait shop?"

"Once a week. We chat and he tells me not to smoke too much, and then he goes home."

"How does he pay for groceries?"

"With medical services. Bartering is a win-win."

"For sure." Pilar felt a pinch on her neck and she reached up. She heard buzzing noises near her ears and suspected that a mosquito had bitten her.

She swiped away the sound, but didn't catch the mosquito.

Pilar tried to remember that bank and path they had just passed by. Unfortunately, after they boated away, the banks all looked the same. Alligators everywhere. How could she return to this spot where she could run to Doc Sam's house to get help?

Nearby, a couple of dragonflies with their semitransparent wings darted here and there by the boat. Even as Pilar enjoyed the visual feast, she still smelled the swamp.

"The swamp smell is strong," she said.

"You get used to it." James navigated the boat to who knew where.

When Pilar looked back, she could see the huts on stilts scattered throughout the resort.

"What is this place called?" Pilar asked.

"You're vacationing here and you don't know?" James laughed.

"That's enough," Laphonso said.

Pilar turned toward him. That was when she saw that Zuriel's hands were shaking.

"Are you okay?" Pilar adjusted her seat so that she faced Zuriel and Laphonso.

"Can we go back now?" Zuriel tapped her foot on the aluminum bottom of the boat. She rubbed her arms repeatedly. She looked a bit jittery.

"What's going on?" James asked.

"She needs her fix every six hours." Laphonso didn't bother to hide it. "Mr. Braun-Dean is the keeper of her pill bottle."

"Where's my pill at?" Zuriel grabbed Laphonso's arm. "I just need one!"

"You'll need more than one pill." Laphonso laughed. "You'll need a handful just to stay normal, but you knew that."

"When was the last time you took it?" Pilar tried to move toward her.

"You stay put." Laphonso pointed a handgun at her with his free arm.

God forbid that this gunman was ambidextrous.

"Whoa." One hand on the tiller, the other hand up, palm facing out, James tried to calm him down while still driving the boat. "No need for that, right, Laphonso?"

"Felix. I need to go back to Felix. I think he gave me fake pills before we left the resort." Zuriel's voice was more shrill as her eyes darted here and there. She grabbed Laphonso's arm a lot. "I need to go see Felix now."

Laphonso pushed her back. "Stop scratching me."

Pilar dared not say anything. She glanced at James. Lifted her eyebrows as if to say, "He just pushed a woman. Whatcha going to do about that?"

"Hey, let's calm down," James said. "Laphonso, you tell me. Turn back now?"

Zuriel clawed at Laphonso, seemingly unafraid

that he was brandishing a weapon, which was no doubt loaded.

Laphonso was about to push her back one more time, when a loud explosion in the distance froze him with his hand in the air.

"What was that?" James asked.

Pilar wanted to know too. The explosion seemed to have come from the east, where the huts were—

Cade!

Lord Jesus, please let Cade be safe and sound.

All around them, wings flapped as birds flew away. Water splashed as alligators—probably—took cover underwater.

"Gators are sensitive to loud noises," James explained, as though he was still conducting a tour. "They're going to hide in the water until the coast is clear."

Loud helicopter noises covered the swamp, startling Pilar.

Choppers? Are we being rescued?

Pilar's heart skipped a beat. She was about to thank God when Laphonso spoke.

"They're early." His eyes widened.

Pilar heard it loudly and clearly. "Who?"

"Take us back to the dock now." Laphonso pointed his handgun directly at James. "Where we came from. Now!"

"Okay, but don't point that thing at me."

Pilar heard James's voice behind him. She stared directly at Laphonso, wondering what was going on as a second explosion swayed the boat.

Without warning, James jerked the boat forward, throwing Laphonso off balance. As he fell back, armed hand rising in the air, Pilar saw her opportunity.

With one MMA kick, she knocked the weapon out of Laphonso's hand. He held his wrist, falling back.

"You broke my wrist!" He charged toward her, screaming a bunch of expletives that Pilar didn't want to hear. Pilar was ready for the fight, but James threw his whole body in front of her.

James?

Who is driving the boat then?

Pilar's eyes snapped toward the unmanned tiller. She lunged toward it, narrowly avoiding the two entangled men fighting in the rocking boat.

She took control of the boat just when she heard a giant splash. She turned to look, and saw James catching his breath on the floor of the jon boat, a bloody paddle in one hand.

Laphonso was nowhere to be found. Where did he go?

Above the motor and a third explosion, Pilar heard a shrill but trembling voice. It cut through the morning like a chainsaw.

"Where's my pill at?" Then she threw up over the side of the boat.

CHAPTER THIRTEEN

Pilar carefully navigated the boat away from the edges of the swamp where she spotted endangered pitcher plants. Those looked like mature hooded pitchers that were about two feet tall, nestling near cypress knees in the acidic soil.

Oscar, Pilar's brother who was majoring in plant biology in college, knew all about pitcher plants—yellow, purple, and all kinds. In fact, he had a few pitcher plants growing in containers outside their house in Miami.

From Oscar, Pilar had learned all about conservation of these pitcher plants. No way was she going to ram her boat into them, if at all possible.

As soon as they cleared cypress knees on both sides of the channel, she could see the resort straight ahead, maybe two hundred feet away.

Half the huts were burning.

At this juncture, she couldn't begin to imagine what happened there, why it looked like that, and who did what. In fact, the fundamental question hadn't yet been answered: Who were the hostages and who were the actual hostage takers?

However, none of that mattered if she couldn't get Cade out alive.

Pilar gunned the throttle. The boat was going at its top speed of eight miles per hour due to the swamp conditions. Not enough, but what to do?

"Why are you going back to the resort?" James climbed over the cross bench seats toward Pilar. "It's burning!"

"My friend is still—"

"No! We're not going back there!" He tried to take over the tiller, but Pilar wouldn't let him.

It was then that Pilar realized she was not physically stronger than James, but he was half-hearted in his attempt to take back his boat.

"Don't make us go back there!" James pleaded.

"No worries. I'm going to drop you off." Pilar remembered where that path was that James had shown them earlier.

"What?" James yelled.

"Zuriel, tell James who we are," Pilar said.

"Us? We?" Zuriel seemed to be out of it.

James stepped closer to Pilar. If he wanted, he could potentially wrestle Pilar. However, he looked like a lighter bantamweight, and Pilar was a trained MMA featherweight who could take him down if she put all her muscles to it.

"James, we're hostages," Pilar explained while pushing him back. "We're not tourists on vacation. Six women plus one man are held hostage in that resort you bring groceries to every morning. That man is my friend. I can't leave him behind."

"If I go back there with you, they will ask where Laphonso is," James said.

"I've been meaning to ask you where he went." Pilar hoped he heard her over the motor noise.

Zuriel pointed to the water outside the boat.

Oh.

Pilar could think of a few scenarios that could incriminate James. For example, he could have fought Laphonso. In self defense, he could have thrown him overboard.

However, Pilar hadn't seen it with her own eyes. She had been busy steering the boat. So she couldn't assume.

Truly, Zuriel and James were the only eyewitnesses, weren't they?

"We fought. He was going to kill me. He had a second handgun," James said.

"I saw it. Very dangerous." Zuriel squirmed and didn't sit still, but she still tried to participate in the conversation. Here she was defending James. What on earth?

Had Zuriel known James prior to today?

"We struggled, and I fell back into the boat. Hit my head on the bench," James continued. "I was on the bottom of the boat when he lost his balance and fell into the water all by himself."

"Right." Zuriel nodded. "The boat was rocking. That's why I threw up. I felt nauseous."

"Was that in your mind or was it for real?" Pilar wanted to ask.

"It's the way you drove my boat," James said. "Amateur!"

"What!" Pilar tried to keep her cool. "Who stepped away from the tiller? You. Is this a self-driving boat? No. We would've crashed if I hadn't taken over the boat. I didn't even know Laphonso was no longer in the boat until I did a headcount."

"It's too late to go back to get Laphonso," James said. "It would take too much time to find him in the water. With ten- or twenty-foot gators all over this swamp, it would take time that we don't have."

"I can't believe we're just going to leave him—"

Another explosion in the distance rocked the boat, sending ripples all around the tannic brown swamp water.

As it subsided, Pilar heard a shrill voice, cutting though the morning like a chainsaw.

"Where's my pill at?" Zuriel whimpered. "Is this boat rocking too much?"

And she threw up again overboard. She sat down on the boat in between the benches, moaning. "I feel sick."

Zuriel needed more help than Pilar could give her.

"James, didn't you say that there's a doctor nearby?" Pilar asked. A doctor would be the best bet for Zuriel. No way was Pilar going to send her back to Braun-Dean.

"Sure did. Doc Sam is his name." James nodded. "He can even deliver babies, although the last time he did that was some thirty years ago when he lived in the city. Hardly anyone lives in this area. We only have hunters and day visitors."

Pilar thought that even though Doc Sam was a rural doctor, his cabinet might have some sort of medicine that could help Zuriel until she could get to a hospital in the nearest city, wherever that was.

"A doctor?" Zuriel's fingers clawed her arms. Her feet tapped the bottom of the boat. "A doctor can give me something."

"Is she an addict?" James's eyebrows rose. Clearly he was talking to Pilar.

Pilar didn't reply. She didn't want Zuriel to hear them talk about her in front of her.

"Oxycodone?"

"I'd rather not say. Patient privacy, you know." Pilar supposed that if Zuriel was having withdrawal at this time and Laphonso had been right about the six-hour interval, then Zuriel last took her pills at around four o'clock in the morning—four hours before Pilar showed up at her hut with breakfast.

Pilar wasn't sure what to make of it. "Were you awake at four in the morning?"

Zuriel cast a shadowy look at her. "Whatcha asking?"

"Did you try to find the pill bottle at four in the morning?" Pilar wanted to find out if Zuriel had been planning an escape by way of the swamp tour, taking her pills with her.

Zuriel raised her voice and got up jerkily from the bench. "Felix has my pills. I have to go to Felix—"

"Sit down!" James ordered her. "Unless you want to be like Laphonso."

Zuriel sat down, but she didn't look good. Her arms were covered with goosebumps. Her eyes were wide and she looked like she was going to claw at

James the same way she had clawed at Laphonso earlier.

"Take me to the doctor or take me to Felix." Zuriel's twitching hands grabbed James's arms. "Please, I beg you. I can give you anything you want."

Pilar didn't wait for James to decide. She steered the boat toward the clearing at the bank of the river where the alligators had been sunning themselves before the explosions scattered them into the bushes and underwater.

"Anything?" James asked.

Zuriel lifted her shaky hand in the air. "You want this ring? Three hundred thousand dollars. Take me to the doctor, and it's yours."

Firstly, it wasn't lost on Pilar that Zuriel had chosen a doctor over the former senator. The clouds might have parted for the poor woman. Pilar wondered about Zuriel's faith, but until she was clean, it was probably not a good time to talk to her about her soul.

Secondly, Zuriel was trying to barter with James. That told Pilar post-rehab, Zuriel's brain might be returning to normal. This mini relapse that was making her jittery could be short-lived, prayerfully. Maybe with one more round of rehab she'd get over this painkiller addiction altogether.

"Three hundred thousand dollars?" James's eyes were salivating at the hunk of rock on Zuriel's finger. "Drop us off. I'll take her to Doc Sam."

"I'll drop y'all off," Pilar said. "You take her to Doc Sam. She pays you three hundred thousand dollars."

Pilar said the dollar amount with emphasis to drive home the point.

"I'd have to work ten years or more to earn that much." James rubbed his hands together.

"I take that as a yes." Pilar could barely hear herself as the wind blew through her hair. She seemed to have lost her hair tie that had kept her mid-length hair in a bun on top of her head since Miami. Now it was gone, and her hair whipped in the wind.

They were close enough to the muddy bank for her to decelerate the boat. It went from eight miles an hour down to almost zero when they hit the bank. The bow slid up the mud and stopped.

Zuriel took off the diamond ring and handed it to James.

James rubbed it on his shirt. Then tried to put it on. It fit his pinky. "I can buy a thousand jon boats with this ring."

Pilar didn't have the heart to tell him that if this boat was three thousand dollars per, he could only purchase a hundred boats, not a thousand.

"For that amount of payment, can you please stay with Zuriel at the doctor until I come to get her, okay?" Pilar asked as James got ready to get out of the boat.

James barely nodded. Pilar feared that he would drop Zuriel and run off.

"Tell me again where Doc Sam is." Pilar kept the boat motor idling. There was no need to cut off the engine altogether.

James pointed. "Half a mile straight up that path. You can't miss it. It's the only house for miles around —except for the bait shop."

"Do you have a cell phone I can use?" Pilar asked on the off chance that James might throw in a phone for the fee he was getting.

"Cell phones don't work inside the resort." James made a face. "Come to think of it, I always wondered why. Now I know that it's not an ordinary resort."

"It's a prison."

"But Ted called me this morning at the bait shop, so someone has a special phone that could call outside."

"So where did you leave your phone?" Pilar asked, realizing that the explosions had stopped.

"I don't own one. I work at the bait shop and use their phone for free."

"Does Doc Sam have a phone?"

"He's the last person to have one. Said it's bad for your brain or something. He won't hold a cell phone to his ear. He has an old ham radio that stopped working forty years ago."

"What kind of a doctor is he?" Pilar glanced at the fidgety Zuriel.

"A medical one. You think he's a vet?" James laughed and rubbed his new ring.

"I mean... Could he treat Zuriel in her condition?"

James tilted his head. "Doc Sam can treat anything."

A vote of confidence.

Pilar wasn't sure at all whether she should leave Zuriel with a total stranger such as James—who would then take her to another stranger, Doc Sam—but Zuriel certainly couldn't return to the resort with her. Zuriel would slow her down and impede her rescue effort.

"James, a word of advice for you." Pilar hoped she wasn't making this up. "You respect Ted?"

"Oh yes. He's the goat. Meanest, toughest guy I know." He sounded like he looked up to him.

"You know who Ted's boss is?" Pilar asked.

James shook his head.

"Former Senator Braun-Dean." Pilar wasn't a hundred percent sure, but the data pointed to that, especially what Zuriel had casually said this morning before breakfast at the hut.

When are they paying the ransom so that we can go sailing on your new yacht?

Josephine Callahan might be right after all. Braun-Dean might have staged his own captivity in order to extract money from someone.

Why? Was Braun-Dean cash poor?

"This is Braun-Dean's girlfriend." This much was true.

"Oh." James's jaw dropped. He wiped his palm on his shirt. Extended a hand. "Ma'am, nice to meet you."

Zuriel did not shake his hand.

"If you try as much as touch me, my Felix will quarter you and feed you to the rats—after I shoot you fifty times." Zuriel was fidgeting but her voice was harsh.

What on earth did she mean? Even Pilar got worried. Was she just trash talking or was she serious? She sounded violent.

James's jaw dropped.

Yeah, Pilar wondered too. Here was Zuriel,

wearing red stilettos to a swamp boat tour, threatening a lightweight tour guide.

"You take good care of the boss's girlfriend and you might be rewarded even more," Pilar said. "Buy all the boats you want."

James nodded. "I might even get that new trailer that I've been saving up for."

"But first, take her to Doc Sam. Tell him she has a relapse and needs help." Pilar prayed that James would really do so. "When you get to the bait shop, please call 911. Tell them there are hostages in the resort."

"And get the resort swatted?" He seemed amused.

Pilar wasn't.

It wasn't time for her to tell James who she really was or to disclose her associates. It was enough for her to ask James to call the police, and if that didn't tell James that she was serious, then none of them might ever get out of the swamp alive.

"Got a pen?" Pilar asked.

"No, sorry."

"I need to write a number down for you to call." Pilar looked around.

"Say the number," Zuriel said. "I'll remember it for you."

Pilar recalled Tanaka saying something about Zuriel having a good memory.

"You'll memorize it?" Pilar asked.

Zuriel nodded. Her hands were shaking, but maybe her brain was still working.

Pilar rattled off the ten-digit number. "Either one of you can call this number."

There was a knowing look on Zuriel's face when Pilar gave her the number.

How come?

Pilar couldn't disclose that the number goes to FBI Special Agent Ruby Tanaka's cell phone. This was also not the time to tell anyone that Tanaka had deputized her as a Task Force Member in her operation which overlapped Pilar's work for Roxanne.

"Please call 911 and that number as soon as you get to a working phone," Pilar repeated.

"I will."

It would seem that James was a good kid—at least for now.

Sometimes in life, Pilar had to learn to trust strangers. Usually a good reader of people, Pilar hadn't made a mistake by misjudging people yet.

A Gen Z who seemed to be working hard for the money, James was technically a businessman. In this transaction, a half-mile walk would yield him three hundred thousand dollars. He would come out a winner.

Still, Pilar hesitated. Maybe she should take Zuriel with her. But it was too late to be indecisive. Zuriel had already paid James to do a task for her.

"Hurry! Let's go!" Zuriel seemed determined to get off the boat.

"Maybe this is a bad idea..." Pilar started to say.

Zuriel stepped forward toward Pilar, her cross-body purse in front of her. She opened it slightly so that only Pilar could see.

And sure enough, Pilar saw it as Zuriel palmed the polymer frame before she slid the five-inch long .380 Ruger LCP pocket pistol back into her purse.

"Don't worry about me, sister." Zuriel smiled.

It still didn't help.

Pilar's older-sister vibes emerged. She second-guessed her decision to let Zuriel go with a total stranger. "How about we all stay in the boat? Maybe I made a mistake to let you go."

"No mistake." Zuriel was firm. Her face was sweating and her hands shook. "I need my pills—or something to help me endure this until I go back to rehab. As soon as I get to a working phone, I will call 911 and the number you gave me."

James helped Zuriel off the boat and told her to stand where it was dry. Then he stepped over the cross benches toward Pilar at the stern, being careful not to rock the boat.

"Sometimes you have to trust strangers," James said. "If you need to go rescue your friend, you better go now."

He leapt over the side of the boat. "I'll give you a push."

Pilar nodded.

She put the motor in reverse, and the boat slid free of the soggy mud and peat underneath the hull. James hardly had to push the boat out to water.

James stood rooted at the bank, as if realizing that his boat had left without him.

"I'll bring *Destiny* back," Pilar shouted over the motor.

"I don't care!"

Pilar pointed behind him. Zuriel had started walking up the path alone. James turned and chased after her.

Pilar prayed for God to keep them safe.

Already, she had to thank God for the explosions. Sensitive to loud noises, the alligators had submerged, allowing James and Zuriel to climb out of the boat onto the bank safely.

Now she prayed that God would give Cade and her safety and mercy. Once she picked him up, they would leave the resort. The boat only seated three people officially, but James put four people aboard without sinking the boat.

What about the other five women hostages? She knew where their hut was, but there was not enough room in the boat.

Somewhere in Pilar's heart, she knew that she couldn't morally or consciously leave five people behind. If something should happen to them, she'd feel terribly guilty.

Well, one way she could rescue them was to get help ASAP. She had reliable transportation—the boat —that could get her out of this ten-acre swamp and toward civilization.

Right now, she had to find Cade. They could figure it out later. Two brains were better than one.

Should she try to find other means of transportation out of the resort? Some van that could seat seven hostages? If so, she'd have to get to the front gate where the vehicles were parked. Then she'd have to get them out of the compound.

It seemed like an impossible task.

Well, Luke 1:37 reminded Pilar that her God specialized in the impossible.

For with God nothing will be impossible.

At the same time, Pilar also knew that the Bible did not contradict itself. It was true that God could do the impossible, but it was also true that God called Christians to make wise decisions. Matthew 10:16 was Grandma's favorite verse.

> *Behold, I send you out as sheep in the midst of wolves. Therefore be wise as serpents and harmless as doves.*

Pilar knew that she had to choose one of two options: leave with Cade to safety first and then get help to rescue the other hostages, or round up all the hostages and take them to freedom together.

Pilar knew herself, that she had a tendency to overthink a situation, only to end up doing something else later. For example, she had thought about how to use steak knives to defend herself, but Cade had reminded her that those captors had firearms instead. Unless she could get them in a close-contact combat, a thrown knife could only go so far.

Cade knew to meet her at the kitchen, but Pilar had lost time dropping off Zuriel and James. Then again, getting them off the boat meant that she could focus on her work without them tagging along. That was the least she could do for James, who had told her the route out of this swamp.

The explosions had subsided, which bothered Pilar. Well, if they continued, it could mean more danger for Cade. If it stopped, at least that was one less way for Cade to be injured.

Why had the explosions happened in the first place?

So many questions, so few answers.

CHAPTER FOURTEEN

The kitchen door flung open and Max staggered into the kitchen, one shoulder bloody. From his hiding spot behind a steel counter, Cade could see Max sway and he could hear the intermittent blasts of firebombs that had peppered the resort.

At least now the door was unlocked and he could escape.

In the momentary silence, Cade heard boots on the boardwalk, men shouting, and small firearms discharging.

The door was still open.

It was too late for Cade to close the door. A big person whose face was indiscernible raised what looked like a shotgun and pointed it in Max's direction.

"Get down!" Cade yelled instinctively, but Max didn't hear him.

If Cade were to reach out to get him, he'd put

himself in the line of fire, endangering himself. Then again, if Max died, he wouldn't be able to see his two-year-old daughter, Anastasia.

Cade barely made it to Max when a shot rang out, and the gunman at the door collapsed onto the sidewalk.

Interesting.

Cade wondered if the resort had been invaded by a second party. Who might they be?

Boots entered the kitchen.

"Max!" Ted yelled.

"He's been shot!" Cade said to Ted.

"Where's Skeeter at?" Ted asked.

Skeeter was in the crowd, and he came forward. Apparently he was their medical guy, and he went to work on Max right away. Cut away the jacket near his shoulder where blood was still soaking through.

Cade saw red blood pulsing out of Max's shoulder near his collar bone. The bullet must've nicked an artery. Max's face was turning ashen and his lips were bluish.

"Need some cloths, towels, something!" Skeeter said.

Cade was still in his chef coat. In his front pocket was a slightly used kitchen towel. It was highly absorbent. He handed that to Skeeter. "I have some clean towels in the pantry."

"Go get them." Skeeter wadded up the kitchen towel and jammed it into Max's collarbone area.

Cade rushed to the pantry and returned with a stack of towels.

"What's going on?" Ted squatted down on one knee.

"Looks like a bullet shattered his collarbone and cut his subclavian artery." Skeeter's hand still pressed down on the wad of towels, now soaked with Max's blood. "We need to get him to the hospital or he'll die."

"I don't know when we can get out of here. How much time does he have?"

"He's already passed out. I'd say he might have lost at least twenty percent of his blood already." Skeeter pointed to Max's gray face. "He's in hypovolemic shock right now."

"Meaning?"

"Meaning he doesn't have enough blood or oxygen. He needs surgery and a blood transfusion. ASAP."

Poor Max.

Cade prayed for Max. He had no idea whether Max believed in Jesus or not. If he never regained consciousness and passed on from this life right there and then, where would he go?

If Max had believed in Jesus Christ to save his soul, then he'd have salvation assurance and an eternal abode in heaven with God.

If Max had never accepted Jesus as his Lord and Savior, then after death came an eternal separation from God, the Creator of the universe.

The people Max would leave behind on earth included his little daughter.

Cade prayed for Max to recover from his gunshot wound. If he woke up, he might have a second chance to believe in Jesus.

Cade felt sorry that he hadn't taken the only

opportunity he had back at the Callahan Hotel to tell Max about Jesus.

A barrage of gunfire outside caught Cade's—and everyone's—attention. They were closing in.

"Why didn't they just firebomb this kitchen too?" someone asked. "It's not like they're not trying to destroy all the huts."

"What are they up to?" another person asked.

They?

"You mean it's not your people doing it?" Cade asked Ted.

Ted ignored him.

"Not us," someone else replied.

"And here I thought y'all locked me in the kitchen while you had some fancy fireworks out there." Even though Cade tried to portray a sense of humor, his heart was heavy.

From the last words by Ted's people, Cade gathered that another group was blowing up the huts. Pilar could be in one of those huts.

Cade had last seen Pilar this morning when she pushed the food tray cart out of the kitchen. He thought they'd see each other again when they sent her back to help him prepare lunch.

It would break his heart into a million pieces if that had been the last time he'd seen Pilar alive.

Cade quickly prayed for Pilar's safety. But he had to know.

He'd been locked up in the kitchen the entire time that he'd counted about half a dozen explosions, big and small, in seemingly rapid successions.

"So what happened to all the other hostages?" Cade asked.

"You're asking about Maria."

Cade played it down. "Hate to lose good kitchen help."

"Is she the one who went on the swamp tour with Mr. Braun-Dean's girl?" someone offered. "I saw Laphonso escort them to the dock. James came back for them."

The dock? Which dock? James usually docked behind the kitchen when he delivered groceries. If so, would Pilar return to the same dock? After all, they had a pact to rendezvous in the kitchen. Cade's hope rose.

"What tour?" Another person slapped the man's back. "You're fibbing."

"Just telling you what I saw, is all." The first person smacked his lips. He was chewing tobacco.

"Let's secure this kitchen." Ted bit off the words and started looking around. "Monty, is there a way out of here besides the front door?"

"Yes, sir." Cade was at attention. "The back door leads to the loading dock, where James brings in the grocery carts every morning."

Ted nodded. "You didn't try to escape?"

"It's locked from the outside. Max opens it whenever James shows up." Cade was telling the truth. He knew that Ted would verify it, so it was pointless to lie.

Ted checked Max's jacket and jean pockets and found the key. He looked around the room.

Cade counted three other men besides himself, Ted, Skeeter, and Max on the floor. He couldn't remember if all those men had been around since

Miami or if they had just joined the captors at the swamp.

"I need a volunteer to go outside and unlock the back door so that we can get out of here." Ted lifted the key in the air. "We padlocked it last night from the outside."

"What's the reward?" one of the men asked.

"You get to live," Ted said.

"I'll go," Cade volunteered. "I know where the door is."

"You'll run away." Ted chuckled.

There was some truth to that. If Cade could break free, he'd run toward the hut where Pilar might be to rescue her.

"From what I understand, those people who are blowing up the resort are your enemies." Cade pointed to Ted. "Since you're holed up in here with me, that tells me your enemies have won."

"What are you saying?" Someone pointed a shotgun at Cade.

Cade tried not to look afraid. "I'm saying that, considering that you're professionals, there's a chance you might survive this. If I run away from you, you might return later on to hunt me down. I don't want that. I am a man of peace and want to live my life in peace. So I would ensure my own survival if I help you to escape."

Cade prayed that Ted would see the logic in his commitment.

"I only ask that once we get out there, you let me go, because I'm only a cook. I'm not a billionaire like the former senator or his estranged wife. I give you no benefit or profit. But if I help you escape and you let me go, we're even. We won't see each again for the rest of our lives—unless you need my help later on. I can make gator burgers, for example. It's a useful skill."

Ted stared at him like he had horns on his head. "Are you for real?"

Cade didn't reply.

Ted handed the key to one of his men. "Butch, you take Cade out there."

Butch nodded, slyness in his eyes.

And Cade could guess what the secret message was. As soon as Cade opened the door to the dock, Butch might kill him. Which reminded Cade that he had nothing to offer these captors—who were now captives themselves.

Either way, Cade wasn't about to stick around to find out.

Butch was a heavyset man with a tight shirt and baggy pants. His belly jiggled when he walked. Cade remembered him as the same guard who had escorted Pilar out of the kitchen this morning.

A deafening explosion rocked the kitchen.

"Now!" Ted yelled.

One man opened the front door carefully. Then he hurried Butch and Cade out of the door, slamming it shut behind them.

Cade shimmied along the side of the building. Butch was next to him.

The air was thick with black smoke, but activities seemed to be far away. Cade had no idea what was happening at the resort, but since the intervals of the explosions had grown longer, he ventured to guess that the enemies had gotten what they were here for.

At the back of the kitchen, Cade pointed to the door, expecting Butch to go first since he had the key.

That was when Cade heard a distinct sound of a boat motor. He looked in the direction of the noise and saw a jon boat coming his way. A person with long hair blowing in the wind was at the tiller.

He could spot her a mile away, as he had done so in Dubai the year before.

Pilar!

She's alive!

Cade was maybe ten feet from the edge of the top deck. There were just a few steps down to the lower deck, and maybe another ten feet to the end of the deck, where Pilar's boat could dock.

As Butch fumbled around in his pocket for the key to the giant padlock on the door so that they could free the people inside the kitchen, Cade tried to make a dash for it—

Ooomph!

Something strong caught his ankles, and he fell chest down on the boardwalk. His chin and elbows hit the wood. He kicked, but a heavy object had pinned down his legs. When he heard grunts, he guessed right away that Butch had caught him.

With all his might, he twisted his feet until Butch's big tree-trunk arms loosened up a bit. Then he kicked free and kept kicking until Butch lost his grip.

Cade sprung up to his feet and noticed that Butch's handgun was at least five feet away from him. With one quick move, Cade dove for the gun, but the three-hundred-pound Butch reached him first.

Immediately a sharp pain shot through his left

thigh. He went down as he spotted the glint of a blade in the sunlight, coming down hard on him.

Slash! Slash!

Cade writhed and rolled to avoid the knives, but the sun was in his eyes, and he was temporarily blinded and couldn't see where Butch was coming from. Butch was silent this entire time, like he didn't need to speak or something.

A searing pain in his right calf told Cade that Butch had slashed at him again. Somehow he had to get up on his feet, or he'd be mincemeat on the wooden deck. He squinted, put his arm over his eyes, and finally saw Butch with a halo around him as he stood between Cade and the morning sun.

For the first time he saw the two four-inch switchblades that Butch gripped in his hands. He was moving them back and forth like a figure eight, as if he could scare Cade.

"Wow, Butch. You sumo wrestler, you."

"Not sumo." *Slash! Slash!* "I'm your worst ninja nightmare!"

What kind of people had Ted hired?

As soon as Butch moved slightly to the left or right, the sun glare blinded Cade again. His legs were in pain, his eyes couldn't see, but he refused to wait for death.

Cade backed up some more, and then realized he was at the edge of the deck. One more shuffle on his bottom and he'd be at the edge of it. The stairs were over there somewhere.

Lord, help me.

Cade didn't have the upper hand. Something had to give—

Thwack! Thwack! Thwack!

Butch's eyes rolled back, his knees wobbled, and he fell forward like a giant Matryoshka doll. The switchblades popped out of his hands.

Cade shuffled out of the way quickly before he could get smashed by Butch's sumo body. He squinted, a hand over his forehead to provide shade from the sun so he could at least see who had helped him.

He saw an aluminum boat paddle, the shaft slightly bent. Then he saw the person wielding it.

"Your legs are bleeding. Can you walk?" she said.

Sweetest voice he ever heard.

CHAPTER FIFTEEN

At top speed, the jon boat skated over the swamp, leaving the resort behind. No more explosions ensued, which made Pilar worry about alligators returning to the bank at which she planned to dock.

She turned to check on her only passenger in the boat. Sitting on the closest thwart bench seat to her, Cade was ripping the sleeves off his chef coat to tie around his thigh and calf to stem the bleeding.

"Sorry I don't have a belt." Pilar's housekeeping uniform had an elastic waist.

"A belt? No need. I'm not making a tourniquet," Cade shouted above the engine noise. "I just need to stop the bleeding until I can get to a doctor."

"How bad are your cuts?"

"I'm not sure, but it hurts. He slashed me twice—in my thigh and calf." Cade winced. "Could've been worse."

"Can you walk after we get off this boat?"

"I'm going to have to." Cade leaned back and closed his eyes. His fingers and palms were covered with blood.

Pilar turned away to see if anyone else was chasing after them. Apparently nobody did. No one cared? She thanked God for that reprieve.

When they were far enough away, Pilar debated whether to ask Cade if it hurt. Of course it did. Duh. However, if he had to answer her, it might play a psychological mind trick on him to make him toughen up a bit. It worked for her brother, Oscar, even though he was fifteen years younger than Cade.

Let's try.

"Does it hurt?" Pilar asked above the wind.

"It might hurt more later. I think I'm okay for now." He scooted closer to Pilar and sat down on the same portable bench that James had set up earlier. Now they were a few feet away from each other and could talk over the wind.

"You need to see a doctor," Pilar said. "I can't carry you if you pass out."

Cade nodded. "I think I have a few hours."

"The sooner we get you fixed up, the better." Pilar tried not to show her worry. "We're going to Doc Sam's cabin, where Zuriel should be getting treated for her relapse if she hasn't been already."

"Doc who?"

"He's a rural doctor who lives half a mile from the swamp."

"You know him?"

"Never met him. James said he's a retired physician."

"Who lives in the woods, off the grid?" Cade's eyes widened.

"Feel free to ask for his credentials when we get there." Pilar laughed.

"I can't believe you just trusted anyone. Who is this James dude?"

Was he concerned about her safety or was he jealous?

"James owns this boat and let me use it," Pilar said. "Although I must add that Zuriel paid him with a three-hundred-thousand-dollar diamond ring. He let go of this boat right away."

"Let me get this straight. You left Zuriel with James."

"They both willingly went together."

"Two strangers on a walk in the woods," Cade observed. "What could go wrong?"

"Are you concerned about Zuriel?" Pilar asked instead.

Cade didn't reply either way. Pilar didn't know how to read that silence.

Then again, she also didn't know her own self right at that moment. Was she jealous of Cade's attention to a woman he just met? Zuriel was an attractive woman, after all—although her profession as a mistress was not a novel one—and Cade was a single warm-blooded man.

"She was in relapse, Cade. I couldn't have her return with me to the resort. I couldn't guarantee her safety and look for you at the same time." Pilar wasn't happy that Cade had questioned her judgment, nor could she give him any other reason beyond that one.

Cade was silent for a moment.

"Zuriel is an adult. She needed her fix. She made a deal with James to get her to a doctor because that was the next best thing. She couldn't return to a burning resort to look for a potentially deceased Braun-Dean."

"What a mess."

"So if we can get to Doc Sam ASAP, you are free to check on Zuriel. She's very pretty." Pilar didn't know why she added those last three words, but she wasn't going to apologize for it.

More silence.

Pilar had been down this way twice, so she knew where to go. She slowed down the motor and cruised among the cypress trees with their protruding knees. She pointed out more pitcher plants and explained their ecology to Cade.

But Cade's mind seemed to be elsewhere.

"Doc Sam. James. Zuriel. All three are strangers to us, aren't they?" Cade asked.

Oh, he was using the inclusive "us" to tamper down his concerns.

"Sometimes we have to accept the kindness of strangers. We don't have to necessarily trust the people per se, but we trust God, don't we? He sends people like James."

"But you don't know James from Adam."

Pilar nodded. "You're right about that, but I prayed for God to send help, and here came James with a boat out of nowhere."

"Hmmm. You have a point. I also prayed to God for help, and He sent you with this same boat."

"See? Sometimes God sends strangers. Now, if

they turn out to be bad afterwards, we'll have to cross that bridge."

"Like if that Doc Sam person doesn't really exist."

"Then Zuriel might be in very bad shape. And we might be stuck in the forest. Apparently, the bait shop is within walking distance from Doc Sam. That's the only place we could call the outside world."

"According to James."

"Right." Pilar had nothing more to say.

"Thank you for rescuing me," Cade said.

Pilar barely nodded.

Cade tugged the hem of her sleeve. "I said thank you."

"God protected us," Pilar replied. "If you hadn't wiggled away fast enough, Mr. Belly might have stabbed your vital organs, like your stomach or heart or lungs. I saw it happen."

"Mr. Belly?" Cade's eyebrows rose. "Ah, Butch."

"We're not out of the swamp yet." Pilar looked ahead. She didn't see any alligators in the water or on the bank. She wondered where they went. The explosions had subsided, so wouldn't they get back to whatever they were doing?

"You know boats," Cade said.

Maybe he was making small talk. Pilar didn't want to think unkindly of him.

"Dad is an outdoorsman," Pilar explained. "My brother and I would go fishing with him all over Florida and Georgia every chance we got. I haven't had time lately, but Oscar still goes with Dad. They'd bring home bass, catfish, whatever, and Mom would cook it."

"I thought you lived with your grandmother."

Pilar nodded. "Oscar and I do. But my parents live an hour north of Miami. We go there for dinners every now and then. Oscar more than me, but we try to keep the family together."

"I should go home more often."

Pilar didn't answer. She knew he'd originated from Wyoming, but right now she didn't feel like talking. She felt bad about what they had discussed earlier.

She had indeed left Zuriel with James, a stranger to them both. However, Zuriel was an adult and made her own decisions to go with James. Pilar wasn't her babysitter and had no time to think of anything else but to rescue Cade.

The same man sitting in this boat who had now ironically questioned Pilar's decision to let Zuriel go. Pilar wasn't happy, to say the least, but she decided to reserve her judgment for later.

She had to give it to Cade for being comfortable enough with her to question her judgment. The only other men who'd dare to question her were her brother and father.

On the other hand, it was a good thing for Pilar to weigh all the pros and cons. Earlier, she had worried about rescuing the other women locked up in the hut, but when she docked the boat and saw Mr. Belly attacking Cade, Pilar totally forgot about everyone else.

I wonder what that means?

Pilar had collaborated with a number of people in her line of work, but Cade felt different. She had worked with Ming a lot, but Ming was family to her. Nothing more. She was on very good terms with Ming and his wife, Sabine, and they were close.

However, Cade was not like that. When they had met in Dubai, they hit it off right away. Granted, Ming knew Cade, so the introduction was friendly. Pilar implicitly trusted whoever Ming trusted.

Months later, Pilar found out that Cade had returned to the States and gotten a job with Helen at Hu Knows, Inc. He had volunteered when Ming called Helen for backups in the Miami project.

Miami had begun with Pilar. When she signed the contract with Roxanne Braun-Dean to spy on her estranged husband in the Callahan Hotel, she didn't want to go alone. Ming was free, so they both ended up in housekeeping.

She deeply regretted not leaving the hotel with Ming that day.

Now she had to deal with Cade. Since she was inside the arena, she didn't know what happened outside of it. What deals were made between the Miami Police and Helen to cause Cade to enter the hotel as a cook?

The clues were there though. Ming had said he suspected that a mole inside the Miami Police—or the FBI—was informing the hostage takers. That had meant that someone outside the police department had to infiltrate the hotel. Why couldn't the FBI do it? Why did it have to be Cade, a private investigator?

"Why are you here, Cade?" Pilar asked. "I sent Ming away because it was getting dangerous for him. You shouldn't be here."

"So you do care, after all." Cade winced when he moved a leg.

"I don't want you dying on my assignment."

"Is that all?"

Pilar didn't reply. The motor had slowed down to an idle before Pilar maneuvered the bow to slide up over the boat tracks in the muddy bank. The hull gripped the mud, and the boat was stuck.

There were two sets of shoe prints—Zuriel's and James's supposedly. That told Pilar that no one else had come here after she had left earlier.

"I need you to pick up that paddle, get out of the boat, and hold the bow gunwale," Pilar said. "I'm going to put the boat in reverse, and we'll push it out. We can't let anyone see the boat here or they might come after us along the path."

"Even though we're not high value targets or the targets at all."

"Are you trying to argue with me?" Pilar snapped. She wanted to cry. She had risked her life to rush back to the resort to save Cade, and he had questioned her judgment about not keeping an eye on some former senator's mistress—who might not be as dainty as everyone thought—even as he thanked Pilar for rescuing him.

"I'm not—"

"Look. I'm tired. I haven't showered. I feel sticky. I don't know if everything I did in the last six hours was right or wrong. I just knew that I couldn't leave you behind. Now get off the boat and hold the bow!"

"Yes, ma'am." Cade disembarked, hissing as he climbed over the side of the boat. His legs were probably still in pain, so Pilar felt bad that she hadn't given him leeway to say whatever he wanted.

Nope!

Perhaps it was Cade's inexperience in the type of work that Helen of Hu Knows, Inc., often sent its people to do. Pilar did the same things too, except on a smaller scale with smaller clients that Hu Knows might not accept.

The only reason Pilar hadn't merged her company with Hu Knows was that she preferred to call the shots and be an independent investigator. She could turn down any job she didn't want to do and take time off to spend with her family.

Pilar was still sitting at the stern at the back of the boat, her hand on the tiller. Beneath her was maybe a foot of muddy water. She glanced around and saw a tiny baby gator peeking from the bushes. Yeah, they were coming out now.

Cade hobbled to the end of the boat and grabbed the bow gunwale with all his strength. "Got it!"

"Okay!" Pilar didn't need to run the length of the sixteen-foot boat. She just needed to leap off the boat far enough to land on the bank instead of the swamp water where she might have to fend off swimming alligators.

Pilar put the motor in reverse, then sprinted to the middle thwart. She saw the slightly-bent paddle she had used earlier, grabbed it, and threw it like a javelin over the boat onto the bank. The paddle clattered and the little baby alligator scampered away.

Then Pilar jumped off the bench, over the side of the boat, and onto the mud. Her shoes sank a bit, but she was able to run to the bow.

She looked at Cade. He was gritting his teeth. "Ready?"

He nodded.

"On the count of three, we push the boat out to the water." Pilar didn't wait for Cade to say anything before she started the countdown. "Three, two, one!"

They pushed the two-hundred-plus pounds of empty boat into the swamp. The mud was slick and the slope was just right. The boat slid effortlessly into the water.

Cade almost fell forward into the water, and he winced again, favoring one of his legs. Pilar grabbed his arm to steady him.

"We have to get away from the gators in the water." She pulled him along and they rushed up the bank to the drier footpath.

Before she could pick up the aluminum paddle, she saw it. A ten-foot alligator about twenty feet behind Cade, coming out from under a clump of saw palmetto with their serrated leaves that could saw through skin. About a dozen little hatchling eyes peeked out of a nearby beautyberry bush, and a few more under a red maple tree whose extended branches almost dipped into the water.

It dawned on Pilar that it was October when eggs had hatched, and here was a mama gator protecting its nest.

"Can you still run?" Pilar asked Cade.

"I suppose."

"When I sprint, you sprint. Okay?"

Cade was still facing away from the mama gator.

Pilar grabbed the aluminum paddle from the ground. "Run!"

Cade did as he was told, following after Pilar. Every time Pilar looked behind him, he was limping, but he tried to keep up. When she looked past him, he also glanced back, and he freaked out.

"That's a big one!" Cade sprinted like his legs worked perfectly.

He'd feel the pain later, but for now Pilar didn't stop him.

Fortunately, the female alligator didn't give chase. She probably made a decision to guard her babies instead.

When they were far enough away from the swamp's edge, Pilar slowed down to catch her breath. She was surprised she was still holding on to the boat paddle.

She handed it to Cade. "You can use this as your walking stick. Also useful to whack people who try to stab you."

"But it won't work on crocs."

"Crocs? They don't live in this area. Crocodiles prefer salt or brackish water, so they're most likely to be closer to the coast," Pilar said. "Gators are freshwater creatures, and they live in inland swamps like this."

"Ah." Cade inspected the paddle. "I hope I can take this home as a souvenir."

"You'd have to ask James for permission."

"Will he demand a compensation for his lost boat?" Cade asked.

"I don't know. It's only lost if the boat capsizes. I sent it adrift, so it could end up stuck by the cypress trees. He can always retrieve it."

"Good point. He only let you use the boat because he wisely chose to get off the swamp to save his life instead of clinging to his boat."

"Whatever you say." Pilar didn't want to argue with him.

Cade followed her up the footpath, but Pilar actually didn't know precisely where she was going. All she knew was that James said Doc Sam lived half a mile up this path. She would assume he lived in a house of some sort that she could recognize when they got there.

"What's half a mile?" Pilar wondered aloud. If limping Cade was not able to do a brisk walk, their strides might be shorter. "Maybe two thousand steps? Can you help me count?"

"Sure." Cade hung on to the boat paddle, using it as his walking stick.

"If we need a break, we'll stop. I might find a stick too." Pilar looked around, and prayed that they wouldn't run into snakes. She disliked snakes more than alligators because the latter stayed in the swamp and close to it, so there was no danger of them wandering around the forest. Snakes, on the other hand, could be in the bushes.

As they walked up the cleared path, Cade suddenly said, "Wow. Did we just outrun a gator?"

"She didn't chase us—probably because she was guarding her new babies—but I wasn't taking any chances."

"Whew. I'll write this in my report when I get home." Cade seemed impressed.

Pilar lifted her face to the sky, where sun rays shone down through evergreen slash pines. The temperature had warmed up, but the pine trees as well as the spreading live oak trees provided shade for the hiking duo.

A whiff of the cypress swamp they'd left drifted in with a humid breeze, as if not letting go of the visitors. Otherwise, the smell of woody slash pine resin was strong in the air as the sun got warmer.

Pilar looked down at the ground where they walked, the flat sandy soil—damp in some places from yesterday's rain—emitting its own earthiness. On both sides of the path, decaying leaves had their own unique smell.

Pilar felt at home in the outdoors, though she preferred to live in the city where more business came her way. In some fashion, she was like Dad. Dad preferred to live in the suburbs, but he often drove a long distance to go fishing or deer hunting. After getting his rustic outdoor fix, he'd drive home and take Mom to dinner at a James Beard restaurant. The best of both worlds, Pilar supposed.

"In a forest like this, there must be snakes," Cade said.

"Funny. James and I were chatting about snakes when we were on the boat."

"What did you and James talk about?" Cade winced.

"If he could outrun snakes."

"Oh? Such a sophisticated question. I only wanted to know what kind of snakes might we have to deal with. A basic question." Cade was hobbling but he seemed to want to keep talking, perhaps to get his mind off the pain in his legs that required a doctor's attention as soon as possible.

Pilar prayed that Doc Sam could treat Cade as an interim measure before they took him to a hospital.

"From the weather in the area and swamp characteristics, I'd say we're somewhere in the south side of Florida. So I would expect rat snakes, garter snakes, racers, and maybe cottonmouth."

"What about rattlesnakes?" Cade hissed, likely due to the pain.

"Isn't that the go-to snake to scare people? But yes, there are rattlesnakes in Florida." Pilar glanced behind her shoulders. Nobody was following them. "Back there in the swamp, you might also get water moccasin. Oscar's friend was bitten by one once. He nearly died."

"Yikes." Cade sounded like he was interested. "Copperheads?"

"I don't know about those. Aren't they more prevalent in Georgia where you live?"

"Probably. I usually work in urban cities, so I'm not out in the rural areas much."

"Nice to be able to pick and choose your assignments," Pilar said, even though she could too, on a smaller scale than the international private investigative firm that Cade worked for.

"And we have different kinds of snakes in the city, for sure." Cade laughed.

"Yeah."

"In any case, it's best to avoid all types of snakes in the grass, right?"

"Stay on this cleared path and you should be okay. Look at the ground occasionally," Pilar said. "If we have to hide in the forest for whatever reason, just stay close to me."

"Did you learn all this from your days in the Girl Scouts?"

"No. My dad is an avid outdoorsman, and my brother and I hung out with him a lot on weekends."

Cade stared at her. "You know that you're the bravest woman I've ever known?"

"You must not know too many women."

"Maybe not, besides my mom and Helen Hu."

Pilar decided not to ask him about the clients he worked with overseas, like that billionaire socialite in Dubai with whom he worked for a number of months—

"Uh-oh." Pilar grunted.

"What?"

"Were you counting steps?"

"I forgot."

"So did I." Pilar sighed.

Cade laughed.

And just like that, they were friends again.

CHAPTER SIXTEEN

Casting a glance behind him every now and then, Cade brought up the rear of their hike through the forest. He hoped that Pilar knew where she was going, but she was more familiar with swamps and forests like this than he ever was, growing up in almost treeless Wyoming.

Pilar was a native of Florida, and Cade trusted her to take them to safety.

As they walked up the beaten path, Cade heard something that didn't fit into the forest ecosystem. "Sirens?"

Pilar perked up her ear. She looked cute, but this wasn't the time to tell her that.

"Maybe the fire fighters finally arrived at the resort to put out the fire." She kept walking.

"Good. Even though they held us captive, I don't wish ill upon them." Cade caught himself off-hard by his own remarks. Pilar personality had rubbed off on him. A year ago, he didn't care if the enemies lived or died. Now he did.

"Before we go on, shall we pause to thank God for delivering us from the resort?" Pilar said. "We could still die in the forest, but at least we're not in captivity any longer."

Captivity?

Cade's mind went to biblical events of epic proportions, but then he reeled in his thoughts. Pilar probably just meant that they were now free from being held hostage.

"Okay. You pray?" Cade asked.

"How about if we both pray?"

"Sure." Cade wasn't a stranger to prayers.

So they did, taking turns to praise God for taking them across the swamp safely. They also prayed that God would get them out of the forest and return them home safely to their families.

Cade realized that while Pilar's prayers were short, they were always to the point. A good Christian woman was hard to find, and Pilar sounded like she was a rare gem. Cade's mom would be delighted if Cade met someone like Pilar.

They closed by saying "amen" in unison.

Cade almost reached out to hold Pilar's hand, but his desire was interrupted by the knife wounds in his legs. They hurt something fierce. But he had to keep his cool and tried to keep up with Pilar who tried to walk alongside him, not ahead of him.

"Do you need to rest?" Pilar asked.

"When we get to Doc Sam's, I will." Cade wondered why Pilar easily believed that a retired doctor lived in these woods. He started to voice it but wasn't sure how to ask.

"Are you concerned about this potential hermit, whether he would harm us more than hurt us?" Pilar spotted something, stepped to the side of the path to grab it. It was a stick about five feet long. It wasn't completely dry thanks to the recent rain.

Pilar broke off the smaller branches on it. The crooked stick was enough for Pilar to use as they continued their trek.

"Yes, I'm concerned about Doc Sam and James," Cade said. "However, more bizarre was why they even let Zuriel and you go on a swamp tour. Wasn't that odd to you?"

"Well, Laphonso came with us. He was armed." Pilar related how James and Laphonso fought in the boat and the latter fell into the water. "I actually didn't see how he fell, but James and Zuriel both corroborated each other, that Laphonso did it by himself. An accident, if you will."

"Interesting." Cade panted. Rivulets of sweat flowed down his forehead. He wiped them off on the back of his palm. "Who made the decision to let you all go on your three-hour tour?"

"Actually, it was supposed to be half an hour one way and then back again. It wasn't meant to be a long tour." Pilar paused a bit. "It happened quickly and I didn't have time to process it. Looking back, I believe that whoever was in charge felt sorry for Zuriel and understood that she was cooped up indoors and needed to go outside."

"There's hardly fresh air in the swamp, right?"

Pilar shrugged.

"Contrast that with the five women held in the hut with you. Did the captors have any compassion for any of you?"

"Good point, Cade. No complimentary tour for us. Neither did we get any hot breakfast, like Zuriel and Braun-Dean did. They were definitely VIP hostages, like you said."

"I think we're missing some stuff." Cade leaned on the boat paddle for a moment. "We're not seeing the entire picture."

The road wound around some sabal palm trees and saw palmettos.

"Look at all those palmetto plants." Cade pointed.

"Yes, the soil here is shadier and less wet, compared to the edge of the swamp behind us." Pilar looked around. "You don't see any red maples here."

"Maple trees?"

"Didn't you see one by the swamp? Several gator hatchlings were under it."

Cade shook his head. "I only saw the big gator. How long was she?"

"I thought she was about ten feet long."

"Wow. Remind me to stay in the city."

Pilar smiled. "Which reminds me of the Callahan Hotel. Two days ago, when I was cleaning the penthouse suite, Braun-Dean was pitching a fit and calling the people around him names. Those people were more like his bodyguards than captors."

"When I went upstairs to deliver their mid-afternoon snack, when you were summoned to the third floor, I felt the same way. That Braun-Dean was in charge."

"In the women's hut, sometime after we were

brought to the gator resort, Josephine Callahan told me that she believed the entire hostage situation was staged and that we were not in any danger."

"Oh?"

"She gave me the impression that the estranged Braun-Dean couple was playing a game."

"What game?" Cade had his own conjectures but he wanted to know what Pilar thought.

"I don't know. Another piece of the puzzle."

"Take a stab at it—no pun intended. Give me your best guess."

"At first glance, it looks like Braun-Dean was being held hostage for ransom. The ransom would come from someone—maybe his estranged wife or a business associate who didn't want secrets revealed to the world."

Cade could tell that Pilar had put some thought into it. "What secrets?"

"You might not know this, but the Braun-Deans are being investigated for money laundering. They probably don't know it yet because the FBI is not telling anyone."

"So how did you find out?"

"I have my sources." Pilar stopped there.

"You can't say now?"

"I might later but not right now, no."

"Okay. So based on that information outside the box, you think that..." Cade waited.

"I gave you the extra dot. You put two and two together." Pilar lobbed the ball back into Cade's court.

"What would it be?"

"You think about it and we can discuss."

All of a sudden, Cade felt like he was truly a

rookie in the business. He could eat the humble pie and admit that he had no idea. Or he could think about how the dots connected.

What dots? He barely saw them.

His legs throbbed. The adrenaline he had earlier in the boat had worn off. His cloth bandage helped a little, but he really needed to sit down and rest a while.

"How much longer do we have to go?" Cade asked.

"I'm not sure since we lost count of our steps, but I am going to guess that we should see something soon. James said that Doc Sam lived off this road. If he lied to us, then we are stuck deep in the forest."

"You think we might die here if nobody finds us?" Cade slowed down a little bit.

"It's not that fatalistic. I think there are people here. Somebody made and maintained this path, for example, which tells me that people use this narrow path—even though it's not wide enough nor does it have enough markers for me to call this a trail."

"Like who?"

"Hunters. It's October, which is archery season in Florida." Pilar slowed down to keep in sync with Cade. "If this is Zone C, as I suspect, we should be seeing hunters looking for white-tailed deer. We can ask them for help."

"Should we be looking out for deer stands then?"

"I guess we could, but right now I'm looking for Doc Sam's cabin. Failing that, we can fall back to Plan B: look for hunters."

"With crossbows?" Cade asked.

"Not necessarily so because crossbow season

starts at the end of October, and it's not quite that time yet. Right now we're just looking for compound bows and maybe longbows."

"But they're quiet, so we can't hear gunshots."

"We might if this was private land. If so, then you can hunt year round with your weapon of choice." Pilar stopped mid-walk. "Let's take a few minutes."

Cade felt a great relief. He fussed with the bloodied cloth tied around his leg wounds. Blood was seeping through. He probably needed stitches. And maybe a tetanus shot.

"Cade?" Pilar's voice was soft.

"Huh?"

"You don't have to be a macho man in front of me. If we're tired, we rest. We're human."

"I can keep going." Cade knew it wasn't entirely true, but he didn't want to be a wimp in front of Pilar.

Then again, he wasn't sure what he was trying to show off. Pilar was the least pretentious woman he had ever met. She didn't wear makeup, didn't care if she impressed anyone. She only wanted to do her job well and return alive to her family.

"I need rest too, but I might keep going until I run down and pass out. So help me take breaks, right?"

Whoa.

Pilar sounded really good at this people diplomacy. She wanted him to take a break, but she spun it into a job for Cade to do for her sake.

As for Cade, he didn't always think of the most polite way of saying things or whether his words might hurt somebody. Most of the time he didn't care. He remembered his first quarter performance evaluation, when his direct supervisor, Earl Young—who was also his mentor since Helen Hu wasn't around that much stateside anymore—told him that he needed to have a heart.

His conversation with Earl not nearly a year ago had seared into his memory.

> *"Don't I have a heart?" Cade asked Earl.*
>
> *"Sensitive people might call you heartless right away," Earl replied.*
>
> *"Sensitive people like women, maybe?"*
>
> *"Not all women, but some men might be sensitive too."*
>
> *"There are five boys in my family, and none of us is sensitive. Neither is Mom or Dad, for that matter."*
>
> *"So you grew up tough and in-your-face and with pride on your sleeves. No biggie when you're at home, right?" Earl asked. "But out here, we have a variety of people working at Hu Knows, and some have said that you can be rude—in spite of the fact that you're a rookie compared to them."*

Cade had played Earl's words over and over in his mind in the following months until now.

It had taken Cade a while to understand. However, the Bible helped him—which made him glad that he spent time with the Lord almost every day and committed verses to memory, such as James 1:19-20.

> *So then, my beloved brethren, let every man be swift to hear, slow to speak, slow to wrath; for the wrath of man does not produce the righteousness of God.*

Cade felt bad that he had put on an air about him since the very first day he'd joined Hu Knows. Perhaps Earl had tried to tell him that they all knew. Helen had not only refused to fire him, but she had asked Earl to mentor him.

Lord, forgive me for my pride.

Truly, he wanted to keep up with the elite investigators in the company as well as their associates, such as Ming Wei, and of course, Pilar.

Speaking of whom, she now pointed with her stick. "You ready to go the last leg of our walk through the woods? I think we should be nearly there, don't you think?"

"You don't seem to be afraid that we might get lost in the woods and nightfall would come and we'd be surrounded by snakes chattering about how to outrun us?"

"Is that what you're thinking of?" Pilar chuckled. "Why don't you focus on connecting the dots? That exercise might take your mind off your pain."

"Dots..." Cade mumbled as he leaned on his boat paddle. He tried not to put his entire weight on it because it might snap.

"Dots, my friend. Dots."

Cade felt touched that Pilar had called him her

friend. Truly, at work, hardly anyone wanted to team up with him except for Helen Hu and Earl Young. Now Pilar had extended a hand of friendship to him. Or was he overthinking it?

He had already fallen in love with Pilar back when they worked in Dubai. Some day, if he was brave enough, he would tell her about that first moment their eyes had met.

Right now, he couldn't say it aloud because it might affect their working relationship. She might look down on him for being unfocused.

Of all the people he had worked with, Pilar was the most focused. She could compartmentalize everything, shove aside all low-priority tasks, and determinedly do that one thing that moved toward the goal of her mission.

That tenacity had attracted Cade to Pilar.

Another reason he couldn't tell Pilar that he'd fallen for her was that he didn't want Pilar to think that it was due to her having saved his life. He could simply send her Christmas gifts every year if he wanted to show his gratitude. Or contribute to a charity of her choice. Or return her kindness somehow later on.

However, he wanted Pilar to fall in love with him. If the feeling was mutual, then he had a glimmer of hope for a life together.

If Pilar rejected him, then he might still continue to work at Hu Knows, but he would have to ask Helen for overseas assignments where he would never see Pilar again. That way, it wouldn't hurt as much.

"Well?" Pilar asked.

"Well what?" Cade had been lost in thought.

"Are you in deep contemplation about the dots?"

Oh, those dots.

Right now, Cade wanted to connect the dots between him and Pilar, not the dots in the increasingly bizarre hostage situation that they had just escaped from.

"If we know what is going on, we will be a few steps ahead of them," Pilar said.

"You know, when I was holed up in the kitchen during the firebombing, Ted's men said 'they' a few times."

Why didn't they just firebomb this kitchen too?

It's not like they're not trying to destroy all the huts.

What are they up to?

"What they said was jarring enough for me to remember," Cade added. "Ted was speaking about the attackers as outsiders to their organization."

"Funny you should mention it." Pilar paused to think. "On our swamp tour, Laphonso said that 'they' were early. He didn't specify who. But I assumed he meant the attackers."

"Let's label them, shall we?" Pilar drew several circles in the air as she walked. "Let's use people's names to mark our groups. Let's say Felix Braun-Dean is one group. I'm going to call this group Felix. Ted and his men are another group. 'They' or the outsiders or newcomers are the third group."

"Does Felix include Mrs. Braun-Dean?" Cade asked.

"Maybe not. How about we make her the wildcard? Roxanne is in her own group."

"Sounds good. Putting all these dots together, we

have a myriad of possibilities." Cade started to get what the private investigators at Hu Knows enjoyed: solving problems. "Let's list them."

"Now we're talking." Pilar looked excited. "Felix could have staged this entire mess. Ted could be working for Felix."

"Or Ted could be working for Roxanne," Cade suggested.

"Oh?" Even though Pilar had drawn a check from Roxanne, she still had to be objective about it. "At this point, I must tell you that the reason I was at the Callahan Hotel was to spy on Felix for Roxanne."

"I know."

"You do?"

Cade nodded. "Ming briefed Helen and me after he got out. You can be sure that Helen's investigating Roxanne even as we were held captive in the hotel."

"I'm sure she is." Pilar rehashed what they had discussed.

"Ted couldn't be working for the unnamed newcomers to the scene because he looked shocked when the resort was bombed."

"Laphonso wasn't. He gave me the impression that he'd expected them to arrive but not that early."

"Did Laphonso work for Ted?" Cade asked.

"Good question. I met him in the inner sanctum of the huts. He was the last guard I saw when I delivered breakfast to Braun-Dean. He went right up to the table to make sure everything looked fine when Braun-Dean sat down to eat."

"Interesting. So there are people who worked for Felix who might not really be working for him." Cade drew a deep breath.

"So many unanswered questions."

"Ted's men seemed to know who the attackers were," Cade reminded them.

"Rival groups, perhaps?"

They walked in silence for a little longer. Cade enjoyed being this close to Pilar, but he didn't want to see her being so serious all the time. They seemed to have escaped their captors, so why wouldn't she enjoy the respite? The worst was not over yet until they got out of this forest.

Cade prayed that he'd survive. He hadn't bled out because Butch's switchblades hadn't cut a femoral artery. However, he still felt pain every time he lifted his legs since they left the boat.

He was thinking of sitting down and resting a while when Pilar spoke again.

"What if Felix and Roxanne were working together?" Pilar asked.

"Now that would be odd. You mean like use the hostage situation for their money laundering operation?"

Pilar laughed. "I know. Sorry I went to the land of bizarre plots."

"Not too far-fetched considering that both parties still do business together even after Roxanne left Felix due to his infidelities."

"Are they?"

Cade nodded. "It was in the extensive profiles of them I had to read on the flight from Savannah to Miami. It said in there that in spite of their contested and protracted divorce, in spite of their lack of a prenup, they still continued to partner in their venture capital business. Fifty-fifty split, they were able to gobble up midsize companies and turn them into multimillion-dollar profits."

"All the while being at each other's throats because Felix kept a string of mistresses—one at every port, so to speak—and finally landing with Zuriel, who had been with him for a while." Pilar shook her head.

"Something like that."

"That ruled out one of them holding the other hostage, right?"

"You know, maybe not."

Slowly, a smile crept up Pilar's face. She nodded. "Good thinking outside the box."

"We make a good team."

Pilar stepped back. "I wouldn't go that far."

"We made a great team in Dubai." Cade drew a deep breath and prayed away his pain. He was feeling a bit lightheaded, but kept walking.

"One time only." Pilar put a finger in the air.

"Enough for me to know."

"Know what?" Pilar's eyes widened. She looked all innocent-like.

Cade wanted to grab her and give her a tight squeeze, but of course he couldn't. Firstly, he smelled like swamp and smoke. Secondly, he didn't want to scare her off by being too forward. Thirdly, he was feeling slightly dizzy due to exhaustion and possibly dehydration. He hadn't had anything to drink since the coffee he had at breakfast at the resort.

They had to keep walking to reach the destination or he might not make it if they stopped and got distracted. He tried to press on, not wanting to appear wimpy in front of the woman he'd been secretly loving for a year.

Pilar stopped mid-step. Her nose was in the air. "Smell that?"

"Yeah, a whole forest. Decay, rot, pine, oak, the works."

"More than that."

Cade looked around but saw nothing except an endless dirt path that went deeper into the woods.

"If the scent carried here, I'm going to guess we're within three hundred feet of the smoker—and hopefully a cabin that goes with it, and thus Doc Sam." Pilar sniffed and kept walking.

Cade was fascinated by the way Pilar's mind processed the situation. She was over there now, and Cade tried to keep up.

He hobbled along, praying that his legs wouldn't bleed more. Every time he lifted them to walk, he could feel his muscles pull. The injured area pulsated. He could see that his legs were shaking now.

The path started to widen a bit, and Cade could see tire tracks. Perhaps they were closing in on Doc Sam's house and the bait shop somewhere in the vicinity.

They better be close to stopping because he was getting lightheaded. He hadn't had a chance to take off his chef coat—which was sleeveless since he'd repurposed the sleeves as bandages—so he sweated a bit in the late morning sun.

Around the bend, Cade smelled lunch. "A smoker. Maybe charcoal. Also hickory?"

The smell was strong.

"Plus ribs. Smelled like pork ribs at first but..." Pilar glanced at Cade. "Stronger. Maybe a wild game. I'm guessing boar."

"A boar? I've never eaten a boar before." Cade looked amused. "Will they invite us to lunch?"

Pilar almost answered—

Cha-chuck.

Cade recognized the noise. It sounded like someone racking the pump of a shotgun.

He turned his head slowly. So did Pilar, who might have heard it too.

In front of them was a 12-gauge Mossberg 500, and they were at the wrong end of the killing machine. Cade looked beyond the shotgun to its bearer. He was tall, wore a camouflage outfit.

His sidekick was shorter. His poker face looked bored as he spat tobacco on the ground. He carried a semi-automatic AR-15 with a scope. Did he hunt boars with that?

"Monty and Maria, aren't you?" The first man said in a low and slow voice. If he were the host of a midnight radio show, he might put people to sleep.

He had a slight drawl, but it wasn't Southern. It had a hint of him being a transplant. An import from another state. Montana or Wyoming, perhaps.

His arm was still extended, the Mossberg practically staring down Cade and Pilar. Considering how loud it could sound, the bearer of the gun might be someone who liked to show off. Cade made a mental note not to cross Mr. Ego.

Mr. Sidekick didn't speak at all. He was busy chewing tobacco.

Mr. Ego repeated his question.

Cade nodded. Standing next to him, Pilar looked like she was on the verge of tears.

Wait. What?

From the corner of his eye, he positively saw Pilar's lips quaver. With a cracked voice, she started speaking in Spanish. Words that he didn't understand.

Cade wondered about her versatility as an investigator, able to put on a cover so realistic that he almost believed she was truly scared of the two men—real game hunters or not—who had found them walking in the woods.

Mr. Ego didn't move his weapon of choice away from Cade's face. He began to speak again, his words in measured cadence. "Our boss wants to have a talk."

"We'll talk if it comes with lunch." Cade couldn't believe he'd blurted out those words.

Without warning, Mr. Sidekick stepped forward and whacked him in the solar plexus with the stock of his AR-15, sending Cade reeling backward onto the dirt path. His aluminum paddle clattered away.

Cade doubled over in pain from the gut punch. He gasped for air. He hadn't expected to get the wind knocked out of him.

Next thing he knew, Pilar was on her knees beside him, cradling him in her arms. It dawned on her that she had rushed to him while a loaded shotgun was still pointed at them.

Cade never felt more loved.

CHAPTER SEVENTEEN

The rustic wood cabin was small and looked like maybe two people could live comfortably in it. The front door was closed and the curtains drawn at both windows.

Pilar followed Cade in a single file in front of the two men with their hunting weapons pointed at their backs.

Around the hut they went until they reached the back of the cabin. Right in the middle of the clearing between the cabin and a toolshed were two 22-inch vertical Weber Smokey Mountain cylindrical smokers. They were the same exact ones that Pilar's parents had in their backyard.

So they were where all that gamey smell had emanated from.

The scent was so much stronger now that it momentarily made Pilar forget that her hands were tied behind her back. She walked slowly, savoring the smell.

A white-haired man who looked like he was in his eighties was at the smoker. He tossed what seemed to be a cup of hickory chips into the firebox on top of the burning charcoal. He closed the fuel door.

For a man his age, he was steady on his feet and walked unassisted. His eyes widened when he saw Pilar and Cade. He didn't smile, but his plump and ruddy cheeks reminded Pilar of the jolly man in old Coca Cola commercials from the 1920s.

"I don't know if I have enough boar for more guests. I only caught a forty-pounder last night."

A forty-pound wild boar? It would seem to Pilar that the meat from such a boar could fit into one smoker. So what was in the second smoker?

The old man might have seen her stare and guessed her thoughts.

He pointed to one smoker. "This has the boar I caught last night. I was hoping that could last for two meals." He pointed to the other Weber. "This one contains the boar that some hunters caught this morning. They paid me to smoke their boar."

Ah, so that was how he made his living in these woods. Pilar didn't say anything. She didn't feel like talking right now. The sweaty housekeeping uniform was sticking to her skin, and she felt uncomfortable with her wrists tied behind her back.

"These two don't need to eat." One of the two men snarled.

Pilar and Cade were pushed inside the hut.

Oooh, the air stank.

To one side of the hut was a small dining table with a kerosene lantern on it. At the edge of the table sat none other than Felix Braun-Dean.

The former senator looked disheveled in a white robe that had turned ashen. Parts of his arms and legs were wrapped up in white gauze bandages.

Why was he in a robe? Pilar guessed that maybe he had been taking a bath when he had to be evacuated from the resort, or he'd changed into this oversized robe after he had arrived here.

Pilar wondered when he had arrived. She had been on the boat in the swamp earlier and hadn't seen any other boats. That meant Braun-Dean hadn't come by boat and hiked here.

Could Braun-Dean have reached the same cabin via the main road that led out of the resort? If they had, might they have encountered James and Zuriel on their way to the bait shop?

Pilar looked around but did not see either one of those two. She prayed that they had escaped, gotten away to safety, and called 911.

Braun-Dean was drinking something in a stainless steel camp mug. Next to it was a bottle of whiskey. Perhaps he was drinking that to dull the pain of his burns.

"She doesn't just want to get my money." He bit out the words. "Now she also wants me dead."

Wait a minute.

Pilar's ears perked up.

Did that mean Braun-Dean hadn't staged his own hostage crisis? Then was Josephine Callahan wrong? Or had Braun-Dean said that to add confusion to the matter? Maybe he wanted Pilar and Cade to hear that now and testify later in court if it came to that.

Pilar knew that she could not objectively see the entire situation right now, but must continue to collect data. Once the fog of war was over, she would see things more clearly.

Pilar tried not to look surprised. She kept a poker face. She stole a glance at Cade next to her. He was almost bending over now. His leg must be attended to, but how could Pilar ask for medical help for him? Also, he shouldn't have gotten himself punched in the gut.

Braun-Dean's phone rang.

According to James, all phones started working once they were at the bait shop, which was somewhere down the road from this cabin. That told Pilar that this cabin was outside the cell phone dead zone.

"You changed the terms of our agreement!" Braun-Dean yelled into the phone. "You firebombed the huts. I could've died. Then who is going to pay you the billion dollars? Did that ever cross your mind or are you just stupid?"

Pilar wondered who he was talking to. He seemed to have a sense of familiarity with whoever it was on the other end of the phone. His words told Pilar that he wasn't afraid of the real captors.

What were they up to?

And the amount of a billion dollars wasn't small potatoes.

The more Braun-Dean listened to whoever it was on the phone, the angrier he got. He kicked the leg of the table and yelped loudly, startling himself so much that his phone fell to the wooden floor.

"Get the doctor in here!" Braun-Dean screamed. "Joe, pick up my phone for me."

Joe turned out to be the name of the man who had

pointed the Mossberg shotgun at Pilar and Cade earlier on the walking path.

Joe obediently did what he was told.

"Hello? Hello?" Braun-Dean cursed into the phone. Then he slammed it down on the table. "I can't believe she hung up on me."

There, another clue.

She.

The captor with whom Braun-Dean had an agreement was a woman.

Still, the dots were not connecting for Pilar...

Unless the woman was Roxanne Braun-Dean.

Somehow, Pilar could imagine Braun-Dean being rude to his estranged wife. Not that Pilar had any proof of it, but according to Roxanne, they didn't get along. They'd often have shouting matches even at work.

However, their love of money overrode their personal grievances, which included Braun-Dean's dalliances and extramarital affairs. Oddly enough, Roxanne paid Pilar to spy on Braun-Dean's business meetings at the Callahan Hotel, not on his relationship with Zuriel, which was an open secret.

Braun-Dean recorded an audio message. "Send her ten million dollars of bitcoin. That should make her happy until we figure out what to do."

Who was he sending the message to? Pilar wondered but had no answer. She guessed that it could be Braun-Dean's accountant. He had mentioned bitcoin. That meant he knew that his captors would accept cryptocurrency payment."

His phone pinged. Pilar supposed that was a

reply from whoever Braun-Dean had sent the message to.

"What do you mean it will take two days?" Braun-Dean fumed. "Is this a game to you?"

He threw down the phone onto the table.

"Where's the doctor?" Braun-Dean lifted his leg a bit to see what was going on. He frowned and made a face.

"Coming! Coming!" The old man bounded in—the same guy who had been at the smoker outside.

"Doc, I'm in pain." Braun-Dean moaned.

Doc Sam.

"What about the other hostages?" Pilar dared to ask. "Do they also need medical attention?"

"All dead," someone walking into the room said.

Ted.

Pilar's heart sank. Five women in the hut. Burned to death? Or murdered by other means?

Behind him came Mr. Belly, also known as Butch. As soon as he spotted Cade, he exploded with expletives and charged at him, knocking Cade to the ground.

With his hands tied behind his back, Cade had no chance against two giant fists.

"Stop! Please stop!" Pilar screamed—even though she wasn't sure if that did any good.

With her own hands tied behind her back, Pilar wedged herself in between Cade and Butch.

Butch's fist froze in mid-air. His eyes widened in shock, and then his eyebrows drooped as did the edges of his mouth.

"Maria..." His voice trailed off.

Pilar realized what she had done, and was now

filled with fear. What a stupid move she had made. She was clearly and absolutely no match for Sumo Butch.

She tried not to blink, or Butch might see through to her trepidation.

Behind her, on the floor, Cade was shouting. "I'm Senator Braun-Dean's cook!"

He repeated himself loudly. More than for Butch, Cade probably wanted Braun-Dean to hear it.

Everyone knew that Braun-Dean was no longer a senator. However, Cade could still use the title out of respect, even though Pilar suspected he was going for a different impact.

"Step aside," Butch ordered Pilar.

Pilar blinked away tears in her eyes. The tears had come on just like that, probably because she was exhausted and this entire event had worn her down.

Butch stepped back. Just one step. But it was enough.

"Thank you," Pilar whimpered.

Butch drew a deep breath. "Thanks for the biscuit."

He remembered. Pilar was overjoyed. Truly one good turn deserved another.

Pilar gathered her strength to have a mini conversation with Butch. "Wasn't the bacon good?"

Butch shook his palm in the air. "Well, it was a bit salty, but at least it wasn't gator meat."

"I know, right." Pilar chuckled nervously.

Butch had nothing more to say. He left the room, fists clenched as though saying that if not for Pilar's good deed, he would've smashed Cade's face to the floor and stepped on it. Or something like that. Pilar had no idea what Butch would do, but she could just imagine the drama Cade would have to go through.

"Let the cook cook!" Braun-Dean's voice started to slur. "Send him to the kitchen!"

What kitchen? The cabin looked a little larger than a lean-to. Maybe there were bedrooms behind those walls. Maybe a kitchen too. But as Pilar recalled from their approach to the house, this building was small.

"Yes, sir." Joe tried to pull Cade to his feet, but Cade wobbled and collapsed to the floor.

Pilar wanted to help, but had no hands.

Pilar could see that Cade's legs were bleeding again. She looked around to see if she could catch Doc Sam's attention. The old man was standing near Braun-Dean.

"Senator, sir! Your cook is injured." Pilar prayed for compassion. Even old secular kings in the Bible, such as Darius or Nebuchadnezzar, had compassion on God's people. Maybe Braun-Dean could spare some heart for Cade.

"What?" Braun-Dean leaned forward. "Why is my cook injured?"

Pilar opened her mouth and nearly said "Cade." Good thing she stopped herself just in time.

It's Monty.

"Um, Monty got stabbed in the legs pretty deeply by switchblades. It's been over an hour and he's still bleeding." Pilar didn't accuse Butch of the deed, not because she didn't want to place herself at the scene, but because this was not the time to accuse anyone. The problem would remain no matter who had stabbed Cade.

"Doc Sam?" Braun-Dean waved his arms.

Doc Sam nodded. He picked up the remaining bottle of whiskey from the table near Braun-Dean and walked towards Cade on the floor.

"No! No!" Braun-Dean pleaded. "Not my Woodford bourbon!"

"Sir, technically, it's my bourbon. I bought it to go with the smoked ribs I'm making for dinner—which I'm now sharing with all of you."

Braun-Dean looked spaced out.

"Now I need a bit of this whiskey to sterilize the area and numb the pain. I don't have any lidocaine or other types of anesthesia." Doc Sam waited.

Pilar thought that he was not only a patient man, but he must take his physician profession seriously enough to defy Braun-Dean, who had armed men at his disposal.

Braun-Dean started to sway in his seat. "Where's my Zuriel? I want her to pour me a drink!"

He pointed to Pilar. "Maria! Weren't you with Zuriel on the boat tour? Where did she go?"

What was she supposed to say?

"The explosions scared us. We got off the boat. We got separated." It had come out of her mouth like that, but there were more details to it.

"My baby needs her pills. She will die without them." Braun-Dean snarled at Ted. "Didn't you send two men to find her? Where is she?"

"Yes, sir. They're out there looking now." Ted didn't sound like he was confident they would actually return with Zuriel.

Pilar wondered if those two men might have fled instead. Clearly, the resort bombing would make anyone believe that being with Braun-Dean was dangerous. Why would they return to him?

"Zuriel, my Zuriel."

Ted pointed to Doc Sam. "He gave her some pain pills this morning, didn't he?"

Doc Sam nodded. "She should be okay for a little while."

Braun-Dean ignored him. He pointed to Ted. "Your people are useless. You yourself go find Zuriel. Bring her back!"

Did Braun-Dean think that they could find Zuriel? Pilar feared for her.

"Yes, sir. Butch and I will go." Ted motioned for Butch to follow him. "We have to walk back to the bait shop to get the pickup."

Braun-Dean then descended into a cacophony of "Twelve Days of Christmas."

Why that song and why Christmas? Pilar didn't care. As long as Braun-Dean was distracted, Pilar figured Doc Sam could give some attention to Cade.

"Is he going to be okay?" Pilar asked Doc Sam as they both crouched on the floor by Cade.

Doc Sam came over with a cup of water for Cade to sip.

"He's lost blood." Doc Sam inspected the crude bandage that Cade had wrapped around his wounds. "Can you talk?"

Cade didn't reply. He looked weak and he was grimacing. Pilar could only pray for him.

Doc Sam pulled out a clean pocket knife and cut away a part of Cade's pants around the crude bandage, now soaked through in blood.

He made a tsk-tsk sound.

Pilar started to cry. Part of it was for show, but the other part of it wasn't. She knew in her heart that she didn't want Cade to die. What would become of them, she didn't know, but she had thought about this man for a year since Dubai, but she hadn't had the time to do something about it.

Now she might not have a chance.

In the background, Braun-Dean was still singing.

"We need to stitch up this wound," Doc Sam said. "I have some antibiotics, but that's all I have."

Pilar realized then that Doc Sam had known from across the room—before he even walked toward them—that Cade was in bad shape. Perhaps he could see that Cade's face had paled.

She didn't know anything about Doc Sam, but James had reminded her that sometimes she had to trust strangers. In fact, if she'd hauled Cade to an emergency room, she would have to trust the physicians and nurses there without even knowing their names and backgrounds.

Doc Sam took Cade's pulse. Then he turned to Pilar. "Do you know first aid?"

"Yes, sir. Not too much, though."

"Good enough." Doc Sam turned to Joe, whose Mossberg was pointed at Cade. "I need her to assist me as I stitch up this man's leg."

When Joe didn't say anything, Doc Sam added, "We're just going down that hallway to my home clinic. You can come watch if you want. Just stitching him up so that your boss doesn't lose his cook. Okay?"

Pilar's stomach rumbled at the inference of food. She could still smell the smoker outside the door.

"If we get this over and done with, this man here

might be up and about, cooking for your crew. Otherwise, he could be dead in about eight hours, and the police will hunt you down for his murder."

Pilar gasped. Was Doc Sam making all that up to scare Joe, et al?

"What are you planning to do besides stitching him up?" Joe sounded like an insurance agent asking for specifics.

"I just told you." Doc Sam kept this voice calm and grandfatherly. "I'm trying to get him back on his feet so that he can cook for us. If he's going to be held hostage, he might as well do something useful, right?"

"Wasn't he the cook at the resort?" Joe asked.

Pilar nodded.

"There you go. He can help me cook." Doc Sam pointed to Cade. "I can share my boar with you, but the only sides I can offer you are baked potatoes."

"I like baked potatoes." Joe turned to a guard walking by. "What do you think, Arnon?"

The guard said nothing, as though he was ignoring Joe.

"If we're going to be holed up here for a while, we might as well make the best of it," Doc Sam continued. "You see why I haven't lost weight even after my darling Samantha passed away? Because I can't let grief prevent me from eating. If Sam were alive today, she'd tell me to eat up no matter what happens."

When Joe didn't say anything, Doc Sam continued in his southern grandpa drawl. "Son, you need food. No matter what your profession is, a man's gotta eat. Let me tell you. I put some delicious dry rub on the ribs and meat. Back when my wife was a young woman in Tennessee, her mama taught her a secret family recipe. Wait until you try it. It's delicious! Oh how I miss Sam. My dear Sam. Gone too soon."

"Sam?" Pilar asked. "Your wife's name is also Sam?"

"Short for Samantha. Mine's short for Samuel." Doc Sam sounded heartbroken.

"All right. All right!" Joe turned to the guard who had been with him on the path earlier. "Arnon, help me get Monty to the clinic."

Pilar and Doc Sam followed behind.

The "clinic" was no more than a converted room smaller than Pilar's own bedroom at home. To one side was a small consultation table with chairs on both sides of it. Across from it was an old hospital bed from another era.

After Joe and Arnon had lifted Cade onto the bed, Doc Sam asked them to free Pilar's hands. "What can she do? We're surrounded by paramilitary."

Paramilitary? That was a stretch, but who was Pilar to argue with Doc Sam's opinion of these captors?

Joe rolled his eyes. "Obviously she can't help you if she's all tied up."

He ordered Arnon to untie Pilar as well as the injured Cade. He then told Arnon to remain there to stand guard. "If they cause trouble, shoot to kill."

Arnon nodded. He hadn't stopped chewing tobacco since they'd met on the path down the road.

The room was small, and Doc Sam kept bumping into Arnon. So Arnon stepped out of the room and waited there with the door ajar. He leaned against the door frame, watching Doc Sam work.

"Please wash your hands at the sink over there," Doc Sam asked Pilar.

She did as she was told and dried her hands on what looked like a clean-enough towel.

"If my daughter were alive, she'd be your age. Are you forty?" Doc Sam asked.

"I'm thirty-one." Pilar began to wonder if she looked that much older than her age. She loved her work, but it did take a toll on her physical health.

"Close enough."

Close enough? That was a nine-year difference.

Pilar dared not question Doc Sam about his imprecision, and whether that "close enough" attitude extended to his medical practice.

"I'm retired, you know," Doc Sam added. "The last time I worked in a medical center with pay was twelve years ago."

Pilar nodded, not being sure why he had told her that. She only had one answer for him.

"Close enough."

CHAPTER EIGHTEEN

How much pain Cade could tolerate depended on the situation he faced at the moment. He would like to think that he could rise above the circumstances, just as Paul could in Philippians 4:13.

I can do all things through Christ who strengthens me.

However, when the rubber met the road, his human nature stepped onto center stage and he cried like a baby. Not for attention, but because of the sheer agony of it.

Granted, he wasn't losing his legs. They were still there. They were not crushed. Just slashed.

All that being said, it had been almost two hours since he'd tried to stem the bleeding. He had hiked over two thousand steps up the beaten forest path, dragging his legs along.

He had enjoyed his conversation with Pilar in the great October outdoors, but now he couldn't remember what they had talked about. Right now, he had more important things to worry about. Like his dignity.

Here, all laid up on an old hospital bed, his pants cut off up to his upper thighs, and his legs in full display before Pilar's eyes, Cade was feeling shy about his own physique. He wished he had lifted more weights and appeared muscular. There was nothing he could do now.

Doc Sam had removed the crude bandages. "We need to irrigate these wounds. Clean it really good."

"With water?" Pilar asked.

Doc Sam nodded.

"I have some clean drinking water in the kitchen, but water's gotta go somewhere, and I don't want it all over my clinic."

The octogenarian turned to Arnon. "We should rinse his legs outdoors. In the backyard, the water can water the grass. Nothing wasted."

"Doc... At a time like that, are you still thinking of protecting the environment?" Arnon shook his head.

"You heard your boss. His cook is injured. You see how Mr. Braun-Dean pitched a fit over his missing girlfriend? Now what if he pitches another fit about his missing cook. You and I know he likes to eat."

Pilar stood by Cade's bedside, watching Doc Sam chat fearlessly with Arnon and his AR-15.

"Just outside the door. You have the bullets. We don't."

Arnon thought for a quick second. "Nope. You

stay in here. Find a tub or something. You're not leaving the room."

"A tub. Now that's a good idea." Doc Sam pointed to a shelf. "Maria, please grab a couple of clean towels from over there. I'm going to the kitchen to get water and a tub to put his legs in."

"Yes, doctor." Pilar washed her hands in the sink nearby and then collected the towels. She searched high and low but could not find something else in particular.

"What are you looking for?" Cade asked.

"Gloves." Pilar kept looking until she found a box of old gloves. They were latex, and Pilar was allergic to latex. "Oh no. I can't wear these."

She gently put the plastic sheet under Cade's legs.

Cade watched her the entire time.

"You okay?" she asked.

"I'm alive."

"Good."

Doc Sam returned with a container of water on a cart. He placed an empty jug on a table next to the hospital bed. "I'll be right back with the tub. I need to get it from my laundry room."

"Your laundry room?" Arnon spat out tobacco.

"Just a corner where I wash laundry. Nothing fancy."

Pilar asked him if he had other gloves besides latex.

"Sorry, no." Doc Sam put down the cup of water on the rolling tray table next to the hospital bed and put on the gloves that Pilar handed to him. "Are you allergic to latex?"

"Yes." Pilar eyed the gloves.

"Then don't wear them," Cade said.

"I'm the assistant though." Pilar looked at Doc Sam for a solution.

"You just wash your hands really good in soapy water," Doc Sam said. "Wash everything from fingertips to elbows. Make sure you get soap under your nails. I'll do the work, so you're going to support me. Don't touch anything I tell you not to touch."

Cade was impressed that Doc Sam sounded so serious, especially since the good doctor himself had forgotten to put on gloves until Pilar found them for him.

"Are you also allergic to latex?" Doc Sam asked Cade.

Cade shook his head.

"He's only allergic to pain," Pilar said from the sink. She was vigorously washing her hands.

"No, I'm not," Cade protested.

Doc Sam disappeared and returned again with a tub.

It wasn't lost on Cade that Doc Sam seemed to be able to come and go among the captors. Why wasn't he afraid of them?

Pilar and Doc Sam helped Cade to get up and sit by the edge of the hospital bed, which Doc Sam lowered as far as it could go. That way, Cade's feet could step into the laundry tub.

Behind them, Arnon was still watching the sideshow.

"This is boiled water that I cooled down earlier." Doc Sam filled a jug. "My drinking water, which is cleaner than tap or well water.

"It's going to sting a bit, okay?" Doc Sam sat down on a plastic stool beside the tub.

"What do you mean 'sting a bit'—owwww!" Cade's left thigh flinched as Doc Sam poured a jug of water slowly over his wounds, letting the blood and grime and swamp and forest run off down his legs and feet into the plastic tub.

After a few minutes, Cade thought that the pain had redistributed to his arm—until he saw that Pilar had gripped it so tightly that her knuckles were white.

"Are you okay?" Cade asked her.

"Shouldn't I be asking you that?"

Cade stared at her grip around his arm. "I think I'm losing circulation in my arm."

"Huh?" Pilar followed his gaze. "Oh. Oh. Sorry."

Pilar released her grip.

Doc Sam was patting Cade's legs dry. Pilar handed him another towel. Then both of them helped Cade to lie back down on the bed.

Under the single light bulb, the wounds on his legs looked raw.

Pilar was by his side, but her palms were on her chest.

"Don't look," Cade said to her gently.

"Are you in pain?" Pilar asked, her voice low. She looked like she was about to cry.

It was then that Cade realized how soft-hearted Pilar was inside. Perhaps she was like roasted marshmallows, a bit crusty on the outside, but soft on the inside.

Cade didn't like to see her cry.

"Pain? Not at all. Why do you ask?"

"Liar." Pilar gave him a playful slap on the shoulder.

"I was being sarcastic."

"Because clearly you were in pain and I asked the obvious?"

And they both chuckled. Pilar still held Cade's hand. Somehow it made him feel better about his predicament.

Suddenly, Pilar let go of Cade's hand. "I forgot. Now I have to wash my hands all over again!"

Cade laughed. "I don't know what to do about you except to marry you."

Pilar froze. She seemed to be at a loss for words.

"I can see you two are madly in love, but let me give you a warning. That was only the beginning." Doc Sam looked up from Cade's legs. "Good news and bad news."

"Bad news first." Cade prayed he could handle it.

Doc Sam ignored him. "The good news is that the wound on your thigh is not deep. Maybe half an inch into your muscle."

"And the bad news?" Pilar asked.

"The slash is not clean. The edges are jagged. I need to stitch them up so your thigh can hold together, especially when you walk. Otherwise, it'll pull apart and you'd be in some royal pain."

Doc Sam moved to the smaller cut on Cade's right calf. "So... how did this cut get on the side?"

"Maybe because I was wiggling to get away from him and he slashed however he could." Cade didn't realize that his forehead was covered with sweat until Pilar wiped it with a towel. "Thanks."

"When was the last time you had your tetanus shot?" Doc Sam asked.

"Can't remember. Maybe a few years ago?"

"I don't have any tetanus vaccine left. I used it up last week when some hunters came by. One of them got gored by a boar, and the other fell onto some rusty nails as they fled to their tree stand."

"Where's the closest local hospital where they might stock tetanus vaccine?" Pilar asked.

"Thirty minutes west in Everglades City at a medical center or an hour away in Naples at the bigger hospital there—that has a trauma center. Alternatively, you could go east to Miami, but you might have to drive for an hour and a half." Doc Sam gathered his materials. "If you can get the shot within three days, you should be okay."

"Nobody's going anywhere!" Arnon shouted from the door. "Just stitch him up, Doc Sam. Make it fast!"

Doc Sam ignored him. "Miss, look in those drawers over there and gather some gauze, sports tape or any tape you can find, scissors, and whatever you think is needed to dress the wounds."

"Okay."

"I'm going to the kitchen to get some ice."

Cade watched Pilar wash her hands all over again, and then collect the things that Doc Sam had told her to get. Pilar did not touch Cade after she dried off her hands.

Cade wanted her to hold his hand again, but it was too much to ask.

They were back to their old selves. If Pilar had any feelings for him, she wasn't showing it.

Doc Sam came back carrying a bucket of ice, a

dish towel, and a long twine. He put maybe two cups of ice onto the center of the towel, and tied it up with a piece of twine. The pack fit into his broad palm. It looked like a ball. He tied up the ends.

"As I said earlier, I'm out of lidocaine. You can thank the hunters who came by." He lifted up what he had in his hands. "So these ice packs will have to do. We're going to ice your wound so you won't feel too much pain when I sew you up."

"What about the whiskey?" Cade asked.

"That comes next, but first, this." Doc Sam placed the homemade ice pack directly on Cade's thigh, directly on top of the wound.

Cade gritted his teeth as the cold seeped into his wound.

"Don't move. The ice pack will sit there for ten minutes." Doc Sam busied himself looking for his sutures. "Needle and thread, needle and thread, where are you?"

Cade rolled his eyes. The sooner they returned to Miami, the better for them all. He made a mental note to get a tetanus shot and to ask Helen for two weeks off. He deserved the time off, even though he had used one week about six months ago when Dad fell off a horse and broke his tailbone. All five sons went home as a show of support.

One week left of his vacation. Maybe that was enough. Would Helen give him an extra week? He could call it sick leave. Doc Sam could write him a note he could give to Helen. Or the hospital could.

"While we wait for the ice to numb your wound, we should pray." Pilar sat closer to the hospital bed but didn't touch Cade.

He missed her touch. "Can we hold hands while we pray?"

"Focus, dude. Didn't you hear what Doc Sam said earlier? If you had left your wounds the way they were, you'd probably be dead in about eight to twelve hours."

"It's by the mercy of God that I survived."

"So let's pray." Pilar closed her eyes.

Cade wanted to watch her pray, but he decided this was no time to be distracted. He put his hand on Pilar's shoulder as she bowed her head. He closed his eyes and listened to her quiet voice.

"Father God, we come before You today in a state of need. We are needy, Lord. So needy that we will not survive today without You. That's how much we need you, Lord." Pilar drew a deep breath. "The air that we breathe, the blood that courses through our bodies, and everything we need to survive as human beings have been given to us by You, creator God."

Pilar paused. Her voice caught.

"We come before you now to pray for Ca—uh... Monty. His wounds need to close up and there is no hospital anesthetic. He'll have to make do. Please hold back the pain and let him recover from this so that he can go on to live the rest of his life serving You, Lord."

Cade thought it sounded like he was preparing for the seminary. As a Christian, he wanted to serve God more than ever, but he wasn't a pastor or a counselor or a ministry worker. He also didn't do much at church, only attending Sunday morning services. He didn't sign up to usher or organize events or anything. Sure, he tithed, but he had done the minimum at his church.

How could he serve God as a private investigator? He was certain that there were Christians in every profession, but he wondered if his contribution to God's kingdom might be smaller than, say, someone who was actively serving at church.

He wondered which church Pilar attended in Miami. Maybe he could go to church with her and serve in whatever capacity she was in. Then they could be together even on weekends.

"I pray for a peaceful resolution to the conflict so that we can all go home safely to our families," Pilar nearly whispered her last words, but Cade had heard it.

"In the holy and matchless name of Jesus, I pray," Pilar said.

Cade and Doc Sam both said "amen."

Arnon snickered at the door. "You believe all that nonsense?"

Cade chose to ignore him. Doc Sam lifted the pack of ice from his thigh. Cade felt numb in that area and hardly felt the ice pack move.

"Feel anything?" Doc Sam touched the skin near the gaping wound.

Cade shook his head, but Pilar made a face. So he admitted it. "A little."

"Good. The ice numbed the area. I'm going to sterilize it." Doc Sam poured a couple of ounces of whiskey on top of the wound.

It burned so badly that Cade let out a short howl, then grimaced. His balled fists hit the bed. He shut his eyes tightly and saw flashing white stars.

He felt something warm pressing against his chest.

His eyes sprung open. It was Pilar's palm. Only his shirt separated his pounding heart from Pilar's touch.

"Are you okay?" Tears welled in her eyes.

Cade nodded.

Please just keep your palm on my chest.

CHAPTER NINETEEN

"Everyone okay?" Doc Sam asked oh-so-casually.

Cade wished the doctor hadn't asked that question because Pilar looked self-conscious. Still, they continued to hold hands. Her hand was warm, and Cade could feel his pain meter drop several pointes.

Cade felt a curved needle threading through his flesh. It still stung a bit, but holding Pilar's hand, Cade felt that he could endure this. When he saw the tears in her eyes, he knew he had to survive this.

"I'm not dead yet." Cade squeezed Pilar's hand.

Pilar squeezed it back. "Just look at me. It will be over soon."

Cade tried to focus on her, trying not to think or feel the pain on his thigh muscles. Yet, he still winced and hissed as Doc Sam sutured his thigh.

"Aren't the stitches a bit loose?" Pilar asked.

"Glad you noticed." Doc Sam nodded. "We just

want the skin and muscles to hold together. If I suture it too tightly, we risk infection. Tight stitches can trap bacteria underneath. Loose stitches also let the area continue to breathe and for fluids to drain."

"Interesting." Cade watched Pilar watch Doc Sam work.

"Once you get to the hospital, they're going to put antibiotic ointment on the wound—I don't have any left—and they can give you medication, for example, Cipro."

"Is that an antibiotic?" Cade asked.

"They might give you more than one antibiotic." Doc Sam continued to stitch Cade up.

Even with Pilar near him, he could still feel every poke of the needle. There was nothing he could do but endure this fiery furnace. He was certain it would be worse if Pilar wasn't nearby.

Pilar leaned over to Cade and whispered in his ear, "I'll give you a kiss for every stitch."

Cade's eyes widened. "You said it, Pilar."

"I thought your name was Maria!" Arnon said from the door.

Uh-oh.

In his pain, Cade had forgotten their fake names.

"Maria is on my work name tag." Pilar looked down at her blouse pocket. "I guess I lost it between the Callahan Hotel and here."

She turned to Cade. "Monty calls me Pilar because he doesn't like the name Maria."

What a save!

Cade felt relieved. The pain in his thigh continued as Doc Sam worked his suture needle and thread, but he was more focused on trying to prevent Arnon from doing anything to Pilar.

Not that he was prejudiced against criminals, but the fact that Pilar was the only woman in the entire cabin bothered Cade a lot. It was by the wisdom of God that Doc Sam recruited Pilar to work with him, thereby sparing her from being out there, at the mercy of Braun-Dean and his merry men.

"My girl is like that," Arnon said. "She hates the name Arnon, so she calls me Aaron."

"Well, whatever name she calls you is the best name for you," Pilar said.

Arnon pointed to her. "I will tell her that."

"You going to marry her?" Cade asked.

"She wants to have a big wedding, invite all the family," Arnon said. "I just want us to elope. She thinks that's not romantic."

"Whatever she says," Doc Sam said. "My wife and I got along for sixty years until she passed away two years ago. You heard of the old adage, 'A happy wife, a happy life?' I can tell you that's true. My wife was always happy."

"I'm sorry she passed away," Pilar said.

"She was very ill the last few months. She was suffering. Brain cancer, you know. But she didn't want to die at the hospital. She wanted to sit on a chair and watch me smoke them boars." Doc Sam's voice caught. "So after she passed, I still kept it up. I put an empty chair in the backyard and cooked ribs in my Weber smoker. In fact, I was doing just that when you came here and took over my cabin. Can't you let a retired old man be?"

Arnon didn't say anything. He was busy chewing tobacco.

"How did you come to stay here in this cabin?" Cade asked.

"This private land belongs to a friend of mine. I saved his life in Vietnam, so he thought he owed me something. He didn't have to do anything, really," Doc Sam explained. "I worked as a general practitioner for many years in Everglades City. My friend found out I liked to fish and hunt, so he bought this land and let me come and go anytime. When my wife and I retired, he let us build a cabin free of charge anywhere we wanted and let us live off the land."

"No kids?" Pilar asked.

Cade liked the question. He also wanted kids. When he saw his nieces and nephews, he longed for children of his own. Then again, he was probably thinking too much. Just because Pilar asked about kids, it didn't necessarily mean she was thinking about having one—unlike Cade's mindset.

"Our only daughter and her husband died in a car wreck almost twenty years ago." Doc Sam sounded sad.

"I'm sorry."

Cade wanted them to stop talking about sad things as Doc Sam was sewing up his legs. However, Doc Sam seemed to be able to compartmentalize the conversation as he worked the sutures.

"You must have made many memories with your wife," Pilar said.

Doc Sam nodded. "It's lonely without her."

What could Cade say? He felt the pain of the

needle again and turned to face Pilar. When he stared at her, his pain level went down.

What was going on between him and Pilar? Was there something more than just a one-sided crush?

Without saying another word, Pilar rubbed his arm.

Cade wanted to know what she was thinking. Was she showing general compassion for him, or did she have genuine feelings for him? When had it all begun? Dubai, perhaps? He knew that had been the time for him.

If the feelings were mutual, why hadn't they figured it out sooner? They had lost a year apart. Sure, they had texted each other and talked maybe once or twice on video, but each had been busy with their jobs. Sometimes they went for months without communicating with each other.

He missed her. Greatly.

That had been why Cade had volunteered right away the moment his boss had told them that their associates were in trouble in Miami. He didn't care what kind of crisis it was, as long as he had a chance to work with Pilar.

So he must survive this.

For Pilar.

Yes, Cade had the will to live. His mother would weep if he died. Would Pilar too? He wasn't sure.

Something else niggled at his conscience now. Pilar had mentioned serving God in her prayer. Cade knew that she hadn't said it casually.

He realized now that he had to go on a quest to seek out God's calling for his life. There must be a place of service for him. If so, what was it? Knowing he had more work to do meant that he could pray for God to keep him alive, right?

Lord, I know so much about You. And yet there is more for me to learn. What is it that You want me to do? What is my calling to serve?

Getting well and moving on meant that he could ask Pilar out to dinner. He thought about how he could do that without scaring her. Just minutes ago, he'd blurted something about marriage.

Soon enough, he should tell Pilar how he felt because their careers seemed to be unpredictable. Their jobs would be less so if he could work with her all the time. Perhaps when this was over, he could suggest that Hu Knows, Inc., open up a field office in Miami. Would that be selfish of him to ask for such a thing? It would only benefit him.

"Done." Doc Sam straightened up. "Now we repeat the same process for the other wound. We'll bandage them both afterwards. Plus I have some antibiotics for you to take."

"I'm not allergic to any medication," Cade said.

"Good. I only have one kind of antibiotics." Doc Sam rolled his chair to the other side of the hospital bed and swapped sides with Pilar.

The ice pack was not cold anymore, and water dripped from the dish towel. Doc Sam repackaged it before he put the cloth bag of ice on top of Cade's smaller wound on his right calf.

Cade was worried that Pilar would stop holding his hand.

Pilar was busy staring at his thigh wound. "Wow. These stitches are neat and tidy. The suture thread looks thick."

Doc Sam nodded. "Yes, because of the thigh muscles."

"I once had to have stitches on my foot, and my doctor used thick thread too," Pilar said.

"When was that?" Cade was concerned.

Pilar brushed it off. "I was in high school. Dirt bike."

"Were you a tomboy?"

"No. My brother dared me. He should have known better than to dare me." Pilar shook her head. "We were both injured, and Dad banned dirt bikes from ever being mentioned again in the house to this day."

"Do you know how to ride a motorcycle?" Doc Sam asked.

"Yes." Pilar didn't volunteer any information.

"As long as your dad doesn't know about it?"

"He's gotten over it, I think. Ironically, Mom was okay with it. She lives vicariously through me. All the things she didn't get to do as a kid or adult or when she married, she let me do." There was a mischievous glint in her eye that Cade dared not ask about.

But it was on his mind throughout the second ordeal of getting his right calf stitched up.

Doc Sam made quick work of it. For a retired physician, he seemed to remember a lot of skills from his former profession. He worked the curved surgical scissors deftly.

"There." Doc Sam got up. "Now we bandage him up. You need to wash your hands again so that we can keep a sterile environment where the wounds are."

Pilar nodded and quickly went to the sink.

"But the psychology of touch helped you get over

the threshold of pain, didn't it?" Doc Sam seemed to have approved of their public display of affection.

Cade nodded.

Doc Sam tore off his gloves and put on a new pair. Then he bandaged Cade up with Pilar's help. She mainly held the bandage scissors to cut the gauze, tape, and bandage.

"How many stitches did he get?" Pilar put her hand on Cade's right calf—it was nearest to her—then realized where her hand was, and retracted it. "Sorry. Sorry."

Cade didn't mind at all, but what could he say?

"No problem." He sounded so businesslike that he surprised himself.

"Eight on the big cut." Doc Sam stretched. "Six on the smaller cut. It was jagged so I put an extra stitch on it."

"Fourteen stitches?" Pilar nearly fell back in her chair. "What!"

"Fourteen kisses for fourteen stitches." Arnon at the door laughed so boisterously that he nearly dropped his AR-15.

Cade's heart soared, and he couldn't feel the stitches anymore—what pain?—and he was over the moon. He tugged Pilar's hand and pulled her back to his bedside.

He stared at her. "Are you going to keep your word?"

Pilar couldn't answer him.

At all.

CHAPTER TWENTY

While Cade napped on the hospital bed in the small room that Doc Sam had called his clinic, Pilar helped to put away the suture needles, gauze, tape, gloves, and so forth.

"Put this bottle back in that drawer over there." Doc Sam handed Pilar the antibiotics that he had dispensed to Cade earlier.

Cade had fallen asleep on the hospital bed. Pilar suspected that the ordeal of getting stitches without anesthesia—not the kind that hospitals generally used—had worn down Cade's body.

He wasn't moving at all. He looked comfortable under the thin and old blanket that covered most of him. His socks peeked out a bit.

Thank You, Lord, that Cade is now out of danger.

Pilar pulled the knob on the drawer that Doc Sam had directed her to. Inside were prescription and pill bottles of all kinds. All jumbled up. Was there something that could...

"Doc Sam?" Pilar wondered how to ask her question with Arnon still watching from the door.

"Yes, ma'am?" Doc Sam was sweeping the floor.

Pilar didn't know whether he was doing that as a matter of routine or that, like her, he was looking for an excuse to stay longer in the clinic so that they could come up with an idea to defeat their captors.

"These bottles are not in alphabetical order," Pilar said. "Wouldn't it be easier for you to find the right medicine if they were in order?"

"My wife used to do that for me." Doc Sam chuckled. "Feel free to rearrange."

"Okay." Pilar read every label on the medicine bottles and arranged them in alphabetical order. Somewhere in the middle of her quest to make the drawer look neat and tidy, she saw it.

Ambien.

She had personally never taken it, but some of the associates and clients she'd worked with in the past five years had.

This bottle had expired six months ago. Would the medicine still be effective? It was worth a try.

"Doc Sam?" Pilar called out.

Doc Sam came over with his broom. He stood over the drawer of partially arranged bottles.

"Where does this one go? It has two names," Pilar said.

"Put it under the brand name. I usually don't remember the generic name."

Pilar picked up another bottle. "Which one is the brand name?"

Doc Sam told her. By now Pilar was standing shoulder to shoulder with him, effectively blocking Arnon from seeing the medicine in the drawer in front of them.

"This one?" Pilar lifted it slightly so that Doc Sam could see the name.

Ambien.

Pilar tapped Morse Code on the lid, soft enough for Doc Sam to sound out the dots.

Three short taps. Three long taps. Three short taps.

Even though SOS technically didn't stand for "save our souls," that was Pilar's intended message. She wanted Doc Sam to make the connection between the Morse code and the bottle in her hand with a potential way to rescue themselves.

Doc Sam's bushy eyebrows rose. He stared at the bottle label with a knowing look. "That's mine, but I don't take it anymore. It's in the wrong drawer."

He picked it up and made a show of opening and closing drawers below the one that Pilar had opened. Then the bottle disappeared from Doc Sam's hand. He closed the bottommost drawer.

"What time is it?" Doc Sam looked around, then asked Arnon.

Arnon checked his phone. "Noon."

"I better make the barbecue sauce!" Doc Sam declared. "The ribs should be ready by now!"

Pilar glanced over at Cade. He stirred a bit, but didn't open his eyes.

"Just let him sleep," Doc Sam told Arnon. "He ain't going anywhere."

"I have to tie up his wrists though."

"It won't be necessary. He's out like a light.

What's he going to do with all those stitches and pain? Hobble his way to freedom? I think we just lock him in the clinic if it makes you feel better."

Arnon thought about it for a moment.

"You like ribs, don't you? This one has my signature dry rub, famous the world over." Doc Sam ushered Arnon and Pilar out of the clinic, closing the door behind him. He pulled a key out of nowhere and turned the lock on the door. "Look. I'm locking the door."

Then Doc Sam turned to Arnon. "How much barbecue sauce do you think I need to make?"

Arnon thought for a minute. "Five of us plus you three. We might have more people coming later."

Five of us.

Pilar caught it. Arnon had put Braun-Dean as one of them. More and more, Pilar believed that Braun-Dean hadn't been a real hostage in the first place.

Then again, what about the argument he'd had with another person on the phone? Their agreement of some sort? It was clear that Braun-Dean hadn't staged the crime alone.

"I'll make enough sauce," Doc Sam said. "But first, I need to check the ribs. See if they're done. You need to escort us, right?"

"Right." Arnon pointed his AR-15 at them.

He hadn't been like that earlier, so Pilar guessed that Arnon was doing it for show so that Joe could see that he was doing the work. Perhaps he wasn't a professional bad guy, if at all. He and her girlfriend had already talked about getting married. That meant he needed money if he wanted to raise a family. So it was possible that Arnon had taken this job for the money.

Pilar didn't want to get into a conversation with him for a deep dive into the why and wherefore. She just wanted to go home safely—and take Cade with her.

In the backyard, Doc Sam checked the smoker. Nodded approvingly. "Lunch is almost ready. I need a few minutes to make the sauce, and then the ribs will fall off the bones and we can eat."

Pilar would be lying if she didn't admit that she was salivating at the thought of eating ribs slathered with barbecue sauce. However, wild boar was not her thing. In fact, she rarely ate pork ribs. She preferred beef brisket.

Nevertheless, she was famished. All she had all morning was coffee. She had given her bacon biscuit to Butch on her way to serving Braun-Dean and Zuriel.

Speaking of Zuriel, Pilar wondered where she'd gone and if she had been able to leave the private land. At the back of her mind, Pilar worried that she might have made a mistake letting Zuriel go with James.

Pilar followed Doc Sam into the kitchen. He used a pot holder to lift the lid off a big pot on the stove. Steam rose into the air. "Looks like the potatoes are boiled. You know how to mash them?"

"Yes, I do." At home, Pilar hardly cooked, but she sure could mash potatoes.

"Salt and pepper are on the counter next to the stove." Doc Sam pointed to a vintage refrigerator that looked like a Frigidaire from the fifties. "Butter and milk are in the fridge. I'll get you a masher and a mixing bowl."

"I don't know the proportions of butter and milk, but you will tell me, won't you?"

"Sure. But I'll tell you a secret." Doc Sam smiled. "I just eyeball it."

"You sound like my grandmother. She can cook anything, but if I ask her how much this or that is, she doesn't know—until she cooks it."

"How old is your grandma?" Doc Sam drained the potatoes and put the pot on a small kitchen table where Pilar would work.

"She will be seventy-nine in May." Pilar carried butter and milk to the table.

Doc Sam gave her instructions for the mashed potato. "Keep the skin."

While Pilar did her part, Doc Sam started on his special sauce. It looked like he was making two or three cups of it. Arnon hovered over them like a food inspector.

"You want to help also?" Doc Sam asked him.

"I'm just the taste tester." He inched his way toward Doc Sam, who was gathering his sauce ingredients.

Doc Sam put a saucepan on the stove top, then turned to Arnon. "No, no. Don't come here. This is my family's secret recipe that was handed down to me which I absolutely cannot share. If you stand here looking over my shoulder, I will deliberately skip a few ingredients to protect the integrity of the secret."

"Whatever." Arnon made a face.

"Have a potato," Pilar offered. "I can put butter on it for you."

Arnon made his way to Pilar's table. She did what she could to keep him there, facing away from Doc Sam. She prayed that Doc Sam would be able to complete his sauce without much ado.

"You and your girlfriend thinking of kids?" Pilar asked casually.

"She wants five kids. Can you believe it?" Arnon dug into the potato that Pilar had put on a plate for him.

"How many do you want?"

"Two or three. Kids can get expensive."

"I bet. Not just when they're young, but also when they go to college."

"I ain't thinking that far." There was a look in his eyes that was somewhat sad. Pilar couldn't pin it down, but she might be breaking through to Arnon.

He wasn't at ease though, his AR-15 was strapped on his front, and he ate with one hand, as if ready for action at any moment.

Pilar mashed the potatoes, all the time wondering how Doc Sam was going to mix in the expired sleeping pills when the sauce was still hot on the stove. Surely he'd know how much dosage to put into the barbecue sauce to knock out at least five grown men.

As far as Pilar was concerned, she only wanted a humane sedation. She didn't want to kill anyone or cause them to have serious medical side effects. She'd rather solve problems through peaceful means.

Yes, she knew how to shoot a firearm and throw knives, but if she could avoid them at all, she would.

In this case, if she had to wrestle that AR-15 from Arnon, she had the skill to do it. However, once she acquired the weapon, if she had to shoot to kill, then what? How could she kill or maim Arnon, who had a wedding to plan and children to look forward to?

It was Pilar's firm belief that the only one who could give and take life was God. Murder was a way to take life, and the Ten Commandments spoke of it specifically in Deuteronomy 5:17.

You shall not murder.

Pilar prayed that the men wouldn't die from the sleeping pills, and that Doc Sam would put just enough to make them pass out so that Cade, Pilar, and Doc Sam could escape from the cabin.

Sauce simmered on the stove. Pilar could smell apple cider, molasses, garlic, and more. She sniffed the air. "Is that Worcestershire sauce?"

"I can't tell you." Doc Sam continued to stir.

Arnon laughed. "I smell it too. Come on, Doc."

"It's a secret ingredient."

Arnon pointed to a bottle on the counter next to Doc Sam. "That's Lea & Perrins. As clear as day."

"I guess you caught me. But I can't say more."

"I'm sure you put salt and pepper in it," Pilar said.

"Nope. Not saying."

"Plus ketchup, brown sugar..." Pilar chuckled. "You better put away the ingredients on your counter or we will know your secret recipe in a minute."

Doc Sam stirred a bit longer and then turned off the stove. "All right, I'll let you in on a secret. I put a bit of water in it."

Arnon was on his feet. "Can I taste it?"

Pilar glanced at Doc Sam.

"Sure." Doc Sam found a spoon and dipped into the sauce. "Careful. It's hot."

Arnon blew at the spoon and then ate the sauce. "Mmm. Very good. You sure you can't share the recipe?"

Doc Sam shook his head. He took the sauce off the stove to let it cool down. "Not unless you give me a million dollars."

"Then who cares about family recipes, huh?" Arnon joked.

"It's time for me to get the meat out of the smoker," Doc Sam said. "You helping?"

"Not my job," Arnon said.

Doc Sam stacked up two large rectangular stainless steel trays that were about four inches deep. Arnon escorted him and Pilar out to the backyard.

Somehow Doc Sam recruited Arnon to help him carry the roasted meat and ribs into the largest room in the cabin which doubled as a dining room. Doc Sam placed the meat on the dining table to the cheer of Joe, Arnon, and Braun-Dean.

Pilar noticed that Ted and Butch still hadn't returned from their mission to find Zuriel. Pilar prayed for Zuriel's safety and then felt bad that she had left her in James's hands. Well, not necessarily. From the briefing that Agent Tanaka had given her, Pilar knew that Zuriel knew a few things, like Krav Maga and the handling of weapons.

And she had willingly gone with James, which told Pilar that Zuriel had believed she could handle him. But the opioid relapse... Would that impair her ability?

Doc Sam opened a sideboard that revealed rows of whiskey, vodka, and rum. It was his own little bar.

"Where did you get all these, Doc?" Arnon rubbed his hands together.

"Sometimes the hunters pay me to smoke their deer or boar or whatever. I take payments in cash or they could give me what they have. Sometimes they bring me these. I can share a few bottles with you."

"A few bottles?" Arnon made his selection. "We'll take them all."

Doc Sam and Pilar returned to the kitchen to get the mashed potatoes and sauce. Arnon frowned and complained that he wanted to eat too.

Pilar made a show of not being able to carry the five pounds of potatoes in the serving bowl, and being the gentleman that he was—or desperate to get back to the dining room—Arnon helped the lady in distress. That way, his attention was on her and not on Doc Sam.

Doc Sam was stirring his sauce in the pot that he'd taken off the stove earlier.

"Whatcha doing, Doc?" Arnon asked. "Isn't the sauce done?"

"Adding a bit more brown sugar in it—oops. Didn't mean to tell you the secret ingredients."

Arnon rolled his eyes.

The deed might be done at this point, but Pilar wouldn't know.

She had to think ahead. After the men had passed out, she had to get Cade. Then they would have to run into the forest. Doc Sam would have to come with them as their guide. He knew how to get out of the forest. Neither Pilar nor Cade had been in this part of Florida before.

If they could get to the bait shop to find a vehicle, it would save them time. Otherwise, an elderly man in his eighties and a thirty-something man with fourteen stitches in his legs might not be able to run like the wind before the men woke up.

Fifteen minutes into watching the three men eat and drink and be merry, Pilar prayed that Ted and Butch would not return before Pilar, Cade, and Doc Sam escaped.

"Can we eat too?" Doc Sam asked Braun-Dean.

"Sure. Have a seat... Oh, there's no seat. Where can they eat, Joe?"

Joe was busy nibbling a bone. "They can eat after we finish, sir."

"If there's any left." Arnon slathered a spoonful of sauce on his ribs.

"Serve us," Braun-Dean said.

There was not much to do because all the food and drinks were on the table.

"More sauce!" Braun-Dean yelled.

"I'll go get it, sir." Doc Sam waddled down the hallway. He seemed to be deliberately not in a rush so that he didn't alert anyone to their plot.

No one stopped him, so he kept going, disappearing down the narrow hallway that led to both the kitchen and the clinic.

Pilar stood by the sideboard with her bowl of mashed potatoes. She wanted some but was afraid to eat any. Instead, she looked around the room to find exit points.

Doc Sam returned with more sauce. He placed the bowl on the side table. He said not a word to Pilar.

Pilar preferred more coordination. A detailed person, she wanted to know what they were going to do beforehand. However, this episode in her PI life had taught her that sometimes she couldn't prepare for things ahead of time.

For example, she still felt bad that she had let Zuriel leave the boat. She prayed that James was a good man and that he would not harm Zuriel.

Sometimes you have to trust strangers.

James himself had told her that.

Now she had to trust a second stranger on the same day: Doc Sam.

Thud.

It was loud enough for Pilar to look.

Arnon's forehead was on the table.

"Look at him. Passed out already." Joe yawned.

Braun-Dean took another sip of his whiskey, which seemed to be his poison of choice.

Pilar almost held her breath as the two remaining men fell asleep at the table.

It worked!

CHAPTER TWENTY-ONE

Groggy, Cade felt slightly disoriented after Pilar woke him up. Pilar helped him off the hospital bed, and then led him out of the cabin to the backyard. He squinted in the noonday sun, inhaled the smell of smoking boar, and then he heard it before he saw it.

An old Indian motorcycle that looked like it came out of World War II roared out of the toolshed. It seemed to be newly painted in bright red-and-yellow hot dog colors. Its sidecar was equally eye-catching in matching colors. Someone—presumably Doc Sam—had polished it to a shine, and it showed under the Floridian sun.

"What in the world?" Cade was half-amused and half-stunned as Doc Sam circled around the Weber smokers and brought the motorcycle to a low-pitch growling idle in front of his guests.

"Meet my wife's 1953 Indian Chief." Tears pooled in Doc Sam's eyes. He sniffed a little and then pointed to the sidecar. "Monty, you sit there to protect the stitches."

Doc Sam motioned to Pilar. "You sit behind me."

Cade noticed that the Indian seat was continuous, unlike other motorcycles that he was familiar with. That was to say, the rider and the passenger would share an extended seat with only a little contour to separate the two people.

"Nope." Cade was wide awake now.

There was no way he'd let Pilar sit behind another man on a motorcycle, even though Doc Sam was old enough to be her grandfather. Call Cade conservative or whatever, but he wasn't going to budge on this.

Before Pilar could give her opinion, Cade made a beeline for the motorcycle and hopped onboard, sitting on the rear portion of the extended seat. His wounds stretched and the pain seared up his legs, but it was too late to change his mind now. His pride was at stake.

Pilar climbed into the sidecar.

"Do we have helmets?" Cade asked.

"Are you over twenty-one?" Doc Sam replied.

"In Florida, you don't need a helmet if you're over twenty and have insurance," Pilar said.

"I still want to wear—"

The rest of his words vanished into the wind as Doc Sam hit the gas and off they went, rumbling down the dirt road in front of Doc Sam's house in their great escape from their captors—

At no more than fifteen miles per hour.

At this rate, anyone could chase after them and catch up.

Doc Sam took them on a dirt path that was almost too narrow for the motorcycle plus the sidecar. Every now and then, the sidecar rode over grass.

Cade noticed that Pilar was glancing behind her often. She was four or five feet away from him in the side car, which was on the same side as the exhaust pipe with a stock muffler making low rumbling noises.

Cade tried to say something to Pilar, but she was unable to hear him. He wanted to ask her where they were going, but their lives were in Doc Sam's hands now. Obviously, they were going to safety, and even more obviously was that he had missed a lot while he'd been sleeping in the clinic.

He'd find out more from Pilar once they cleared the area to a safe zone, wherever that was.

They turned a corner and the path fed into a wide gravel road that vehicles could probably drive on. There, Doc Sam sped up the old bike, but not by much. Cade guessed that it was going at no more than twenty-five miles per hour.

At this rate...

Whatever. Just enjoy the ride.

Cade glanced back whenever Pilar didn't. He wanted to help, but he wasn't sure what he could do.

Pilar looked worried.

Cade wondered if she'd eaten lunch.

He felt thirsty but he doubted they had brought water with them.

How long was this ride? He couldn't ask anyone.

It was an interesting moment for Cade. He had no idea where they were going and how they had escaped from the captors. He only knew that he trusted Pilar, though he had previously questioned her decision to drop off Zuriel with James.

As far as he knew, neither one of those two people had shown up at Doc Sam's cabin. Cade hoped that they had made it out alive and called 911. That was all they needed to do.

When they turned another corner, Pilar shouted and pointed. Cade saw it too.

An off-white van seemed to have run off the side of the road and smashed into a tree. It made Doc Sam speed up. He went around the front of the van, where someone was lying on the shoulder of the gravel road.

Doc Sam slowed down his motorcycle and came to a complete stop near the person.

"We have to help him," Doc Sam said.

"Him? Can you tell if it's a man?" Pilar climbed out of the sidecar at the same time Cade got off the motorcycle. Doc Sam followed after.

They rushed to the man on the ground.

"It's James!" Doc Sam was on his knees, checking vitals. "Son, can you hear me?"

"Son?" Cade asked Pilar.

"I don't think they're related but they're neighbors. James looks up to him."

Immediately, Cade's thought went to Zuriel, but he didn't want Pilar to be jealous of him thinking of another woman, especially since she had been the reason he'd scolded Pilar this morning.

"Where's Zuriel?" Pilar asked. "Have Ted and Butch found her?"

Cade vaguely remembered Braun-Dean calling out for Zuriel back when they were in the cabin. Cade had almost passed out on the floor, but Braun-

Dean's voice was loud and carried in the small living room.

What Pilar said now made Cade think that Braun-Dean had dispatched Ted and Butch to go find Zuriel.

What he was seeing now made Cade fear that something had happened to Zuriel.

"He's still breathing." Doc Sam looked up from his position near James.

"I'll see if there's a first aid kit in the van." Pilar ran to check. "Nothing!"

"I told him to keep a first aid kit in the van. Kids these days don't ever listen." Doc Sam looked over at James. "He's been badly beaten up and bleeding. I need to stay with him and see if I can treat him before it's too late."

"Does he have a cell phone in the van?" Cade asked. He was about to shuffle his way to the van when Pilar stopped him. "You stay put. I'll check."

Pilar rummaged in the front seat for a good bit, then the back cargo area, but shouted back at them. "No cell phone."

"I hate to leave James here," Doc Sam said. "He's like a son to me—and to my wife too. She always baked him cornbread."

Cade watched as Pilar tried to start the engine, but the van was as dead as a doornail. Not even a noise came out of it. She walked back to Cade.

They both looked back at the road they had come from. There was nobody there for miles and miles.

"Where does this road lead to?" Pilar asked Doc Sam.

"Go straight and you will see the exit out of

Geiger Ixora. There will be signs there for Everglades City." Doc Sam pointed. "Twenty minutes from here."

"Wait. Geiger what?" Pilar asked.

"This private land—together with cypress swamp and the resort therein—is called Geiger Ixora."

"I will go," Pilar said. "Key in the ignition?"

"Yes, ma'am. You know how to ride an Indian?" Doc Sam looked worried.

"What year is this model?" Pilar asked, climbing on.

"1953."

"I've ridden a 1949 Harley Knucklehead," Pilar said.

Cade wondered what else Pilar had done. He wished to go on future adventures with her.

"Left hand shift and left foot clutch?" Pilar asked.

Doc Sam's eyes brightened. "You got it. Don't go too fast. Twenty miles per hour. Whatever you do, don't wreck it."

"I'll do my best." Pilar gave him a quick salute, which made Doc Sam grin. "As soon as we get to a phone, we'll call 911. Help should be coming soon, so I'm guessing anywhere from fifty minutes to an hour for the round trip."

"That's what I think too," Doc Sam said. "We'll hide in the forest until you return."

To Cade, Pilar said, "You coming with me?"

"You already know the answer." Wincing but enduring the pain in his leg, Cade climbed aboard the motorcycle with a grin on his face. Gingerly, he put his feet in the foot pegs, and hugged Pilar from the back, his arms locking around her waist.

"I really think we need helmets," he added.

"I always wear one, regardless of the state law, but today we just pray our way out of this forest."

Before Cade could reply, they were on the dirt road again, leaving Doc Sam behind to tend to an unconscious James.

Who would have beaten him up like that? Was it to capture Zuriel? Where had they gone with her?

Once they left Doc Sam, Pilar sped up the motorcycle. It was going at least forty miles per hour now.

"Aren't you going a bit fast?" Cade shouted into the wind. "Doc Sam said twenty miles per hour."

"No. This Indian Chief can go up to fifty miles per hour on a gravel road. So forty is fine!" She revved the engine to prove her point.

"Okay. Whatever you say, ace!" Cade was slightly impressed at Pilar's skill and knowledge.

Better to be on her good side.

Cade's arms were still around Pilar. He enjoyed riding tandem with her, even though this was not a vacation. The ride was smooth now because the gravel was no longer loose. Cade suspected this road was used often by hunters, whose vehicle tires had packed in the gravel over time.

Logically, Pilar might be right about the speed. Then again, if Doc Sam recommended twenty miles per hour and Pilar wanted to go forty, perhaps thirty was a safe compromise. But Pilar didn't ask Cade.

The early afternoon sun shone in through the pine and oak trees. A breeze in the air swayed clumps of palmetto palms on both sides of the gravel road.

Not ten minutes away, Cade spotted a red shoe on the other side of the road. He tapped Pilar's shoulder and pointed. As they drew closer, Cade noted that it was a high-heeled dress shoe.

"Looks like Zuriel's shoe!" Pilar shouted but didn't stop.

"We're not stopping?" Cade asked, but he knew the answer right away.

"No, we need to get help first. We're no match for Ted and Butch, who are armed. Since Braun-Dean wanted Zuriel back alive, I'm safer guessing that they won't hurt her."

Knowing Pilar, she was probably unarmed. He didn't have a weapon on him either. Ted and Butch, if they were after Zuriel, would probably be armed.

Since there were no other vehicles on the road—except for James's van earlier—Cade assumed that Ted and Butch had fled, with or without Zuriel.

Cade also recalled that Ted and Butch had supposedly walked from Doc Sam's cabin to the bait shop where they'd parked a pickup truck. That meant they were driving.

Five minutes later, they saw another shoe.

Cade started to wonder if Zuriel had thrown them out of the pickup truck. Then it dawned on him that he might have been looking at this in reverse. Ted and Butch had been tasked to bring Zuriel back to Braun-Dean at the cabin. If so, they would have to drive in the opposite direction. So the first pump he'd seen was probably the second pump that Zuriel might have thrown out of the pickup.

No, they wouldn't hurt her. Braun-Dean would kill them if they did.

That might be another reason Pilar didn't stop.

Cade was mulling over these things and almost

didn't hear the rumble of vehicles coming up the gravel road. At first he thought they might be Ted and Butch's pickup truck, but he saw two vehicles, lights flashing on top, coming toward them.

Pilar decelerated the Indian Chief and came to a complete stop by the side of the road. She turned off the ignition, remained in her seat, and held up both arms in the air.

Not knowing anything better to do, Cade did the same.

He watched the two patrol vehicles surround them. Deputies exited the SUVs and came toward the duo with their Glock 17 sidearms drawn.

Cade's heartbeat sped up.

CHAPTER TWENTY-TWO

Finally, the cavalry had arrived.

The Collier County Sheriff's Deputies were a godsend, swooping in like the cavalry to rescue two former hostages without laughing at their hotdog-colored retro Indian Chief motorcycle with a sidecar. Pilar figured that as Florida law enforcement officers, they had probably seen just about everything.

First things first.

"Doc Sam is attending to James about fifteen minutes from here," Pilar said. "James is unconscious on the side of the road. Look for a white van that has crashed into a tree."

Officer Weatherby called for the paramedics. It helped that he knew Doc Sam, who had smoked some deer meat for him and some buddies a couple of months ago. He had also stopped by the bait shop a few times and had met James. So he was able to describe how Doc Sam looked to the dispatcher.

"Ma'am, we did get a call from someone about an hour ago," Officer Weatherby said. "The woman is supposed to meet us around this area. Was that you?"

"It has to be Zuriel." Pilar thanked God that Zuriel had managed to get a phone to call 911. She prayed that Zuriel would stay safe until the police could rescue her. "I asked her to call 911. I also gave her FBI Special Agent Ruby Tanaka's number."

Weatherby's eyebrows rose.

Pilar told him that she had been deputized by Agent Tanaka as a Task Force Member to keep an eye on Zuriel, an asset in an ongoing money laundering investigation. She felt bad that she had lost Zuriel.

"We'll find her," Weatherby said.

"Ted and Butch might have captured her. Her red Manolo Blahniks pumps were on the road. We didn't touch them." Pilar went on to explain that Ted and Butch were armed, and that she felt it was too dangerous for her and her injured colleague to stop and pick up the shoes.

The officer listened.

Pilar figured he was recording the conversation on his body cam.

Weatherby relayed all that information to his team just as more vehicles arrived.

Pilar saw several souped-up SUVs and a Lenco BearCat armored vehicle stopping near the deputies' vehicles. They looked like they all belonged to the Collier County Sheriff's Office SWAT. Pilar wondered about the presence of Miami SWAT, which had cordoned off the Callahan Hotel a couple of days ago. Might this end up being a joint operation, after all? She made a mental note to ask Agent Tanaka the next time they saw each other.

When they parked, a trailer arrived, carrying several all terrain vehicles that the SWAT team would use. Pilar wasn't sure if the ATVs would reach Doc Sam's cabin because the path in front of his cabin was small and narrow. Maybe three feet wide only. They'd have to go on foot to cut down vehicle noise, but that would be the SWAT team's problem, not hers.

The SWAT Tactical Commander in body armor approached them and introduced himself as Lieutenant Taylor. "The caller said that hostages were at the resort, but you're saying you were at Doc Sam's cabin?"

"Originally, we were held hostage at the Callahan Hotel in Miami. Then we were brought to the resort during the tropical storm. Cade and I escaped—only to be held against our will again at Doc Sam's cabin."

Pilar explained what she and Doc Sam had done to put three captors to sleep in the cabin. "You'll have to ask Doc Sam how much Ambien he put in his barbecue sauce and how long the men would be out."

"However, if Ted and Butch are there now, they could wake everyone up," Cade said. "Those two men were supposed to bring Zuriel back to the cabin."

The Tactical Commander asked Pilar and Cade more questions, just as an ambulance flew past them. Its sirens were silent.

Pilar prayed for James to get well soon.

Behind the ambulance, a black Chevy Suburban arrived. And out popped Agent Ruby Tanaka. Pilar was so happy to see her that she gave her a big bear hug—forgetting that she hadn't showered in a while.

"We've been looking everywhere for you!" Tanaka looked happy to see Pilar. "We had no idea where you were until Zuriel called. Glad you gave her my number. Good move."

"I'm grateful, but at the same time, I'm also surprised that she could remember the number. I only gave it to her once. She didn't write it down. If it were me, I can't even remember my own phone number after all these years."

"Now that's pretty bad," Cade ribbed her. "Why can't you remember your own phone number?"

Pilar brushed away his remarks. "Because I don't call myself."

"Zuriel has an extraordinary memory." Tanaka brought the conversation back to Zuriel. "That's why she's an asset and we can't lose her."

"Wait a sec. If her memory is that good, why didn't she say anything when I gave her your number?" Pilar said.

"Because I gave you a different number than the one I'd given her."

Tanaka's explanation made sense.

"But why?" Pilar asked.

Tanaka only smiled.

Pilar had to live with the lack of answer from the agent, but she guessed that Tanaka didn't want both of them to be implicated if they both had the same number that could be traced to the FBI. If that were the case, who would be Tanaka's priority? Zuriel or Pilar?

Pilar knew the answer.

Oh well.

She moved on. "Since she called you, does that mean she gets the reward?"

"What reward?"

Pilar pretended to look disappointed. "You mean we're not important enough for you or the local police to offer reward money?"

Tanaka laughed. "Aren't you just glad to be alive?"

"Seriously, I am. God is good."

Tanaka inspected Pilar's housekeeping uniform. "Grunge looks good on you."

Pilar laughed. "It was cream colored in Miami. The swamp colored it gray and brown."

"Glad you're okay."

The SWAT convoy rumbled past them, no doubt to go to their new staging area, now that the standoff had moved from the swamp resort to the forest cabin.

"Oh, I forgot to introduce you two," Pilar said. "Agent Tanaka, this is Cade Sumter, a PI at Hu Knows, Inc."

Tanaka shook hands with Cade.

"Helen and Earl have mentioned your name before. Nice to finally meet you," Cade said. "I still can't believe that Pilar is deputized. She didn't say a word until just now."

"There was no opportunity," Pilar said. "Besides, I didn't know who might be listening in."

"So you were in Miami for Zuriel?" Cade asked.

"Not exactly. When I agreed to spy on Braun-Dean for his estranged wife, Agent Tanaka found out about it and contacted me. We went from there." Pilar didn't want to say more. She turned to

Tanaka. "How did you get here so quickly from Miami?"

"I flew into Naples. Faster than driving. Borrowed a vehicle from our resident agency in Naples." Tanaka looked around. "Zuriel was supposed to wait for me in Everglades City, but she didn't show up."

Pilar repeated everything she had told Officer Weatherby and Lieutenant Taylor. "She could've been captured by Ted and Butch, and taken back to Doc Sam's cabin now, where Braun-Dean is waiting for her."

"Sounds like former Senator Felix Braun-Dean might not be innocent after all," Tanaka said.

"I don't know for sure." Pilar could imagine that false imprisonment would be one of the charges.

"Either way, he's not going to escape. CCSO deputies are also blocking the east entrance." Tanaka looked up at the clear blue sky. "Soon, we should see choppers and drones overhead."

"There were explosions in the resort this morning," Cade said to Tanaka. "Has anyone reported them?"

"The police department did receive multiple 911 calls about the explosions," Tanaka said. "When the fire department arrived, the bridge was out. The fire trucks could not access the floating resort. They had to wait for air tankers to put out the fire."

"Air tankers?" Pilar asked.

"Choppers with built-in water tanks."

"Oh, I see." Pilar nodded. "Did you find the women? They were in a hut with me."

"Did they find bodies?" Cade asked what Pilar was afraid to ask.

"The resort is entirely burnt down. If not for the swamp around it acting like a moat, the fire could've spread to the entire forest."

"They're still combing through the rubble," Tanaka replied. "However, they did find half a dozen bodies with weapons on their side in what looked like a bombed-out kitchen."

Cade went on to describe how many men he thought were hiding in the kitchen. "Max was near-death. Skeeter was treating him, but Max really needed to get to the hospital."

Tanaka didn't show any emotion.

As long as Pilar had known Tanaka, she was like that. Perhaps the shell had helped her to endure her difficult line of work.

"Somehow Ted and Butch escaped with Braun-Dean." Pilar's voice trailed off. "And then additional personnel showed up at the cabin: Joe and Arnon."

"We have many questions but few answers right now." Tanaka got on the phone with Lieutenant Taylor to get on the same page with him. She made a few more quick calls, letting Pilar and Cade stand there listening. While Pilar was deputized, Cade wasn't. However, they both knew the drill.

Mum's the word.

The SWAT convoy moved past them. Pilar assumed they were heading for Doc Sam's cabin which was twenty-five minutes from there.

"We can continue talking in the SUV," Tanaka said. "This is an interagency and interdepartmental operation, but the CCSO has the most boots on the ground with help from Miami's STR unit."

Pilar nodded.

"As for us, our role is to wait for them to do their work. Meanwhile, we need to do a debriefing. I have many questions about the Callahan Hotel as well."

"So do I," Cade said. "For example, we were holed up in the hotel for hours, with Miami SWAT and CNT outside."

"That, I know the answer to." Tanaka lifted a finger in the air. "Your captors said they had rigged the entire hotel with explosives. Any false move, and the entire building—along with other buildings surrounding it—would implode. Considering that you were in a high-density part of downtown Miami, we couldn't risk it."

"I didn't see any explosives, nor did I hear the captors talk about them," Pilar said. "Did you, Cade?"

"Nope." Cade concurred. "Now I know how we managed to escape in the middle of the night."

"We found the tunnel after you had left—leaving behind the rest of the hostages," Tanaka added. "And of course, after a thorough search of the hotel, the MPD Bomb Squad found no explosives. It was all a smokescreen."

"They must've been relieved not to have to defuse any explosives," Cade added.

Pilar concurred. "Speaking of hostages, I worry that Josephine Callahan plus the other four women might have perished in the firebombing."

At the same time, Pilar also feared that something worse than death might have happened to them.

Tanaka turned to walk to her SUV when she spotted the Indian Chief. "What is that thing?"

"What? You don't like red and yellow stripes on a vintage motorcycle?" Pilar teased.

"Hurts my eyes." Tanaka blinked.

"That's Doc Sam's. Actually, I heard it's his wife's. She has since passed away."

"Not while riding that, I hope."

"No. Brain cancer."

"Oh, sorry to hear that," Tanaka said.

Pilar and Cade followed Tanaka to her vehicle. Cade was still limping.

"How are you doing?" Pilar asked Cade. "How are your legs?"

"I'm okay now. When we get to town, I'll stop by the hospital."

"Everglades City has a medical center. If the case is more serious, they'll take you to Naples," Tanaka said. "Or if you want, we could drive ninety minutes east to Miami. The only catch is that I can't leave without Zuriel."

"I think I can wait," Cade said. "Doc Sam fixed me up good."

"You have to tell me all about Doc Sam. Sounds like a fascinating fellow." Tanaka opened the SUV for Pilar and Cade to climb in.

"Do you think we'll be safe out here on the road?" Pilar asked.

Tanaka nodded. "The joint SWAT teams will stage about half a mile away from the cabin, which itself is half a mile from the swamp resort. We are outside that circle. Besides, you see the CCSO vehicles out here too."

"CCSO?" Cade asked.

"Collier County Sheriff's Office," Tanaka said.

"Ah." Cade didn't say more. He closed the vehicle door.

Pilar felt safe again, sandwiched between Tanaka and Cade. She also felt exhausted, like she could pass out. And hungry. She even thought of eating smoked wild boar from Doc Sam's Weber.

"Want some water?" Tanaka handed out water bottles.

Usually, Pilar avoided drinking water from a plastic bottle because she didn't want to ingest microplastic, but she didn't want to die of thirst. She downed the entire bottle in one go.

"How about some power bars?" Tanaka lifted a ziplock bag filled with protein bars.

"Yes, please. I'm so famished." Pilar took two bars.

Cade seemed content to be with Pilar. And vice versa.

Her shoulders leaned against his, and he leaned back against her. She didn't know what that meant, but he was clearly not rejecting her—unless he was trying to push her away.

Tanaka smiled, watching them. "Something going on between you two?"

"We survived together." Pilar wasn't sure if that was it, but during their being stuck together, they had bonded.

Then again, it could be due to the fact that they shared the same Christian faith.

"How long have we known each other?" Pilar asked.

"One year. We met in Dubai." Cade finished his

water and put the empty bottle in a cupholder in the SUV door. "It's because of Pilar that I moved home to the States and got a job at Hu Knows, Inc."

"For real?" Pilar didn't know what to think.

"For real." Cade nodded. "It's also because of you that I came to Miami however many days ago now."

"Four days ago," Tanaka said.

"It feels like it's been at least a week." Pilar leaned back on the seat.

"Sure does." Cade chewed on the power bar.

Pilar turned to him. "When do you go home to Savannah?"

"If you want me to, I'd stay in Miami permanently."

"You mean you'd find a new job in Miami?" Pilar wondered what he was trying to tell her. "Will Helen be willing to let you go?"

"I'll talk to her about letting me work out of Miami, like a PI at large," Cade said. "After all, I travel all over the place anyway, so what difference does it make if my apartment is in Savannah or Miami, or even Atlanta for that matter."

"If she says no?"

"Then I quit. Are you looking for a partner in your PI company?" Cade sounded serious.

"I can't afford to hire anyone," Pilar said. "I can barely pay myself after company expenses."

"Maybe if we team up..." Cade's eyes tracked hers. "You know, like Mr. and Mrs. Smith."

Pilar's jaw dropped. She had no idea Cade was this forward.

"After all, I'm still waiting for the first of the fourteen kisses you promised," Cade added.

Pilar's face turned red. She had been hoping he'd forget about that silly thing. It had been her idea, but in retrospect, she felt embarrassed she'd even suggested it. Well, at that time, Cade had been in pain on the clinic bed, and it was the only way Pilar could think of to get his mind off his suffering.

"One kiss for every stitch, remember?" Cade pressed.

Pilar buried her face in her palms.

Cade only laughed.

The long wait in Tanaka's vehicle made Pilar sleepy. She couldn't keep her eyes open. She stirred when Tanaka's voice woke her up. Only then did she realize that she had fallen asleep on Cade's shoulder. He didn't seem to mind.

Tanaka laughed, but stopped when a new call came. "Oh, you have her? Good. Thank you, sir."

She hung up her phone and turned to Pilar and Cade. "Good news. They found Zuriel in the cabin like you suspected. Now we can leave."

"That was quick." Pilar stretched.

"It's been over half an hour since we waited in this vehicle." Cade pointed to the dashboard clock.

"I slept for that long?"

Cade nodded.

"SWAT captured the five men, three of whom were still groggy from the sleeping pills." Tanaka made a face. "How much did Doc Sam put into the sauce, I wonder?"

"I wonder too." *Best not to know.*

CHAPTER TWENTY-THREE

After the Collier County Sheriff's Office SWAT had apprehended the five men holed up in Doc Sam's cabin and rescued Zuriel from them, Pilar and Cade rode with Agent Tanaka to Naples, about fifty minutes away from the entrance to the private land, following the ambulance that took James and Zuriel.

Doc Sam gave his statement to the deputies and chose to ride his Indian Chief home to his cabin. He had to take his second boar out of the Weber grill and clean up the mess that his unwelcome guests had left behind.

Softie Pilar bade Doc Sam a tearful goodbye, almost adopting him as her grandpa.

To move things along, Cade promised Doc Sam that he would bring Pilar back to see him as soon as they had time. After all, Miami was only an hour and a half away from the cypress swamp.

Cade wasn't seriously injured, and didn't have to

go all the way to Naples. At the entrance of the private land, Everglades City had its own medical center that was sufficient enough to treat Cade. However, he wanted to follow Pilar, who was going with Agent Tanaka and Zuriel to the hospital in Naples, which had a trauma center that could treat James's very serious injuries.

At the hospital, Pilar stood by Cade's bed the entire time, as he got his wounds checked and properly cleaned in an examination room at the emergency department.

Cade was in a semi-reclining position with his legs stretched out. He felt comfortable only because Pilar was with him. One look at Pilar, and his pain dropped a notch—

Owww!

He had spoken too soon. He hissed and held his breath as the nurse flushed his thigh and calf wounds with saline.

Cade turned to Pilar with a puppy-face look. "You have to hold my hand and give me kisses because it hurts."

"What's wrong with you?" Pilar's face reddened.

Cade knew that she wouldn't have said that to him if they didn't know each other. Maybe they had started out as colleagues a year ago, but now they had progressed to friends and maybe more.

"I have no shame," Cade responded.

Pilar shook her head. "I have no words."

Cade knew that beneath that hardshell exterior, Pilar had feelings for him—at least a little bit. She'd proven it the morning she freaked out when Arnon kicked him on the walking path, and then shortly later when she had held his hand and hugged him in Doc Sam's makeshift clinic.

Without proper anesthesia—the ice pack and whiskey being temporary—Cade had felt the pain of every stitch and yet pretended to be strong and made light of the matter.

He wondered if Pilar had seen through that.

The nurse patted his legs dry and laughed at their banter. "Your boyfriend is very affectionate."

"He's not my—"

An ER physician, Dr. Avramov, came in and put on a pair of gloves. He said that Cade's blood work looked good and that he didn't need a blood transfusion. He then inspected Cade's leg wounds. He pressed around the stitches.

Cade held his breath.

"Your thigh looks good. Some swelling but it will go down." The physician looked up. "These stitches are fine. We don't have to redo them. Who sewed you up?"

"Doc Sam," Cade said. "He lives in the forest hunting ground, about half a mile from the cypress swamp."

"Retired physician, living off the land," Pilar added. "He has a small clinic that seemed to be stuck in time. Injured hunters go to him for emergencies. They pay him with game and booze. Sometimes they pay him to smoke deer or boar."

"Huh. Never had the pleasure of meeting him." The physician instructed Cade to roll to his side so that he could inspect his calf.

After poking a bit, the physician told Cade to lie back down on his back. "The stitches on your calf also look good. I don't think we need to redo these either."

The physician read something on his laptop, which was on a wheeled cart. "Says here that Doc Sam gave you expired amoxicillin. Since you were injured at the swamp, we want to watch out for various forms of bacteria, including swamp *Pseudomonas* as well as *Staphylococcus*. I'm going to give you two types of antibiotics to knock out all the bacteria that might attack you."

Cade nodded. He had been a generally healthy person his entire life and rarely had to go see the doctor for anything growing up. Since he'd been in the security business, he'd been in and out of the doctor's office quite a few times.

However, from now on, all he wanted to do was guard Pilar and no one else.

"You don't recall the last time you had a tetanus shot." The physician typed away at his laptop. "A nurse will come by to give you a shot and put new dressings on your wounds. I'll ask her to put some antibiotic ointment on your wounds."

"Thank you," Cade said.

"Will it leave a scar?" Pilar asked.

A scar? Cade didn't even think about that.

The doctor nodded. "They will eventually fade with time."

"I'm just glad to be alive," Cade said.

"For the next forty-eight hours, no water on the wounds," the physician added. "After that, tape plastic around your legs if you must shower, but no baths yet."

Cade nodded.

"No bungee jumping, skydiving, saving the world, or any superhero stuff. You just rest and take it easy. Elevate your legs."

Cade smiled at the physician's instruction.

"If you have pain, take ibuprofen—not aspirin, in case you bleed." The physician moved toward the door. "In three or four days, go see your own doctor for a follow-up and to make sure there is no infection. If all goes well, you can have your stitches removed in about fourteen days."

"Until then, I guess I need a cane," Cade said.

"The best thing you can do for your legs is to rest." Dr. Avramov left the room.

"Hear that?" Cade asked Pilar. "I have to rest."

"Therefore, rest." Pilar's eyes watered. "I'm just glad you're going to recover. You could've bled to death."

Cade wiped tears from Pilar's cheek. "God protected us. He sent Doc Sam, remember?"

"We need to return his kindness."

"We will. You and me together. We'll help him, okay?" Cade softened his voice. He decided to stop teasing her.

They were alone in the exam room. The door was closed. The nurse hadn't returned with the tetanus shot. He figured he had a few minutes of alone time with Pilar.

"Be with me." Cade held Pilar's hands.

She didn't pull away. Perhaps it was because they had held hands earlier today in Doc Sam's cabin, so she was getting used to their skinship.

Cade would like to think that they were making

headway in their relationship, but he began to feel impatient at their slow burn.

"Okay," Pilar finally said. "I'll make sure you get back to Savannah safely."

"That's business." Cade's hopes dropped a notch. "I meant that I want you to be with me from now on—today, tomorrow, always."

"Always? That's a long time."

Cade waited.

"We'll see."

Cade realized that was all he was going to get from her. But he still had a trump card. "I'll wait for my fourteen kisses."

Pilar covered her eyes. "I don't know what overcame me. I guess you were in such pain that I had to give you an incentive to hold on."

"It worked. I survived, didn't I?" Cade knew that Pilar always kept her word. He hated to burden her with this, but she had given him her word.

Pilar sighed. She tugged his arm a little and then leaned down to peck his cheek.

Cade turned his face just enough so that he could look into her eyes, but now their lips were inches away from each other.

He waited.

He didn't want to beg and he wasn't about to steal a kiss that she was unwilling to give and thereby ruin their relationship forever.

So he waited some more.

Finally, Pilar smiled and pecked him on the lips oh so briefly. She stepped back. "That counts as one."

"Does it? It barely registered." Cade hoped that

Pilar would consider his words a joke and not take it as a push.

He realized now that he had to be satisfied with what Pilar was able to give him at this moment in time. He understood that all these years Pilar had worked very hard to establish a business for herself. She was financially independent because of her job as a private investigator. For someone so driven and singularly focused on her career, it would take time for her to consider adding a slice of life into her daily routine.

Cade wanted to be her slice of life.

So yes, he would patiently wait for her to open up to him in her own time. If that time came, Pilar's decision would be final. If it didn't come at all, Cade decided he would be single the rest of his life.

It was either Pilar or no one else.

He had known that since Dubai. It hadn't been because Pilar had saved his life then because he had also returned it in kind when they had to escape terrorists in the Middle East on their way home to the United States.

They had made a great team, and Cade prayed that some day Pilar might realize that too. Having said that, Cade didn't want Pilar to think of him as merely a business associate. If she went there, he might be stuck in the friend zone.

No. He had already told her that he wanted to marry her. She had brushed him off as unserious.

Pilar had to realize her own heart—whether she wanted anything to do with Cade or not. Until then, Cade had to wait patiently.

Pilar's new burner phone from Tanaka rang. "It's Agent Tanaka."

She put it on speakerphone so they could both hear it.

"Are you done?" Tanaka asked.

"Almost. The nurse is coming back to give Cade a tetanus shot and wrap up his wounds with new dressing," Pilar said. "Whassup?"

"Zuriel wants to see you, but they're patching her up at the moment," Tanaka said. "Could you come here? I'm in the second floor waiting room."

Pilar turned to Cade to see his reaction.

He nodded. "Sure."

"Okay then," Pilar told Tanaka.

One of the things that Cade appreciated about Pilar was her ability to include people. She was a team player through and through. In this case, it was clear that Zuriel wanted to see Pilar, not Cade. Pilar could have just walked out of the exam room on her own and gone upstairs to see Zuriel.

But no.

"Does that mean you want me to go with you upstairs?" Cade asked.

"Isn't that obvious?"

"And that you didn't want to leave me behind."

"Do I have to spell it out for you?"

Cade reached for her hand again. "I'm a literal guy. I can't read between the lines."

Pilar let him hold her hand again. "Let's just say after these few days, I don't want you out of my sight. Something could happen to you."

"And you too if I'm not watching."

Pilar's smile faded. "You mean like leaving Zuriel with a total stranger such as James?"

Cade felt bad. He had indeed given her a hard time about it. "I'm sorry. You had good judgment. I shouldn't have second guessed you."

"Actually, you were right. I had second thoughts about leaving Zuriel behind. I wanted to turn around and get her back on the boat, but I had to get to you. The thought that you might already be dead..." Her voice quavered and her lips quivered.

"You're saying that I was more important to you than Zuriel."

"You were on my mind," Pilar admitted.

"Will I ever be in your heart?" Cade asked quietly, but he knew that Pilar had heard his every word.

CHAPTER TWENTY-FOUR

An hour of waiting later, Pilar could see that Zuriel was stitched up and bandaged in quite a few places all over her body. The two women sat in adjacent armchairs in the waiting room, with Cade lying down on a sofa nearby with his legs raised over a throw cushion. Outside the door, two police officers stood guard.

Pilar understood that they were not protecting her or Cade. It was the FBI asset that they were more concerned about in the joint task force.

"Now that we're all here, let me introduce everyone." Tanaka began with Zuriel, whose real name was Kelsey Murphy. She said very little about who Kelsey really was, but Pilar was quite sure that Kelsey had been recruited out of Braun-Dean's sphere. It was all about catching the money launderers, and at the heart of the operation were Braun-Dean and his estranged wife.

Tanaka let Pilar and Cade reveal themselves.

"I'm Pilar Santiago, a private investigator from Miami," Pilar said.

Cade waved a hand in the air. "Cade Sumter, also a PI, but I work for Hu Knows out of Savannah."

"Nice to meet you all over again." Kelsey extended her hand to Pilar. "I knew you were different but I didn't want to judge you."

Pilar pointed to her uniform. "I can't wait to take a shower and change into some clean clothes."

"I hear you."

Cade let the women talk. He seemed to be taking a nap.

Agent Tanaka's phone rang and she left the room to take the seemingly confidential phone call. She had requested for a couple of police officers to stay with them in the waiting room until she returned.

Kelsey explained that, in her attempt to escape Ted and Butch, she had run barefoot into the forest. Her delicate arms and legs battled the many clusters of saw palmetto, and she had lost to the plant's knife-like serrated leaves that took up their positions among live oaks and slash pine trees in the forest.

She had taken her pumps with her, which had come in handy later when Ted and Butch threw her in their pickup truck to take her back to Doc Sam's cabin in the woods. She used every opportunity—she only needed two—to toss the shoes out of the window as a call for help.

"James's van wrecked a ways from the exit," Pilar said. "We saw his van before we saw your shoes."

"Right. We were very close to the main road when Ted and Butch caught up with us. They hit our van to prevent us from leaving the private land. James tried to stop them while I ran into the forest with my Blahniks," Kelsey explained. "They caught up to me when I fell in the forest."

Kelsey looked like she didn't want to repeat what she had already told the police and FBI, but she went on to answer Pilar's question. "After they put me in the pickup truck, I saw in the rearview mirror that James chased after us with his van. I threw out my shoes one by one in the hope that Agent Tanaka would see it later on and somehow find me."

"You don't have to rehash it if you don't want to." Pilar patted Kelsey's hand.

It was hard for Pilar to think of this woman as Kelsey, but then again, her real name suited her more than Zuriel.

"No, I want you to know that James is not a bad guy. Back at the bait shop, he let me use his cell phone to call 911 and Tanaka."

"Oh. So you knew the phone number I gave you was for Agent Tanaka."

Kelsey shook her head. "Not at first. She answered, so that's how I knew."

"But you worked with Tanaka."

"She gave me another number. I didn't recognize the one you gave me."

"Oh, I see."

Kelsey grabbed Pilar's hand. "I just want to go back to James. He didn't hurt me at all. I wanted you to know that I chose to go with him into the forest. I knew he worked at the bait shop and I knew they had a working phone there. That was why I asked for a boat tour."

"Why didn't you use Braun-Dean's phone?"

"Did you think he'd let me? I couldn't risk getting beaten up again."

"I'm sorry."

Kelsey shrugged. "I'm still alive, so he can't win."

"So you were only pretending to be..." Pilar dared not say the word.

"Ditzy, you mean?" Kelsey laughed. "I know you were ambivalent about letting me off the jon boat to go with James. I couldn't tell you in front of him that he was no match for me. I know a bit of Krav Maga, and I could have taken him down. That is, if my Ruger didn't stop him first."

Pilar remembered the small handgun that Kelsey had stashed in her purse. "Who gave it to you?"

"I bought it myself, but Agent Tanaka didn't say I couldn't have it."

Pilar suspected that there was more to Kelsey than what she could see. She felt bad that she had so easily dismissed Kelsey because she saw her as Zuriel the mistress, a woman of the night, an escort for the sleazebag Braun-Dean.

"James was genuinely trying to rescue me. He got hurt so badly." Kelsey sighed. "He didn't know that Felix would never hurt me. Neither would his people."

His people?

Pilar began to suspect that Ted and Butch worked for Felix Braun-Dean. That might explain why Braun-Dean and Kelsey were "VIP hostages," as Cade and Pilar had called them.

Pilar shot Cade a look. His eyes were open, so he had probably woken up from his nap on the sofa. He nodded, as though he had heard what Kelsey said.

Was Cade thinking the same thing that Pilar was?

"Are Joe and Arnon also Braun-Dean's people?" Pilar asked.

"New hires, I think. Funny thing is, I've seen Joe and Arnon in Felix's Miami Beach mansion that he built with Roxanne. They were in the security detail on the grounds."

Pilar's interest perked. Roxanne Braun-Dean still wintered on that sprawling estate by the waterway, where her yacht docked.

"Maybe I'm mistaken." Kelsey shrugged.

"Have you told this to Agent Tanaka?"

"Yes, but maybe I was misremembering."

Pilar found that interesting. Someone who had a great memory suddenly said that she might have misremembered something? Surely Agent Tanaka wouldn't take that at face value.

Was Kelsey afraid of Roxanne Braun-Dean? Why? Had Roxanne threatened Kelsey in any way?

"Anyway, Ted and Butch just wanted to take me back to Felix," Kelsey said. "In my heart, I knew that I couldn't go back, but when they ran James off the road a second time and his van crashed into the tree, I knew they were going to kill him. I told them to leave him alone and that I'd go back with them to Felix. But they still beat him senseless."

She wiped a tear.

"God kept him alive." Pilar patted her shoulder. "And God sent Doc Sam to stay with him until paramedics came. He's in surgery now, as you know, and maybe we can see him soon."

Even as she said it, Pilar wasn't sure if she and Cade would see James ever again.

Firstly, they had to go back to Miami where Helen and Ming were waiting for a report. However, they couldn't go home just yet. As soon as they were done with the hospital, they had to give their full statements at the sheriff's office. Helen had ordered a private vehicle to drive them around town and then to take them from Naples to Miami. The vehicle should be arriving at the hospital parking lot soon.

Secondly, Agent Tanaka had hinted that she was taking Kelsey away because it was too dangerous for her to be here. Kelsey had to return to rehab for her relapse, but after that she had to assist Tanaka in her money laundering investigations.

Kelsey was silent for a little bit.

"You okay?" Pilar asked. "Want some water or something?"

Kelsey shook her head. "I was just thinking about what you said earlier."

"What?"

"You said that God kept James alive and God sent Doc Sam to stabilize him."

"Yes."

"You look like you believe it."

"Of course. I doubt Cade and I could have survived without God. At any point in time, we could've been killed by humans or alligators, but God kept us alive." Pilar pointed to Cade. "He could have bled out and died if not for Doc Sam. God certainly sent Doc Sam."

"I hear that 'god' is anything or anyone you want it to be," Kelsey said.

Pilar sensed that Kelsey was seeking God. "I'm a

Christian, and in our belief, God is a person, not an object."

"I have been to church before, like for weddings." Kelsey looked down. "But God feels so distant."

"Before I was saved, God was very distant from me as well," Pilar explained. "It's because my sin had separated me from Him. No matter what I did, I couldn't reach God."

"You? Sin?" Kelsey laughed. "You don't know what sin is."

"Yes, ma'am, I do. The Bible says that every single person on earth has sinned and fallen short of the glory of God. That includes me." Pilar recited Romans 3:23 by heart.

> *For all have sinned and fall short of the glory of God.*

"God is holy and will not put up with my sins. The Bible says that those who sin must die." Pilar looked around her, and spotted a Gideons' Bible from The Gideons International on a corner table.

Kelsey started to weep softly.

"Then I must die a million times over because I have broken so many of the Ten Commandments," Kelsey said through tears. "I've stolen someone else's husband and caused him to commit adultery. I want their things. I have lied against so many people. I did it all under the fake name of Zuriel, but it's all me underneath. I did it all."

Pilar was stunned. Kelsey had pegged Exodus 20:14-17.

You shall not commit adultery.

You shall not steal.

You shall not bear false witness against your neighbor.

You shall not covet your neighbor's house; you shall not covet your neighbor's wife, nor his male servant, nor his female servant, nor his ox, nor his donkey, nor anything that is your neighbor's.

Pilar handed Kelsey a box of tissue. "How did you know what's in the Ten Commandments?"

"I heard it in an online sermon somewhere." Kelsey blew her nose. "I've been cursed with the ability to remember most things that I've seen and heard."

Pilar had seen it first hand, when Kelsey remembered the phone number that Pilar had given to her in the boat at the swamp.

"Not a curse but a blessing that God has given you." Even as Pilar said it, she couldn't see clearly how being able to remember more than ordinary people could be a blessing. Maybe it would show itself as she talked to Kelsey.

"It's a curse because there are many things I'd rather forget, but they are all crystal clear to me and I can't erase them from my memory. My own sins with Felix, for example. I remember them all. How can that be a blessing?"

"Because then you'd be more aware of the only person who can wash away all your sins and make you holy and blameless before God." Pilar opened the Gideons' Bible to Romans 5:8. "His name is Jesus."

But God demonstrates His own love toward us, in that while we were still sinners, Christ died for us.

"As I mentioned, a holy God cannot put up with sin. The penalty of sin is death. But Jesus paid the penalty for us when He took all our sins and nailed them to the cross." Pilar read Romans 6:23 to Kelsey.

For the wages of sin is death, but the gift of God is eternal life in Christ Jesus our Lord.

"I know what you're doing." Kelsey wagged a finger at Pilar. "You're trying to replace my bad memories with good ones."

"Salvation in Christ is good news. The best news ever." Pilar placed the Bible on her lap. "Do you want God to wash away all your sins? Then when God looks at you, He sees you through the righteousness of Jesus, and you are blameless. He has paid the ultimate penalty of your sin."

Kelsey almost nodded. But then she said, "What about my past? I was Felix's mistress."

"Was. It's in the past now. The moment you accept Jesus as your personal Lord and Savior, He gives you a new life, a new beginning, a new hope. The guilt of your sin is gone." Pilar knew she had to be careful about what she said. "You still have to go through the repercussions of your actions. For example, Braun-Dean's estranged wife might still come after you. You may have to go into hiding. You need to go to rehab one final time to get rid of this opioid addiction once and for all."

"I get it. But my soul will be free." Kelsey grabbed Pilar's hands. "Tell me. What must I do to be saved?"

"Believe in the Lord Jesus Christ, and you shall be saved. Do you want to receive Him into your heart?"

Kelsey nodded.

"You can pray this prayer with me," Pilar said. "Just repeat after me, but only if you genuinely mean it."

"Okay."

They bowed their heads. Pilar didn't care who was watching–Cade or the two police officers. Kelsey's soul was at stake.

"Dear Lord Jesus, You know all about me and You have seen all my sins," Pilar prayed as Kelsey repeated after her word for word. "Thank You for dying on the cross to save me from my sins. Thank You for forgiving me forever. By faith, I trust You as my Lord and Savior. Help me live this new life in Christ. In Your Holy Name, I pray. Amen."

When they both looked up, Pilar was crying and Kelsey was comforting her.

Kelsey's eyes were bright, as though a dark cloud had vanished. "My heart feels light. I feel free. God has lifted away my burden. Wow. I didn't know this would be how I would feel."

"There is a long road ahead as you study the Bible and learn to live the Christian life," Pilar said.

"A hard road too because I am leaving Felix, and he will never let me go." Kelsey looked determined. "I can't stay with him any longer and live in my old sin. I am a new person now. I have a new life in Christ."

"Where do you live?" Pilar asked.

"Right now, nowhere." Kelsey thought for a

minute, then said, "Maybe I'll do my rehab in Miami. Then I can stay there after it's done. Start over there. Go to your church."

"Sure. My church would welcome you. We also have a mid-week women's Bible study that you might consider attending."

"Good. I need to learn all about the Bible."

"You can start right away." Pilar reached for her pocket for her phone. "I was going to say that you can download a Bible app, and begin reading the book of John in the New Testament."

"Okay. I will remember that."

"You might find John 8:3-11 interesting," Pilar added. "It's the story of a woman who was ostracized by the religious leaders of her time, but Jesus freed her soul and instructed her to sin no more."

"Oh. Sounds like it's for me."

"It's for all of us. We change when we meet Jesus, who transforms us from the inside out."

"That's what I need to hear. Appreciate it."

"No problem. Also, if you decide to move to Miami and need a job, I might be able to help you find one if you send me your résumé," Pilar added.

"Thank you, but for now, I will need to be able to move around in case Agent Tanaka needs me."

Speaking of whom, the FBI agent walked in.

Kelsey sprung up to her feet. "I'm ready to tell you everything."

"No holding back?" Tanaka put away her phone. She looked surprised.

"I'm a Christian now, and I want my conscience to be clean before God."

"When did you get saved?" Tanaka folded her arms across her chest.

"A few minutes ago."

Tanaka looked over to Pilar, who nodded.

"We prayed just now and Kelsey asked Jesus into her heart," Pilar said.

"Very good. Now God will keep you safe and I will worry less." Tanaka turned to Kelsey. "James is out of surgery. He should be awake soon."

"Thank God." Kelsey caught herself. "Whoa. I actually mean it this time."

"Do you want to see him?" Tanaka asked. "You have to be Zuriel when you see him. He's a civilian and not involved."

Kelsey nodded. "I'll just see him briefly, and then we can go."

"You two." Tanaka waved to get Cade's attention. Pilar also listened. "Your private driver has arrived and is waiting for you at the pick-up and drop-off zone downstairs. He has your new phone, Cade."

"Good." Cade slowly got up.

"Helen said he's taking you to a hotel so you can shower and change first. I want to note that she emphasized 'separate rooms' so you don't have to worry about Pilar's grandma asking why you were in the same hotel room together when you're not married...yet."

"What?" Cade looked bewildered.

"I know, right?" Tanaka laughed.

"Then we still have to go to the CCSO to give our statements to the detectives," Pilar said.

"That's right, Miss Santiago." Tanaka looked at Pilar, then Cade. "When you've cleaned up, the driver will take you to the CCSO headquarters, which is ten minutes from here so that you can give your full statements."

As soon as she could, Pilar had to call her grandma and Oscar. She didn't want them to worry, although they were used to her disappearing for days and weeks on end. Perhaps texting them would make them worry even more.

"You'll need to tell CCSO everything, not only about your experience at the swamp and cabin, but also about what happened inside the Callahan Hotel in Miami," Tanaka added. "CCSO will share the data with Miami Police as well as the FBI via their interagency system so that you don't have to repeat yourselves in Miami."

"Good." Cade sighed.

"What time is it now?" Pilar asked.

"It's almost four in the afternoon," Tanaka said. "Half an hour to shower and get ready. Maybe an hour giving your statement to CCSO detectives. Then you're free to go."

"If we finish soon enough, we could still go home to Miami tonight," Pilar suggested. "Sleep in the car and let the driver drive."

"Or we could stay at the hotel overnight–since it's paid for–and leave in the morning," Cade countered.

"Helen is paying for the private driver," Pilar reminded him. "That's an added cost I don't want her to roll to me. I can't afford it."

"So we'll let Helen decide then. If she pays for it, we'll go home tomorrow. If not, we'll go home tonight." Cade sounded disappointed.

Go home?

Pilar found it amusing that Cade would consider Miami—a city he was only visiting—to be his home. She shrugged it off.

She turned to Tanaka. "Any word about the five women hostages who disappeared?"

"The CCSO and FBI are looking for them."

"I hope they're okay," Pilar said.

"Yes. Now get going, you two." Tanaka shooed them out.

"I'll see you around." Pilar hugged Kelsey. "Agent Tanaka has my contact information, but here's the number for my personal phone—not this burner phone. Don't call me until tomorrow. I left my phone at my office in Miami before I went undercover at the hotel."

Pilar gave Kelsey her number. Kelsey didn't have to write it down.

Pilar wondered how the FBI was going to use Kelsey's memory gift in the money laundering case, but it wasn't Pilar's problem, was it?

Her problem now was to get home to Miami as soon as possible and sleep for two weeks.

CHAPTER TWENTY-FIVE

So much for Pilar's best laid plans to take time off. As soon as she told Cade that she was going offline for two weeks, his phone rang, cutting short any plans Cade might have had in joining Pilar on her vacation.

Cade had been happy to get a phone again, courtesy of his boss and delivered to him via their private driver, Remigio. His happiness was short-lived, as the first call he had came from Helen.

Every time Helen was on the phone, it was about work.

"Why didn't she call me instead of you?" Pilar asked as they exited the Collier County Sheriff's Office, where they had given their full and truthful statements to a detective who had the evening shift.

"Maybe because you don't work for Hu Knows, Inc." Cade walked Pilar to Remigio, who had waited this entire time in the SUV in the CCSO parking lot.

"It involves me, doesn't it?"

Pilar was right. Without her, the final phase of the project wouldn't fly.

At the same time, it baffled Cade that this wasn't an FBI operation. How did it end up being handled by Helen, a private investigator?

Liability? Or perhaps their target had a mole inside the FBI as well.

Interesting.

"We can ask Helen to fill in the blanks when we see her," Cade added—not as much for Pilar as for himself.

Pilar nodded.

After they got in the vehicle, Remigio told them that Helen had instructed him to drive them to Miami. "Make yourself comfortable. I'll get you there in two hours plus a few minutes."

"I guess we don't get to stay in town at that five-star hotel after all," Cade joked.

"It only has three stars. I checked." Pilar buckled in.

"But Naples, though."

"We won't be able to see the sunset on the beach." Pilar checked her phone. "Sunset won't be for another hour, just before seven o'clock. You sure we can't stay a little longer?"

Cade knew that Pilar wasn't trying to complain. She just stated the facts. Her words showed how exhausted she was and how much rest she needed.

Cade caught something else. Pilar liked to see sunsets. If he had known that, he would've asked Helen if they could watch the sunset on the beach first before they drove to Miami.

He didn't want to suggest that Pilar stay back in Naples by herself and take another ride home. He wanted her to be with him at all times. It wasn't too late to ask Helen to have some compassion on both of them.

Before Cade could text Helen to ask if they could leave after sunset, Pilar's phone rang. It was Helen. She was calling via video.

"Whassup, Helen?" Pilar asked.

"You look none the worse for wear," Helen said. "Any stitches?"

"Fortunately not. All stitches are on Cade and Zuriel—I mean, Kelsey."

Cade leaned toward Pilar as far as he could go with the safety belt holding his torso back. He wanted to see what was on screen.

Pilar also leaned toward him and held the phone in between them.

"Listen, we have to discuss something," Helen said.

Cade glanced at the driver. "We're not alone in this vehicle."

"Remigio is one of ours," Helen said. "He's been driving Ming and me around in Miami the last few days. He has clearance."

Cade didn't know that.

"What? You think I'd let a random stranger drive you from Naples to Miami?" Helen laughed.

Behind her, someone was saying something. It sounded like Ming.

When his face showed up on camera, he waved. "Glad you're okay, Pilar. Sabine and I prayed for you. Thank God you made it out alive."

"Yes, thank God." Pilar's voice was jubilant. "Please thank Sabine for me."

"Will do." Ming's face moved away from the camera. Helen turned her head to talk to Ming for a minute.

"I think landscaping has a bigger crew, don't you think? They can also stay longer," she said.

"You're right. Only takes a crew of two or three to clean the lap pool. For sure, we need them to stay longer." Ming's voice faded away.

Helen was back again. "Firstly, your friend Alma says hello from the Jackson Memorial Hospital."

"Oh good. I'm happy to hear that," Pilar said.

"The Ryder Trauma Center saved her life. She flatlined twice."

"Wow."

Cade squeezed Pilar's shoulder gently as a show of support.

"Don't worry," Helen added. "Her kids are with her and she's recovering from broken bones and bruises and all sorts of internal injuries. Miami Police is adding attempted murder to the charges against the captors."

"Good," Cade and Pilar said together.

Then they looked at each other and grinned.

"What's going on between you two?" Helen raised an eyebrow.

Nothing so far.

Cade told himself to keep praying. Maybe Pilar would warm up to him and he could take her out to dinner, just the two of them.

Helen didn't wait for an answer.

"Secondly, Braun-Dean and his merry men are

sitting in the Naples Jail Center waiting for tomorrow's arraignment," Helen said. "Their lawyers are making their way to Naples as we speak."

"Okay."

"Contrary to the statements made by the four men during their police interviews, Braun-Dean has vehemently denied from the outset that he masterminded the hostage situation at the Callahan Hotel or imprisoned six women and one man at the swamp resort."

"Let me guess," Pilar said. "Someone leaked all this information to you because their hands are tied but ours are not."

"As usual, you're half a step ahead." Helen seemed impressed. "Really, you should come work for Hu Knows. Let us take care of accounting for you. You can pick any project you want and go anywhere in the world."

With me.

Cade almost said it, but didn't.

"I'll think about it," Pilar said. "But first, what do you want us to do?"

Us?

Cade was happy that Pilar had included him.

"You'll have different tasks, but this must be done ASAP. Otherwise, I'd have told y'all to take a couple of days off." Helen sighed. "Word is, Braun-Dean's lawyers have already set things into motion."

"Figured." Pilar nodded her head. "When you said 'word is,' did you mean you heard through the Tanaka grapevine?"

"No. She's one of the best FBI agents there is, so she's not going to disclose to us civilians what they find. Information flowed one way to her, as you know."

Helen wasn't going to tell them more, and Cade knew not to pry. "What do you want us to do?"

"Remigio is bringing you here to our staging area." Helen paused, as though she was wondering whether or not to drop names.

The phone line was encrypted and secure, but sometimes Helen was paranoid like that.

"Our team is assembled, waiting for you." That was all Helen said.

"Is the team from Hu Knows?" Cade asked.

"A mix."

"Atlanta involved?" Pilar asked.

Helen hesitated and then nodded.

"Bingo." Pilar snapped her fingers.

Cade couldn't read her mind. What did she know?

Helen smiled at the camera. "Like I said, you're a step ahead of us."

"Anything we need to do now? We're less than two hours away." Pilar sounded excited, like she'd caught a second wind.

"Nothing until tomorrow," Helen said. "I called to make sure you're on the way and that you're not out on a date night or dilly-dallying on the beach in Naples watching the sunset. You can do that soon if all goes well."

Pilar didn't respond to Helen.

"Rest now since you don't have to drive. I've set up rooms for you here in Miami."

Cade said goodbye, and Pilar hung up the phone.

Pilar leaned back against the seat and closed her eyes.

Cade didn't want to guess what was on her mind. "Whatcha thinking about?"

"All the things said and unsaid." Pilar rolled her head toward Cade.

Cade wanted to hug her, but this wasn't the time. His hand inched toward hers and held it. Her hand was warm.

"I've already given my statement to the CCSO," Pilar said. "However, I keep thinking we missed something."

"Are we connecting dots again?"

"I think so."

Cade whipped out his phone and opened a blank note. "How about we list all the things that stand out and see what we can piece together?"

"Sure."

"Let's do speech to text. Saves me from having to type on this tiny little virtual keyboard." Cade chuckled.

He lifted the microphone end of his phone closer to Pilar's lips.

"Kelsey told me that she might have seen Joe and Arnon before at Braun-Dean's Miami Beach estate, where Roxanne now resides," Pilar said. "Then she backtracked."

"I'll file that under Kelsey." Cade edited the file and put a header over what Pilar just dictated.

"She's working with Agent Tanaka, so let's put her aside for now." Pilar moved on to Felix Braun-Dean.

Cade typed his name on a fresh document file. "Ready.

"You were out of it when we were at the cabin, but he was talking on the phone with someone," Pilar said into the phone. "I wish I had Kelsey's memory, but it all happened so fast."

"Didn't you recall everything and tell the CCSO detectives?" Cade asked.

"Yes, but I summarized it." Pilar looked thoughtful. "There might be more. I think it'll come back once I get some sleep. I'm super tired right now."

So much for her second wind.

Cade deleted all the personal notes that had nothing to do with the case. Then he pointed the phone at Pilar again.

"Something about a collaboration," Pilar said into the microphone. "The person on the other end of the phone was a woman. They had an agreement, but the other party firebombed the resort and now demanded more money. Braun-Dean called someone else to send her ten million dollars of bitcoin to appease her temporarily."

"Didn't Josephine Callahan say that the hostage situation was staged?" Cade thought that was worth revisiting.

"Yeah, but she didn't say who was responsible. If she's found—I pray that she's still alive—then she might explain. I wish I had made her explain it when we were in the hut, but all I wanted to do was get away from her because she was in my face. In any case, the little she said corroborated with what I heard Braun-Dean say on the phone."

"I've got that down but I think we leave some

space for more later." This was as good a time as any for Cade to bring up Doc Sam. "He lives rent-free on the private land, helps people during medical emergencies, knows a lot of hunters, but doesn't care about the swamp resort that feeds bodies to gators?"

"He might not be aware of any of that. Perhaps Braun-Dean's entourage was the only people who did the macabre."

"Are you ruling out Doc Sam? He wasn't afraid of the captors." Cade waited to see how Pilar would respond. He wasn't jealous of Doc Sam. The man was old enough to be Pilar's grandfather, even though in this day and age, one could never tell.

"That might be because he's been around the block and has a fatalistic mentality." Pilar thought for a moment.

"Oh? What about the Ambien in his medicine cabinet? What did that mean?"

"I didn't ask him why he had sleeping pills in the clinic. Was it because he had problems sleeping after his wife passed away? Unless we talk to him again, we may not know," Pilar said.

"Even if we talk to him, would he talk to us?"

"Good point. Then again, he helped us escape the private land. He treated James by the roadside."

"But is he a good guy or bad guy?"

Pilar's eyes widened. "Good question, but the Bible does say that good trees cannot produce bad fruit."

Cade opened up a browser window and searched for the Bible passage. He found it in Matthew 7:17-18.

Even so, every good tree bears good fruit, but a bad tree bears bad fruit. A good tree cannot bear bad fruit, nor can a bad tree bear good fruit.

"So the jury is still out on Felix Braun-Dean," Pilar said. "There are two people who didn't appear in person these few days. One I've met and one I haven't met."

"Roxanne Braun-Dean," Cade said.

"Right."

"The other is?"

"He or she was on the phone with Braun-Dean and was in charge of his bitcoin account," Pilar said.

"Not Arun Dhillon, because he's dead." Cade knew about the story from Earl Young when he had been tasked to protect Sabine, back when she was an administrative assistant who knew too much.

"Then who could it be?"

"The plot thickens."

CHAPTER TWENTY-SIX

One week later...

Roxanne Braun-Dean was a svelte and lithe sixty-year-old woman who had long, straight, and healthy hair that extended down to her waist. Extensions, perhaps. Or totally real hair. Either way, Roxanne looked like a multi-million-dollar mature model.

She wore a floral taffeta blouse with red flowers all over it and a pair of black tight pants. Her open toe heels went clickety-clack on the old style terracotta floor tiles in the expansive living room.

She didn't look at Pilar before she sat down on a plush cream-colored settee near a long bank of windows and sliding glass doors that opened to a stone patio, a lap pool, green grass, and a dock on the intracoastal waterway.

The living room was long and wide, and ran parallel to the pool that looked like it was a hundred feet long. The room stretched from one end of the pool to the other end. On the other side of a few clusters of sitting areas plus a grand piano, a wide hallway led to what looked like a gourmet kitchen with stainless steel appliances and chandeliers.

This was the first time Pilar had been inside this fifteen-thousand-square-foot mansion, and also the first time she met Roxanne. Their previous communications had been facilitated through her assistant, a balding man in his fifties named Leif. Pilar had seen him briefly when he'd scanned her at the door. His equipment was not very advanced, and it detected nothing on Pilar.

Roxanne didn't ask Pilar to sit down.

While waiting for Pilar to speak, she looked outside. The sky was blue with puffy clouds. If this wasn't still October, no one would know that it was also hurricane season in Florida, though the only big event in Miami and Miami Beach had been the tropical storm last week, which Pilar had narrowly escaped.

Under the sunny sky, landscapers were trimming evergreen hedges and mowing the lawn. The room seemed to be soundproof because Pilar could not hear the lawn mower. At her house, she could hear the low frequency noise all through her neighborhood.

One of the landscapers was Cade, though Pilar couldn't tell which one right away. The landscapers wore wide brimmed hats and covered their mouths with bandanas. One had an old towel over his neck. They were all buff and wore long sleeves that accentuated their arm muscles. If Pilar had paid more attention to Cade's arms, she might have been able to spot him—

Never mind.

There he was, the only man limping gingerly away from the hedges.

That had to be him.

It was enough for Pilar to know that Cade was among them, carrying a portable signal repeater in his pocket that could boost the signal from Pilar's micro radio frequency transmitters embedded into the buttons of her jeans and the rivets at pocket edges.

The technology that hacker Leland Yang-Joule of Binary Systems, Inc., had brought to the table had indeed leveled up their game. Helen was close to Leland, having worked together all over the world. Somehow, the buttons had sailed past Roxanne's security, right into her living room.

As long as Cade was within a hundred and fifty feet of Pilar, everything she recorded in this meeting would be transmitted to the landscaping truck parked on the street, where Ming and Helen would relay to Leland in Atlanta via a laptop.

Agent Tanaka was watching from somewhere. Earlier this morning, before they were deployed to the sprawling one-acre waterfront estate, one of the FBI agents involved in this sting operation had deputized Ming and Helen.

Tanaka had suspected that her team had been compromised because leaks had warned the Braun-Deans of raids. This time, she wanted to keep it airtight.

Roxanne pressed a button on a remote control on

a side table near her. Jazz played softly through the speakers somewhere above them.

"I don't like it quiet." Roxanne made a face. "Activity breathes life, doesn't it?"

Pilar didn't reply. How could she? She didn't agree with what Roxanne just said.

"No?" Roxanne raised her sculpted eyebrows.

Pilar thought they might be tattooed eyebrows, but she wasn't sure. It wasn't the time to pry just to satisfy her curiosity.

"I think it's the other way around. Life breathes activity." Pilar had to say it, but she knew it could spell trouble.

"You oppose me."

Time for damage control.

"No, ma'am. I'm being honest, considering that you raised a philosophical question that could be a master's thesis at universities," Pilar said as calmly as she could.

"Oh?" Slowly a smile crept around Roxanne's plump lips painted strawberry red. She pointed with her long artificial nails, beautifully manicured, to a sofa opposite from where she was sitting. "Sit down."

The compliment earned Pilar a seat across the table.

Making progress.

Roxanne sighed. "Tell me honestly. What did my no-good husband really do at the hotel?"

"He yelled at people, threw things at walls, and ate a lot of food like hamburgers and steak."

"Some things never changed, except now he's doing it with that woman instead of me." She drew a deep breath. "I don't know why I put up with his dalliances. They only got worse and worse in the last ten years. I've had to get tested just in case he gave me STDs or something. In the end I stopped sleeping with him. Now I'm finally getting a divorce, but he's lying to me about being poor. He's not poor. He's worth billions. Where are the billions? I want half!"

Her voice rose, and Pilar pretended to be frightened.

Roxanne chuckled. "You're afraid of me."

"I'm sorry about what your husband put you through. I can't believe he's such a monster."

Roxanne's eyes were deep and dark and drilled into Pilar's, even though they were maybe eight feet away from each other.

"Did you complete the task that Leif gave you?" she asked point blank.

Leif—with no last name—was Roxanne's accountant who had transferred five hundred thousand dollars of bitcoin into Pilar's temporary account, which Agent Tanaka had set up for her.

"The hotel meeting never took place," Pilar said. "I'm not sure if Leif's information was correct."

"What did he tell you?"

"That Mr. Braun-Dean was having a meeting at the Callahan Hotel about his crypto investments," Pilar said. "However, shortly after I arrived, we were all held hostage."

"He did it." Roxanne sounded confident. "Felix did it."

"Did what, ma'am?" Pilar prayed that her micro RF buttons could transmit through the sliding glass doors that she now believed were hurricane-grade laminated glass.

"Oh, don't play coy. You were there. Was Felix suffering as a hostage?"

"I'm not sure, ma'am. I worked in housekeeping and wasn't always in the penthouse."

The only people in the penthouse suite had been Braun-Dean, Kelsey when she was Zuriel, and the captors. If the captors were Roxanne's men, wouldn't they have reported back to Roxanne regularly?

Why would Roxanne ask Pilar about Felix as a hostage?

Wait a minute.

Kelsey had said that Joe and Arnon might be working for Roxanne. Those two men hadn't been at the hotel. As far as Pilar knew, they hadn't appeared at all until Doc Sam's cabin.

Potentially, Ted and Mac were Felix Braun-Dean's men. Those two had run the show at the Callahan Hotel. Whether they also drew paychecks from Roxanne remained to be discovered.

"Then your observation skills are...blah." Roxanne waved her nails in the air. "You look useless to me. Why are you even a PI?"

"I need the money to pay for my brother's college tuition and to support my eighty-year-old grandmother." It was the truth.

"That's why I doubled your fee." Roxanne crossed her legs. "I did some digging. Your office is in a dangerous part of Miami, and you drive a car that's on its last leg."

"Thank you, ma'am. That was very generous of you."

"I give money to charity all the time. This time, I'm helping myself."

"If the Callahan Hotel hostage situation was Mr. Braun-Dean's doing, then who was supposed to pay the ransom?" Pilar tried to look baffled.

"Me!" Roxanne leaned forward. "He asked me for money, that rat!"

Ah. Pilar saw it now. "So you turned the tables on him."

A twinkle in Roxanne's eyes confirmed Pilar's suspicions.

What about the "agreement" that Braun-Dean had talked to someone about on the phone in Doc Sam's cabin?

"The firebombs at Geiger Ixora were clever." Pilar threw her a compliment to see if she would bite. "It flushed out Mr. Braun-Dean from hiding in the swamp resort."

And where Roxanne's two men—Joe and Arnon—could infiltrate the security detail because the rest of his men were dead, except for Ted and Max who had escaped with Braun-Dean.

"The huts on fire also burned Mr. Braun-Dean's arms and legs, putting him in a lot of pain," Pilar added. "You made him suffer."

Roxanne eyed her. "If you keep guessing correctly, you won't be able to walk out of this place alive."

"But I gave you a compliment. Don't you want me to be on your side?" Pilar asked.

"My yacht can sail you out to sea for a burial in the deep." Roxanne continued to stare at Pilar.

Pilar wasn't sure how to react. So far she had succeeded at tugging at Roxanne and opening her up by appearing fearful of her. She continued that stage play.

Roxanne bought it. "I scared you."

She laughed with a strange crackling noise that Pilar couldn't define.

Pilar cleared her throat. "I'm sorry, ma'am. Actually, I asked to meet you to deliver a USB drive containing the only meeting that Mr. Braun-Dean had at the Callahan Hotel."

Roxanne frowned. "You said earlier that the meeting never happened."

"No, but I was only going by what Leif told me—that Mr. Braun-Dean was supposed to meet with some business associates." Pilar dug into her jean pocket—

Click.

Roxanne pointed a handgun at her. It looked like a .380 Smith & Wesson. The fact that Pilar had come here unarmed—due to Roxanne's house rules—put her at a grave disadvantage.

Pilar froze. "I'm only retrieving the USB drive from my pocket."

"Do it slowly."

"Yes, ma'am." In deliberate slow motion, Pilar drew out her USB flash drive.

"It's a lipstick." Roxanne frowned again. "You mocking me?"

"No, no. It's a USB drive. Look." Pilar detached the base of the lipstick and showed Roxanne the USB connector.

"How cute. Where did you get it?"

Pilar wasn't about to tell her that Helen Hu got it from Binary Systems, Inc. "You can find it just about anywhere online. Search for novelty USB flash drives."

"What's on it?" Roxanne put away her Smith & Wesson.

"A conversation between Mr. Braun-Dean and Zuriel about his crypto stash."

That got Roxanne's attention.

"I hate that woman—and every woman out there that Felix slept with." She grunted. "Now that he's in jail, he can stop fooling around. I did him a favor."

Pilar popped the base back into the lipstick and put it on the coffee table toward Roxanne.

"The video is two minutes long, and I can preview it for you on your laptop. However, it's only a short clip. I can send the rest of it once I leave this house and drive away safely." Pilar paused. "And after you deposit one bitcoin in my account."

"What? You want to be paid for the rest of the video?"

Pilar nodded. "Will work for bitcoin."

"Not cash?"

No, because they were catching a big fish, bigger than both Felix and Roxanne combined.

"I suppose I can ask The Steward to wire you one bitcoin, but not until you send me the rest of the video."

"Fair enough. But first, don't you want to see what's on this drive?" Pilar waited as Roxanne got on her phone.

"Leif, get in here with a laptop." Roxanne hung up.

Leif appeared out of nowhere, and placed the laptop on the coffee table.

He sat close to Roxanne. Too close. It made Pilar wonder if there was something going on between Roxanne and the balding Leif, who seemed to be a loyal servant to the queen.

"Darling, I want you to scan the lipstick to make sure it doesn't have malware."

Roxanne said those words with an air that made it look like she knew what she was talking about, and that she knew technical terms and whatnot.

They all waited for Leif to do his job.

He finally looked up from the laptop. "It's clean. It's just a novelty USB drive."

Of course he'd find nothing right away. It was really a cheap USB drive, but the secret sauce was the video itself. It would infiltrate Roxanne's computer systems and do whatever Leland and her team at Binary Systems had set it up to do for Agent Tanaka.

Pilar's job was to deliver the Trojan horse and go home—hopefully, alive.

"I'm not looking for death, you know." Pilar tried to assure them that she meant well.

Roxanne laughed.

Leif played the video on the laptop, and it also showed up on a television mounted on the wall.

Funny how Pilar hadn't noticed the television was there at all. In fact, it looked like a framed picture. Earlier there was some painting on it that Pilar hadn't paid much attention to.

Roxanne might be right. Pilar's observational skills had gone blah.

She could use a few days off to recharge her brain.

Pilar watched the video for the first time with Roxanne and Leif. It had taken Leland's team two days after Kelsey was rescued to produce this AI-generated deep fake video, and one more day for Pilar to secure a face-to-face meeting with Roxanne.

Braun-Dean and Kelsey—as Zuriel—looked so realistic on the video that Pilar was impressed. Their voices sounded like the real people they were supposed to represent. For example, that was how Kelsey talked in real life.

As far as Pilar knew, the data for this conversation had come from Kelsey's lucid recollection of their actual conversation at the Callahan Hotel.

In truth, there was no more video beyond these two minutes. This was all Leland could generate using the highly classified supercomputers that Leland had access to at a military contractor site in Marietta, Georgia.

On the video, the persona of Zuriel was sitting on Braun-Dean's lap. His hands were all over her.

> *"I'll give you a million dollars in crypto every time you please me." Braun-Dean squeezed her arms.*
>
> *"I will take only bitcoin. I don't know all those other types of coins. Alt this and alt that. Just gimme bitcoin, sweet Felix," Zuriel cooed.*
>
> *"If I didn't have to share with Roxanne, we'd have more," Braun-Dean said. "Please be patient with me as I grow my crypto nest eggs. Then we can get married."*

As Roxanne watched the video, her ears turned redder and redder by the second.

"No way is she getting my title and my share!" She was on her feet, stomping the terracotta floor. "I didn't want to divorce Felix for the longest time because I wanted to be the one and only Mrs. Braun-Dean."

"You were willing to put up with all his infidelities." Leif's voice sounded compassionate. He was on Roxanne's side and all that.

"So you didn't want the divorce?" Pilar asked.

"I'll take it if I get half of his crypto. We didn't have a prenup." Roxanne drew a deep breath. "I'll free him at a price."

"But he won't let you go," Leif said. "You're too valuable to him."

Roxanne rolled her eyes. "Because of my contacts and connections."

Pilar wanted to ask who they were but she was afraid that it might raise suspicions. So she didn't say a word.

"Not everyone knows the people you know." Leif closed the video window, and the wall-mounted display returned to its alter-ego as a picture frame. It showed a Picasso.

Roxanne gazed wistfully into the distant waterway and up to the sky. "As strange as it might be, Felix still needs me. He roams the countryside, but he still comes home to me in the city."

She might be dreaming because as far as Pilar knew, that power couple had been separated for months. Perhaps it was Roxanne's wish that Felix returned to her. He was too rich to let go.

"He needs me to make those transactions overseas," Roxanne added, perhaps to remind herself of her status as the most valuable player. "Otherwise, he'll run out of fake charities to funnel his money through."

Money laundering?

Suddenly, Roxanne said no more. "Why am I telling you this?"

"I'm a good listener," Pilar said.

"What was your major in college?"

"History."

"No kidding."

"I was planning to go to law school, but I burned out as soon as I graduated from college and didn't make it that far." Pilar didn't have to explain, but she wanted to keep the conversation going with Roxanne.

"It's almost lunch time. You want a sandwich?" Leif asked Roxanne. "I'll ask Camilla to make your favorite Cuban sandwich."

"With extra cheese."

Leif left the living room with the laptop and strutted his way to the kitchen some thirty feet away from where Pilar and Roxanne sat.

Slowly, Pilar spoke. "I don't want to disturb your lunch. I'll just go."

"Go where?" Roxanne's voice was harsh. "Did you think for a moment that I'd let you leave—after all that I've told you?"

"But you want to see the rest of the video, don't you?"

"I'm changing the terms." Roxanne smiled. Seemed she knew she had the upper hand. "You stay put right here. Ask someone to deliver the rest of the video. Then I'll let you go—"

Boom!

The explosion from the kitchen was so loud that it shattered glass all around the living room. It was so loud that Pilar's ears started to ring.

"Get down!" Pilar yelled as she dropped on all fours on the floor and covered her ears with her hands to prevent further hearing loss.

A second explosion came at the heels of the first, setting off alarms in the house. Thick gray smoke filled the house.

We have to get out of here!

On the other side of the coffee table, Roxanne was screaming her head off. Pilar crawled to her and tried to get her up from her prostrated position.

"No-no-no-no-no...!" Roxanne clawed at her.

Pilar looked around.

The hurricane-grade glass on the sliding door nearest them had spiderwebbed and was cracked in places, the frame buckling. But the doors were still intact. She probably couldn't slide them open. She had to get Roxanne out of the house to safety.

"Let's get out of here!" Pilar coughed and choked in the smoke. She pulled her collar up to cover her nose as much as she could. She firmly held onto Roxanne's arm and got her to her feet.

The thick smoke had nowhere to go but to fill the space in the living room. From her memory, Pilar recalled that there were doors that way—

Or this way?

She could see sunlight streaming through the top of another set of sliding glass doors at the end of the long living room. The doors being closer in proximity to the kitchen must have been why the explosion had wrecked the frame of those doors, letting smoke escape and sunlight in.

She assisted Roxanne to go that way.

Then she heard something heavy fall to the ground, glass shattering on what sounded like a hard surface—outside pavement?—followed by someone calling her name.

It sounded muffled, but she heard it through the slight ringing in her ears.

"Pilar! Pilar!"

In the waning smoke, she saw a figure coming toward her.

Cade.

CHAPTER TWENTY-SEVEN

Sirens swarmed all around them as Cade and Pilar half-carried Roxanne through a broken sliding door frame and into the yard as fire raged in the Braun-Dean mansion behind them.

They had left the haze, but Cade's eyes stung. He blinked a few times. His legs still hurt, especially around the stitches, but what could he do? It was more important for him to get Pilar safely away from the burning house than to worry about his healing muscles pulling.

They passed by firefighters from the Miami Beach Fire Rescue running into the house, shouting at the trio as they dashed by. "Get out of here! Evacuate three hundred feet away from this house! Go now!"

"There are at least two people in the kitchen," Pilar told the firefighters. "Leif and Camilla."

One firefighter nodded and waved. "Got it!"

Cade and Pilar walked as fast as they could, with Roxanne in between them. The house was wide and they had to walk at least a hundred feet to the end of the pool where they could then skirt the house and walk up the driveway and the street. If they went two doors down, that would be about three hundred feet away from the house.

"It's Felix!" Roxanne was beside herself. "This is his revenge!"

She seemed certain of what she said.

Cade glanced over at Pilar, whose face and clothes were smudged with soot.

"What do you mean?" Pilar asked Roxanne.

Even at a time like this, Pilar was working. Cade wondered if Pilar ever turned work off, like a switch. If she could compartmentalize work and rest. Weekdays and weekends.

"He blew up the kitchen that I spent hundreds of thousands of dollars renovating just to spite me." Roxanne didn't seem to realize she was outside, in a public place, with police presence all over the property. "He's trying to get back at me for firebombing his huts! Tit for tat!"

Cade glanced at Pilar. He hoped that her micro RF transmitters were still actively recording.

They waddled under the yellow crime scene tape that the Miami Beach Police Department had hung all around the property and the two houses on both sides of the mansion.

Paramedics ran toward them even before they cleared the tape.

"I need oxygen!" Going all diva-like, Roxanne slumped into the arms of a clean-cut handsome paramedic.

Cade would leave her alone if he hadn't heard the

conversations between her and Pilar. He knew they couldn't let Roxanne ago. After all, she had twice admitted that she had blown up the swamp resort. That was, someone had done it at her behest.

MBPD had cordoned off the road in front of the mansion. There on the asphalt, the paramedics were treating Roxanne and several people, supposedly house staff who worked for Roxanne, and Pilar.

Cade stayed with Pilar as the paramedic checked her for smoke inhalation. They asked her if she was dizzy and if she could hear.

Cade thanked God that Pilar was far enough away from the kitchen that she was going to be okay.

At the same time, Cade kept an eye on Roxanne. She wasn't going anywhere. She was getting a lot of attention from the young paramedics, talking to them, telling them that she felt she was dying.

The MBFR incident commander lifted up his bullhorn and ordered everyone to clear the area. Apparently, curious neighbors had come outside in their shorts and pajamas to have a look-and-see.

Cade thought that the fire department probably suspected a natural gas leak. He looked back at the house three hundred feet away. Firefighters continued to put out the fire that roared through one side of the house where the kitchen probably was.

Cade spotted Helen talking to an officer from the MBPD. They nodded to each other. Then the officer talked on his portable Motorola radio.

The paramedics released Pilar, but she stayed with Roxanne. The paramedics put Roxanne on a gurney to send her to the hospital. She kept asking for oxygen.

Before they wheeled her to the awaiting ambulance, Roxanne waved to Pilar. She lifted up her oxygen mask. "Thank you for saving my life."

"Thank God we both made it out safely," Pilar said.

"Who is that cute guy who came to rescue you?"

Cute guy?

Cade didn't want to be called cute. Neither did he want to disclose who he was. He was undercover as a landscaper and this was how he'd remain.

"Oh, he's just a passerby," Pilar told Roxanne.

A passerby?

Would that be even worse? Cade didn't know what to do with Pilar at this point. He didn't want to be a passerby in Pilar's life.

At the same time, he suspected that Pilar didn't want to disclose his identity, especially before Roxanne was arraigned. It was bad enough that Roxanne had hired Pilar out of her office in Miami—which meant that Roxanne knew Pilar's real name and her place of business.

Whether Roxanne had told her estranged husband that she had planted Pilar as a spy at the Callahan Hotel was a matter for another day, even though it would all eventually come out in future court hearings.

"How can he be a passerby if he knew your name?" Roxanne coughed out the words.

Earlier, Cade had yelled Pilar's name as loudly as he could when he'd entered the house, looking for her in the smoke-filled living room. Obviously, Roxanne had heard it.

Pilar didn't reply.

"Oh, I get it. A passing stranger." *Cough. Cough.* "Two ships in the night."

"No..." Pilar's face turned beet red.

"Well, he's hot. A keeper." Roxanne laughed and choked.

The paramedics put the oxygen mask back on her face.

As the gurney reached the ambulance, an officer spoke to a paramedic and then climbed on board with Roxanne. When the ambulance sped off, Cade heard Helen calling his name. He watched her amble across the lawn toward him.

"An officer is going with Roxanne to the hospital and she will be put on an investigative hold. The MBPD will work with Agent Tanaka on an arrest warrant," Helen said. "She's out of our hands now."

Pilar nodded. "Now we go back to the hotel and sort out some data?"

"I've already sent all that you recorded to Leland in Atlanta," Helen said. "Tanaka will take it from there. Our job is done."

Pilar expelled a sigh of relief.

Helen's phone rang. "You need something, Ming?" She paused. "Okay. I'll be right there."

After hanging up, Helen said, "Ming is in the truck, and he is in a three-way video call with Leland and Tanaka. They want me in the convo."

By "truck," Cade knew that she meant the Ford pickup truck that they had commandeered from the landscaping company that did work at the Braun-Dean yard. Cade had ridden in the extended cab of the truck earlier, but he didn't plan on taking the same ride back.

Ming had stayed in the truck instead of working in the yard with Cade because his wrist and the base of his right hand were in a cast.

"Do you need to go to the hospital?" Helen asked Pilar.

"The paramedics say no need. My hearing is back. I'm okay now." Pilar's knee chose to buckle at that instant, but she leaned against Cade.

Cade stood firm on the grass, trying not to move, acting like a tree trunk. His thigh and calf muscles throbbed, but he wasn't about to look weak in front of Pilar.

"Take Pilar home to clean up. Then go to lunch on me. You've worked hard," Helen said.

Cade grinned. He was on the clock so of course lunch was on Helen. What was she talking about?

"My lunch too?" Pilar asked. "I'm only your business associate."

"Your lunch too. You earned it." Helen patted Pilar's shoulder. "And change out of this outfit. You smell like smoke. Can you be back at the hotel in two or three hours?"

Pilar nodded. "Maybe even sooner than that. We could get a takeout lunch and eat at the hotel."

"A working lunch?" Helen glared at Cade. "No. You two go find a restaurant you like. Sit down and eat like normal people. Not on the run."

"Yes, ma'am." Cade gave her a salute. He knew exactly what Helen was implying.

Could this be their first lunch date? Cade dared not think that far.

Pilar stepped away to stand on her own. Cade bent down to try to lift her up.

"What are you doing?" Pilar asked.

"I'm trying to carry you." He felt embarrassed.

"What are we in? A K-Drama or something?" Pilar pushed his arms away. "I can walk. Thank you."

Although Cade had heard of Korean dramas, he hadn't watched any, so he had no idea what Pilar was talking about. He just wanted to find an excuse to hold her and never let her go.

"Where did you park your car?" Cade asked.

"It's actually on the street right in front of the house." Pilar pointed. "We may have to wait until they let us cross the barricade tape."

Cade pulled a slightly used sports towel hanging off his pocket. "Come here."

Pilar stepped forward.

He wiped some of the soot off her face. "That's enough until you get home and shower."

"Thank you."

As they walked along the yellow tape toward Pilar's old car, Cade kept looking at her. Behind her, a fire truck was parked just inside the tape, blocking his view of the mansion and the waterway behind it.

"What?" Pilar asked.

"Thank God you're okay."

Pilar stopped. "Let's pray and thank God properly."

So Cade did. They both said "amen" in unison after he finished praying and giving praises to the Lord for saving Pilar from the explosion.

"In one week, God has saved us multiple times from danger," Pilar said.

"Exactly what I was thinking." Cade prayed silently about what he was trying to convey. He decided to just say it. "I waited a whole year to ask you this, but this week's events, and particularly today's—when you could have died in the house—are warning me that I shouldn't wait for the 'perfect' time."

"Whatcha talking about?"

"Life is short."

"Yes, it is." Pilar nodded. "Now say what you want to say. No need to hem and haw."

They hadn't walked forward since they stopped to pray. There on the grass, Cade held Pilar's hands.

"Pilar, would you like to walk with me on the beach and watch the sunset over the ocean?" Cade asked.

"Which beach?"

"Any beach." Cade waited. "What's the closest?"

"Well, Miami Beach is, but it's on the east coast of Florida. We can only see the sunrise over the ocean and sunset over the buildings," Pilar said. "To see the sunset over the ocean, we'll have to go to the Gulf side of the state, like the beach in Naples or the state park in Key West. Or any other beaches facing the west."

Cade felt like he had just suffered an epic failure. Any moment now he expected Pilar to let go of his hands.

But she didn't.

"To be fair to both sunsets and sunrises, you'd have to take me to multiple beaches. It could take a while for us to check out various beaches just in Florida alone."

Cade's heart soared. He was almost certain now that their feelings were mutual. He had been right all along that they had hit it off in Dubai. If they hadn't been so busy over the months, they might have gotten together sooner. A year of separation had caused him a lot of heartache, but all that was about to disappear now that they had reconnected.

"I'll drive," Cade offered.

"You said it."

"I meant it."

They were still standing outside the yellow tape beside a MBFR fire truck. A couple of MBPD cruisers were parked outside the tape. Police officers, local reporters, curious neighbors, and firefighters were everywhere.

But Cade didn't care about the noise all around them. In his heart, he had peace about Pilar.

"When we walk on the beach, hold hands, and watch the sunrise and sunsets, I want to do this." Cade stepped closer to Pilar.

"Do what?" Pilar smiled. She probably guessed it.

He lowered his lips to hers.

She didn't protest.

EPILOGUE

Four months later...

With hardly any breaks since her October ordeal, except for a day off for Thanksgiving and another for Christmas, Pilar arrived with a screeching halt in February when her stamina finally gave out and she forced herself to take a whole week off or suffer a shutdown.

Her new workload had nothing to do with the Braun-Dean case, fortunately. As far as that case was concerned, Roxanne was in jail for holding her husband hostage, trying to kill him, blowing up the huts, and selling five women to human traffickers.

It had turned out that Joe, Arnon, Ted, and Max were all working for both Roxanne and Felix Braun-Dean without the warring couple knowing about their double dipping. They figured that they might as well maximize their profits and cash as much as they could out of the situation since the couple was in the middle of bitter divorce proceedings and their jobs were on the line.

Agent Tanaka told Pilar that Roxanne's stay behind bars might be extended now that they had evidence of her money laundering schemes and the illegal sales of firearms overseas on top of everything else. That investigation was not Pilar's problem, but her curious mind liked to have known about it.

As for the former senator, Felix Braun-Dean, he was briefly imprisoned for domestic abuse against Kelsey, which largely happened in Georgia. After a couple of months, he was released on bail with an ankle monitor. Under house arrest at his lake house in greater Marietta, Georgia, he was unable to see Kelsey again.

His lawyers were able to get all the other charges dropped, including supplying Kelsey with highly addictive opioids. They settled out of court, with Braun-Dean agreeing to pay in full for Kelsey's rehabilitation.

As soon as Pilar turned the page on the Braun-Dean case, she landed on one small case after another. Even the Christmas season wasn't spared. Then came the after-Christmas lull when she could take a breather.

And yet Pilar's work was never truly done at the office. Even with a slowdown in contract work during the winter, she still had to do bookkeeping. She told herself not to think about that right now. She would turn on the computer when she returned to the office bright and early on Monday morning. She wasn't in a hurry because she had already filed last year's business taxes at the end of January.

She disliked accounting and bookkeeping, but there was no one else who could do it. Cade had asked her if she would sell her company to Hu Knows so that her employer could take care of her taxes and general accounting for her. Then they could spend more time focusing on doing actual PI work that they were skilled in doing, instead of Pilar using up half her energy dealing with administrative work, funding, accounting, and non-PI tasks.

Ah, she'd think about everything on Monday.

Tonight, on this beautiful Friday evening, all she wanted was to eat dinner with Cade and enjoy his company. Just the two of them. Baby brother Oscar was studying late at the campus library. He had eaten dinner at the college cafeteria. Grandma was on a cruise in Antarctica, of all places, because she wanted to take photos of the penguins with her new iPhone.

Pilar would have the house to herself this weekend and all of next week. Oscar lived at home and commuted to college, but he'd come and go on his own schedule. They might run into each other next week, and if Pilar got up early enough in the morning, she might cook breakfast for them both or maybe just eat cereal or instant oatmeal.

Pilar opened the screen door and stood on the brick patio in her sandals. At the edge of the patio was a hand-me-down gas grill from her parents. Cade was adjusting the knobs on the grill. The smell of hamburgers on the grill was strong.

Pilar smiled a little at the memory of nearly eating gator burgers at the cypress swamp back in October.

"Are you thinking of what I'm thinking?" Cade shouted from behind the gas grill.

"What?" Pilar didn't want to guess.

"Gator grub!" He laughed.

Pilar pointed at him. "Which I narrowly missed!"

"I took a bite."

"Oh, you brave man." Pilar clapped. Then: "Do you need any help?"

"Nope. Got everything here. Clean platter, cheese, burger buns."

Cade sounded honest, and Pilar would like to think he was. However, underlying that, Pilar knew that she couldn't cook hamburgers properly to save her life. She often overcooked the patties—burning them—or undercooked them. There was no in-between for her. The only times she didn't mess it up at the grill was when Dad stood beside her.

In the end, it was best to leave cooking over fire to the experts. Pilar chose to do the dishes instead. She could also set the table. "Salt and pepper are in the kitchen. I can go get them."

"No need. If the bugs come out, we might have to eat inside," Cade said.

"Not to worry. We can eat out here. The lanai screen will keep the mosquitoes out—even though I don't think they're back yet, considering it's only February."

"Won't it be too cold for you?" He closed the grill cover over the beef patties.

"Not cold like winter. It'll just cool down some after the sun goes down."

"I'll get you a sweater if you need one."

How sweet.

"Sun's setting." Pilar pointed to the sky beyond the trees and wooden fence. "Look at the orange and vermillion and red sky."

She retrieved her phone from a side table and took several photos. She didn't realize that Cade had left the grill, stepped onto the lanai, and hugged her from behind. He rested his head on her shoulder.

She turned around. "Let's get a photo of us and the sunset that God made tonight."

"We have taken so many photos of sunsets—and sunrises, for that matter."

Yes, since October they had watched many beach sunrises together on Miami Beach. Less frequently were sunsets over the ocean because they had to drive to either Key West or to Naples to see those.

They had decided they'd go back to Naples again soon, when their busy schedule permitted. It would only be a day trip if they could spare a day. Two hours of driving there to the beach town and two hours of driving back to Miami. They could chat about life all the way there and back. Sunset was free, and they could pack sandwiches for dinner on the beach.

"Each sunset is different though," Pilar said. "One more before it's gone?"

"I agree, but I'm hugging you right now. Don't want to let go."

"Just for thirty seconds before the sun disappears into the horizon." Pilar snapped a few photos of the setting sun while she waited for Cade. She hadn't realized he could be clingy.

"All right. Anything for you, my love." Cade loosened his arms from around her waist.

He took the phone from Pilar, and they turned

around. He extended his arm as far as he could so that the phone could snap a photo of the sunset in their background. Pilar rested the back of her head on Cade's shoulder. They both smiled, teeth showing. He took several more photos, just in case.

Heads together, they looked at the photos.

"Send me this one." Cade pointed.

So she did.

Pilar liked the way they talked with each other. She felt comfortable with Cade. They had known each other for more than a year now, and had grown to enjoy each other's company, more so since they had started dating in October after her near-death experience at Roxanne's house in Miami Beach.

Cade had fallen for her first, and he couldn't keep his feelings contained. He wasn't one to keep a secret from her for long. It seemed to Pilar that he wanted to tell her everything, including his deepest thoughts. At first, she wasn't ready to hear them, but since the day he said he had fallen in love with her on the first day they'd met in Dubai, Pilar opened up to him more and more.

A patient listener, Pilar preferred to hear what he had to say about things than to interject her own thoughts into the conversation. Cade had to make her open up more, to speak her mind, to not hold back anything, thinking she would offend him in any way.

As a result, honesty and transparency permeated their relationship. If they disagreed about something, they'd say it point blank.

It helped that Pilar and Cade saw each other every day of the week. He would drive from his apartment five minutes from her house to pick her up so that they could carpool to and from work. Pilar didn't have to navigate the morning rush hour traffic in Miami at all or drive her old car that sometimes made noises. Cade was good at the wheel, and Pilar felt safe letting him drive.

Cade had somehow managed to persuade Helen to let him work in Miami. After much cajoling, she said yes. Hu Knows, Inc., rented a desk for him at Pilar's office in downtown Miami. That turned out to be a blessing for Pilar as the sublease offset her office rent.

Cade had even transferred his church membership from Savannah, Georgia, to Pilar's church five miles from her house, so that they could go to church together on Sunday mornings for church service and Wednesday evenings for Bible study.

He had moved his world to be with Pilar.

"We could probably eat in five or ten minutes." Cade returned to the grill.

"Don't burn mine, but I don't want it raw either. Nothing oozy, okay?"

"I know."

"Thought I needed to remind you, considering we've only been together for three months."

"Ninety-seven days," Cade reminded her.

"How long are you going to keep up the counter?" Pilar chuckled.

"Until I'm old and gray, but I'll never forget you."

"Awww." Pilar stretched out on one of two wicker outdoor recliners on her lanai facing the backyard and Grandma's garden of bougainvilleas and birds of paradise plants near her blooming lantana that attracted butterflies this time of year.

A couple of days ago, Pilar had sent Grandma photos of her plants, which Oscar and Pilar had promised to water until Grandma came home. In return, Grandma sent them photos of orcas and penguins in the Antarctic summer in the southern hemisphere.

As Cade grilled, Pilar rested, thanking God for Cade and her family. A couple of hours ago, she had talked to Mom on the phone. She was patching up one of Dad's favorite old shirts that he'd refused to throw out even though he could have afforded a thousand of the same shirt. But it had to be that one. Only that one.

Pilar wondered if she was more like Mom or Dad. In many ways, she was a mix of both of them. Oscar, on the other hand, was like Dad, down to his eating habits. They were both meat-and-potato sort of eaters and liked their steaks medium rare.

Around her the air started to cool down some more. It was still in the low sixties. Pilar felt comfortable in her short sleeves and capris in such a temperature, but if she stayed out here too long, she would need a blanket over her ankles and feet.

Miami didn't often get too cold, unlike Georgia, where she had to work every now and then on projects for Hu Knows, Inc., her biggest client.

Sometimes they were her only client when the work dried up. She could always do something for Hu Knows. They had a backlog of unsolved cases and plenty of customer money waiting. Yes, Helen Hu had built up a successful investigative company with branches in Europe as well.

Their company profits enabled Helen to send

Cade to work permanently in Miami. Perhaps a better way to put it would be: God sent Cade to Miami via Helen by blessing her company enough.

And now Pilar had this privilege of getting to know Cade better. She hadn't dated in years, but Cade made her comfortable. It was easier for them, perhaps, because they had started out as colleagues, forced to get to know each other, and then as friends, when they wanted to continue knowing each other.

The pivotal point in their timeline would have to be last October at the Callahan Hotel and cypress swamp, when they didn't know if they were going to live or die. They had such rapport with each other, as though they had known each other for a long time.

They had survived the swamp because God sent Doc Sam to stitch up Cade's legs. Otherwise, he was eight to ten hours from death.

"Maybe someday when we have time, we should go visit Doc Sam," Pilar said.

"We should. What's he up to now?" Cade was separating slices of cheese and putting them on a plate on the small side table attached to the grill.

"He's taken over the bait shop."

"Yeah? Since when?"

"This week. Told me so on his new cell phone when I called this afternoon. He still lives at his cabin and smokes meat in his backyard, but he goes to the bait shop twice a week. If the hunters need him more, they could just call him and he'd be there in two minutes on his Indian Chief."

"James working with him?" Cade sounded careful.

"Not jealous, are you?" Pilar chuckled.

"No. Just asking." Cade kept a stoic face.

"Doc Sam said that James recovered at home at his mom's house in North Carolina somewhere, and decided to join the police academy there in his hometown."

"Oh?"

"Yeah. We'll probably never see James again." Pilar waited to see what else Cade was concerned about.

"Let's go visit Doc Sam soon before the bugs come out," Cade said.

"Okay. How about next week? I'm off all week, even though I'd rather not go anywhere."

"No. Next week is your stay-at-home week. You need the rest. Wear pajamas all day. I will come three times a day to make you breakfast, lunch, and dinner."

Pilar sat up. "You're kidding."

"I'm serious," Cade said.

"Here I am, wondering if this is going to last." It was what she truly felt.

"What do you mean?"

"Our relationship feels surreal," Pilar said. "Sure, we don't always agree with each other on everything and we do irritate each other at times, but for the most part, we get along. We share the same ideals and work ethics. We're like two peas in a pod. Where I lack, you balance me out, and vice versa. It's too good to be true."

"I try not to question God's blessing," Cade said. "We have a lot of difficulties in our line of work. It's a blessing to be able to come home to someone who understands you."

Pilar nodded. "You are right."

"It doesn't mean that we will always have happy times. There will be hard times interspersed with the easy times." Cade pointed a pair of grill tongs in the air. "Sometimes couples have troubles with each other. Sometimes their troubles come from external sources. Which would you prefer? That we fight each other, or that we team up and fight hardship together?"

"Right. I'd rather not quarrel with you," Pilar said.

Cade nodded. "The Bible says that we need to thank God at all times, good or bad."

Pilar knew to which verse he was referring. She could recite 1 Thessalonians 5:16-18 from memory, but Cade beat her to it.

> *Rejoice always, pray without ceasing, in everything give thanks; for this is the will of God in Christ Jesus for you.*

"That's my personal life passage, especially useful when things get tough," Cade said. "However, I forgot all about the verses when I was attacked at the swamp."

"We all live and learn, don't we?" Pilar comforted him. "If you recall, we prayed."

Cade nodded.

"I always go back to Job. Regardless of what happens, he still worshiped and blessed the Lord." Pilar found Job 1:20-22 in her Bible app on her phone and read it aloud.

> *Then Job arose, tore his robe, and shaved his head;*

and he fell to the ground and worshiped. And he said:

"Naked I came from my mother's womb,
And naked shall I return there.
The Lord gave, and the Lord has taken away;
Blessed be the name of the Lord."

In all this Job did not sin nor charge God with wrong.

"I love that we both share the same Christian faith and can talk about that anytime we want." Cade smiled.

"I thank God for you, Cade." Pilar meant it.

"I thank God for you too, love of my life."

Pilar remained in her comfortable seat and watched Cade work the grill. She wondered what it would be like to go on assignments with Cade. Would their relationship affect the mission? If they ended up getting hurt, would she make decisions that could change their trajectory and cause them to miss their goals?

She noticed that it was after 6:30 p.m. and wondered if she should text Kelsey to see how she was doing. Pilar had done that every Friday to keep in touch with Kelsey, who had limited access to phone calls at the in-patient rehab center in San Antonio, Texas, where she planned to stay for six months until she was clean and stabilized.

Whenever they texted, Pilar would share verses with her. One of them was about the adulterous woman and what Jesus said to her in the last verse of John 8:3-11.

And Jesus said to her, "Neither do I condemn you; go and sin no more."

Kelsey was determined to kick the habit, and many women at Pilar's Bible study at church prayed for her. Pilar sent a quick message to Kelsey to remind her of the support she was getting. Pilar did not expect a same-day reply. She put aside her phone and leaned back on the recliner.

Cade walked up to the lanai. Pilar jumped out of her seat to open the screen door and hold it for him. He carried a platter of hamburgers in one arm and a basket of buns in the other. The buttered buns had grill marks on them.

Cade was heading for the wrought iron table to one side of the lanai.

Just then, Pilar realized she hadn't set the table. "I was sitting there and forgot all about it."

"I'll do it," Cade said. "You don't get up until I ring the dinner bell."

"You're spoiling me."

"No, you worked hard all week." Cade had seen Pilar work all week, so he knew.

A merciless client wanted her to help him catch a dog thief. He was willing to pay six figures for the work. It turned out that his ex-girlfriend's new boyfriend's high school stepbrother had kidnapped the Giant Schnauzer to sell it because it had won best in show at a recent dog show.

"I prefer short projects like that and not long-projected jobs, you know," Pilar said.

"Long or short, I don't care, as long as I'm with you." Cade placed their dinner on the lanai table.

Then he busied himself putting two placemats on the table across from each other.

He had remembered that Pilar preferred to sit across from him so that they could have a conversation face to face while eating their meal, instead of next to each other.

Pilar could not sit down again on the recliner. She followed Cade through the open sliding glass door into the kitchen so that she could help get the silverware. Before she could open the drawer, Cade cornered her, placing both hands on her shoulders and turning her around to face him. Her back was up against the counter.

He leaned forward to face her eye to eye. He smelled of hickory smoke and the late winter Floridian outdoors.

"I ran out of kiss coupons a long time ago." He pouted. "Could you please give me a new set?"

It looked like he still remembered the fourteen kisses for the fourteen stitches from October.

Not that they hadn't kissed beyond that. Who was counting?

"You don't need new coupons." Pilar smiled. Instinctively, her eyes dropped to his lips. "How about unlimited kisses for a lifetime?"

His eyes lit up. They sparkled under the kitchen light. "You said it. Do you really mean a lifetime?"

"You know me. I mean what I say, and I say what I mean—unless we're undercover and taking an assumed name, in which case we're actors on stage... What are you doing?"

Cade was on one knee on the kitchen floor. Out of his front jean pocket, he fished out something shiny. It was a round diamond set on a gold ring. Very traditional.

"Pilar, I love you. I fell in love with you the first day we met sixteen months ago, and I've prayed ever since then for God to show me if you're the one for me. I got my answer in October. I felt deeply in my heart that God had given you to me. I was over the moon when you agreed to date me." His voice cracked.

Pilar couldn't control the tears in her eyes. It was one of those times in life.

When you know, you know.

"We might have only been dating for three months, but even back in October, before we dated, I knew that I wanted to marry you and spend the rest of my life with you, to have kids with you, grow old with you, and love you always." Cade was still holding up the engagement ring in his hand.

Pilar wiped away tears from her eyes. If God had blessed her, why would she say no?

"Ever since I met you overseas, I knew you were different, but I was too busy with work to deal with my personal life," Pilar said. "However, you reappeared in my life in October, and I saw that you're a blessing from God. I'm very happy to be with you, Cade. I love you."

"Since we love each other..." Cade blinked away a grown man's tears. "Pilar Mariella Santiago, will you marry me?"

"Yes, I will, Cade McCall Sumter." Pilar didn't hesitate.

Cade nervously threaded the shiny diamond onto Pilar's left ring finger. She pulled him to his feet and gave him the first round of his new lifetime stock of unlimited kisses.

~

Dear Reader:

Thank you for reading *Never a Hostage* (Defender Sweethearts Book 2). I hope you've enjoyed this Christian Romantic Suspense novel featuring two private investigators, Pilar Santiago and Cade Sumter.

Zuriel, whose real name is Kelsey Murphy, tells her story in the next novel in this series. *Never a Fugitive* (Defender Sweethearts Book 3) takes us on a multi-state adventure after Kelsey recovers from her prescription drug addiction and ends up helping the FBI in a cryptocurrency money laundering scheme. But first, she has to stay alive.

Never a Fugitive
Defender Sweethearts Book 3
JanThompson.com/fugitive

Helen Hu is a private investigator and the CEO of Hu Knows, Inc., based out of Savannah, Georgia. Helen makes a cameo in *Never a Hostage*, and appears or at is at least mentioned in every book that her private investigators are in. She tells her own story in *Once a Thief*.

Once a Thief
Protector Sweethearts Book 1

JanThompson.com/thief

Private investigator Ming Wei is in *Tell You Soon* (Savannah Sweethearts Book 3) and *Once Bitten, Twice Shy* (Guardian Sweethearts Book 1). In both stories, his real estate agent wife, Sabine, also takes center stage.

Tell You Soon
Savannah Sweethearts Book 3
JanThompson.com/tell

Once Bitten, Twice Shy
Guardian Sweethearts Book 1
JanThompson.com/bitten

To be notified when new books are published, sign up for my mailing list. I send out newsletters multiple times a month.

Join Jan Thompson's Mailing List
JanThompson.com/newsletter

Continue reading for a sneak peek of the next novel, *Never a Fugitive.*

THE NEXT NOVEL IS NEVER A FUGITIVE

DEFENDER SWEETHEARTS BOOK 3

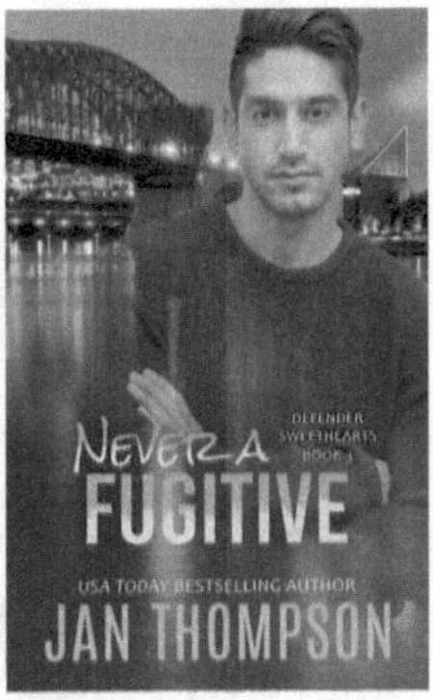

A grieving brother.
A former mistress.
A stash of stolen secrets.

A grieving accountant seeking justice for his murdered brother finds himself on the run with a senator's former mistress who knows too many secrets.

Starting his own investigation…

After his brother is killed by a car bomb, Armin Dhillon quits his job to conduct his own investigation into the murder. His efforts lead him to a former senator's ex-mistress who is now a devout Christian trying to leave her past behind. Only her sordid past won't let her go, and neither will Armin, who thinks she has the answer that will bring closure for his family.

Stuck together for better or for worse…

Kelsey Murphy wants to start over with a new life in Christ, but her old career keeps telling her that she's unworthy and must pay some sort of penance. The FBI finds her and asks for her help to take down some money-laundering criminals related to the former senator. Thrown together for a common cause, Armin and Kelsey find that they have no choice but look out for each other.

Solutions are nowhere to be found…

Thrown together, Armin and Kelsey find that they like each other's company. All around them, mirages appear. Things are not what they seem to be. Friends may not be friends. Enemies may not be enemies. But they all have the same goal: to get to the stash of seventeen billion dollars worth of cryptocurrencies. Will they be able to wade through the fog of misinformation to get to the truth? The winners take all, or do they?

Never a Fugitive is Book 3 in *USA Today* bestselling author Jan Thompson's Defender Sweethearts Christian romantic suspense collection, a sister series to

Protector Sweethearts. While the heroes in Protector Sweethearts search for lost treasures and lost people, the Defender Sweethearts novels focus on protecting the helpless and hopeless. The main characters in Defender Sweethearts come from the supporting cast in Protector Sweethearts.

~

Never a Fugitive (Defender Sweethearts Book 3)
JanThompson.com/traitor

Defender Sweethearts
JanThompson.com/defender

For Book News from Jan Thompson:
JanThompson.com/newsletter

NEVER A FUGITIVE SNEAK PEEK (CHAPTER 1)

DEFENDER SWEETHEARTS BOOK 3

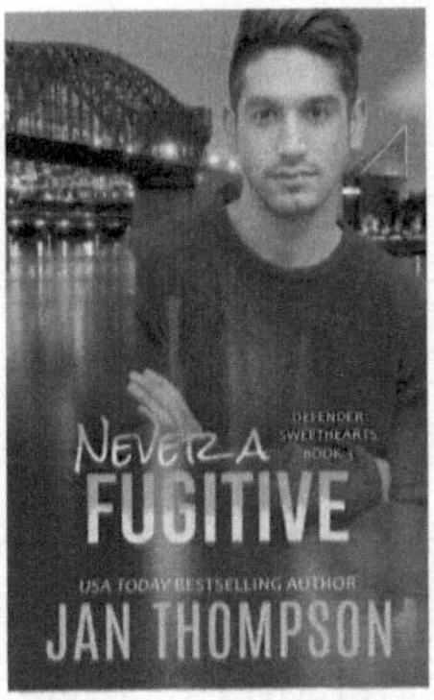

Kelsey Murphy crouched down in the narrow space between the kitchen sink and the small bathroom of the camper van. She resisted looking behind her, where the only thing separating her and the sounds of gunshots in the dark campground outside was an old bedsheet taped over a broken back window.

The other windows had blinds, but the left back window above the full-sized mattress had been shattered hours ago, when Kelsey backed into some protruding rods at a construction site when she was driving FBI Special Agent Ruby Tanaka to the emergency room after their meeting with an informant went awry.

They were ten minutes from the Savannah Memorial Hospital ER, and it was faster for Kelsey to drive Tanaka there than to call 911 and wait for an ambulance. Besides, Tanaka only broke her arm—even though that was awfully painful—and she was still able to walk on her own two feet.

Still, Kelsey couldn't remember how they'd made it to the Savannah Memorial Hospital ER without getting into a serious wreck on the road.

While she was waiting for Tanaka at the hospital, another FBI agent came to see her and told her to drive away to a particular campground and wait.

Here she was, waiting. Waiting for what?

Thinking back, Kelsey had asked the FBI agent for credentials, but how was she to know whether his badge was real? However, there was no time to ask any questions. Kelsey did as instructed, and ended up at this campground between Savannah and Richmond, just as night fell over Georgia.

Kelsey barely sat down to eat a dinner of cheese and crackers when she heard the first popping noise. That made her drop down to the floor, the crackers falling out of the box and onto her head and all around the floor of the camper van.

A second and then a third popping sound made her scream a little, and she reached for the bathroom door and rushed inside. She shut the door tightly, locked it, and sat down on the closed toilet seat cover.

She covered her ears.

Help me help me help me...

Minutes later, the gunfire ceased outside. Now Kelsey began to doubt herself. Were they really gunshots? They couldn't possibly be. After all, former Senator Felix Braun-Dean's ex-wife, Roxanne, usually hired former military henchmen who'd use silencers—just as Agent Tanaka had.

Speaking of whom, Kelsey wondered how Tanaka was doing at the ER. The FBI agent had protected Kelsey with her life in the last twenty-four hours as they fled from Roxanne Braun-Dean, who seemed set on vengeance. Kelsey's testimony had put Roxanne behind bars, but allowed her husband to be out on bail.

Roxanne was still under investigation by both the FBI and the Secret Service for money laundering and illegal arms sales to foreign operatives. In a nutshell, Roxanne had used her husband's position in the Senate Committee on Armed Services to build her multi-billion-dollar empire on the dark web.

Pop! Pop! Pop!

Kelsey checked the bathroom door. Locked. Maybe this was bad news because she had imprisoned herself in this small bathroom.

She wished she had her Glock with her, but she'd left her purse on the... Where had she left her purse?

She couldn't remember. Inside her purse was a burner phone she could use to call Tanaka.

Perhaps she should call her friend, Nicholas Bay, who'd rather be known as The Stylist—although he'd made an exception for Kelsey, whom he had said could call him anything, including boyfriend, if she wanted. Over and over, Kelsey had told him that she only considered him a friend, and if anything, a big brother, but no more than that.

Still, Nicholas had been a great help to her since the Braun-Deans were arrested. In fact, Nicholas had filled in the blanks and answered all her questions about the former senator's dealings. Also, he didn't judge her past profession, and treated her as a friend.

After all, Nicholas owned the vehicle. He had let her use it for free after he upgraded to a more expensive recreational vehicle for himself. He had let her borrow this camper van because she didn't have a place of her own in Georgia, or a job to earn enough income to rent an apartment yet.

To call Nicholas, Kelsey had to leave the bathroom to find her cell phone. She was debating with herself on whether to do that when she felt the floor shifting beneath her feet.

What...?

The camper van was clearly moving. She could hear the engine now.

How had she not heard it before?

She placed a palm over her chest, where her heart thumped wildly against her rib cage.

Calm down.

Logically, she shouldn't fear. FBI agents should be all over the campground, right? After all, she had paid her taxes...

I have to get out of here.

She zipped up her thigh-length jacket, made sure the shoelace on her boots were tied up. She couldn't put on gloves because then she couldn't hold her Glock properly.

She unlocked the bathroom door and peeked out.

No one stopped her. From what she could tell, it was a lone driver, who had the build of a man—even though he could have been an athletic woman. In any case, he was wearing a baseball cap and a leather jacket, and his gloveless hands gripped the steering wheel.

The van picked up speed, and Kelsey fell back against the bathroom door.

She looked back to see if she could jump out of the broken back window. The bedsheet was fluttering in the wind. The van must be going at least thirty or forty miles per hour. It might be too fast for her to jump out without injuring or killing herself.

Well, if she died, she'd go to heaven to meet her Lord and Savior, Jesus Christ, so it wouldn't be a total loss.

Not yet, though. She had to stop Roxanne, who had no qualms about shooting at a federal agent or disabling her own husband. More people would be hurt if she wasn't stopped.

But first, she had to deal with the driver who had carjacked the camper van. If anything happened to the vehicle, how was she going to explain it to Nicholas?

Kelsey spotted her purse on the floor, surrounded by crackers and a tray of cheese. It must have fallen with her earlier.

Slowly she crawled toward her concealed carry crossbody purse. She knew her Glock had a full clip of ammunition, and she had four more clips in her purse.

She yanked the purse toward her, put it over her shoulder, and pulled out her loaded Glock. Since

Glocks had no safety, she hadn't put a bullet in the chamber. Her trembling hand reached for the slide, when the van came to a screeching halt at a stop sign.

Falling forward, Kelsey nearly lost her Glock.

Kelsey regained her balance as the driver put on the blinker to turn right.

Hmm... A carjacker who obeyed traffic laws.

The van itself was was about twenty-three feet from end to end, so standing in the center of it put Kelsey about ten or eleven feet away from the carjacker. At this distance she could shoot the carjacker easily, but then would it cause a wreck if the driver lost control of the van?

Kelsey racked the slide, and shuffled her feet slowly toward the front of the camper van, bending down slightly to prevent the driver from seeing her through the rearview mirror. She pressed her hips against the edge of the kitchen counter for support.

She held the Glock in both hands and pointed at the driver.

"Stop the van!" she yelled.

He ignored her.

"Stop the van or I'll—"

The man slammed on the brakes. He unbuckled his safety belt and leapt off the seat and came toward her. "You'll what, Zuriel?"

Zuriel?

She hadn't used that name in over a year since she'd been rescued, having been held hostage with Felix Braun-Dean. In fact, that had been the last time she'd seen him in person.

Since her escape, Kelsey decided she would call him Braun-Dean from now on. It would save her from remembering the days when she'd called him "sweet Felix" and he'd call her "my lovely Zuriel."

Zuriel wasn't a secret name. Anyone could have read it in the news following the former senator's arrest.

The Glock shook in Kelsey's hand. It was too late for her to change her mind. "Who sent you?"

"You know who." He made it sound like it was a friendly gathering he'd be driving her to.

No way would he confess so quickly.

"No, I don't know who."

The man moved a finger.

"Don't move!" Kelsey yelled. The entire time, she wasn't sure if she could follow through with the Glock. Nicholas had told her that if she couldn't handle the consequences, she shouldn't be pointing the handgun at anyone.

Too late now.

"She sent me to scare you, but I think we can have a little fun before I drop you off." The man smiled.

She? Roxanne Braun-Dean?

Why should she believe him? Yes, it was true that Roxanne had been coming after her because she believed that Kelsey kept cryptocurrency belonging to her husband. Well, if Kelsey had, then why was she still poor, living at campsites?

Even though Roxanne might have wanted to scare her, she wouldn't have sent someone like this traffic-law-abiding carjacker. She'd have sent a professional. And she could have also sent an assassin. However, she hadn't so far because she needed Kelsey to be alive to tell her where the billion dollars worth of Bitcoin was stashed away.

How was Kelsey supposed to know?

Still, not talking was her only ticket to staying alive.

This carjacker declared who he worked for. Was he telling the truth? Would a criminal tell the truth? Maybe, maybe not.

The man stepped forward. "I locked all the doors."

He was bigger than she was, though Kelsey believed she could take him down. The self-defense training that Nicholas had put her through could help.

Then again, fleeing should have been her Plan A instead of B. What was she thinking?

Kelsey stepped back in the narrow passage between the stove and dining table, between the kitchen sink counter and the bathroom. She knew that the bed at the back of the van would impede her movement toward the door. She'd have to hop on it to open the latch on the door.

The man stepped forward, like they were two in a tango—albeit in slow motion with the handgun between them.

There wasn't much space between her and the man. He was still inching slowly toward the nozzle of her Glock, and countering that, she was stepping back.

The Glock shook in Kelsey's hands.

"Nervous? You might miss a shot." No snarl. Just a statement of facts.

If she turned around and made a mad dash for the back window, he'd tackle her from the back, and it would be the end of her.

If I died here, would anyone know? I can't die at thirty-four.

Tears welled in her eyes.

Wait. I texted Armin, didn't I?

What good was that? Armin Dhillon was still in Chicago the last time she had talked to him two days ago. In fact, he hadn't replied to her text at three this afternoon to tell him that the FBI had sent her to wait at this campground. She had taken a photo of the piece of paper with the address scribbled on it that the FBI agent had given to her at SMH and sent it over to Armin.

So now two people besides the FBI agent knew where she was.

Her Glock was still pointed at the carjacker.

"We don't have all day, but I work by the quarter hour—just like my lawyer." He grinned. "Let's play nice and be done with this. I have another job to go to."

"Who sent you?" Kelsey asked again. She wanted clarity so that she could justify shooting him.

Nicholas had taught her to look for body mass when firing, but she couldn't make herself do it. What if the carjacker suffered internal bleeding? What if he died? Kelsey was no murderer.

So she shot him in the shoulder, exactly where she'd aimed.

The man yelled in pain. Expletives exploded from his mouth.

Oh dear. I think I made a mistake.

He reached into his jacket—

And Kelsey shot him again—this time on his

thigh. Actually she had aimed for his other arm, but missed this time because the Glock shook wildly.

"Do you see this? I can't control my trigger finger." Kelsey was blanking out. "You need to...need to...uh... You need to back away."

The man growled and lunged toward her, dragging a leg and an arm. His undamaged hand reached into his jacket again a second time—

Kelsey didn't miss her third try as she shot the handgun out of the carjacker's hand. The handgun went flying.

The man fell back, hit his head on the dining table, and dropped to the ground. He was bleeding from his limbs, but his mouth was still working. He yelled and screamed.

"Look, mister. I don't want to hurt you." Kelsey sprinted toward the back of the camper van, leapt up on the mattress, and reached for the back door handle—

It was stuck.

She jiggled it. It made no difference.

"Told you I locked all the doors." The man laughed. He hissed in pain.

Kelsey wasn't sure which part of the shoulder she'd shot, but she could do it again if she needed to, although rehabilitation on his shoulder might be unpleasant.

She shoved her Glock into her jacket pocket, and yanked the flapping bedsheet off the windows. A gust of January wind slapped her face. There was no snow in most winters in Georgia, but the biting air was chilly. She was a Florida girl, so this was plenty cold to her.

The window was small. It had been modified from the original utility van window into this small porthole, almost, but she could potentially climb out of the van through it.

The carjacker was still screaming and cussing at her.

She didn't know what to do. Her mind went blank, and all she could see was the darkness outside the window. The road was deserted, and there were no street lights in this rural part of Georgia.

Without thinking further on the matter, she started to climb out of the window. She dared not look behind her as she wiggled, barely fitting. She could feel her palm and hands gashing on the broken glass.

Her thick winter jacket snagged at her hip, and next thing she knew, she was stuck.

Oh no.

A strong force pulled at her legs still inside the camper van, preventing her from getting out of the window. Her boots kicked at the mattress and at the assailant, who was cussing at her a mile a minute.

Didn't I shoot his arms? How could he still pull my legs?

Outside the van, bright lights came at her. Headlights of a truck or SUV of some sort.

"Help! Help!"

The high headlights shone in her eyes, but she couldn't see anyone. She squinted and screamed as the carjacker pulled her legs, and he was now gripping her hips to try to yank her back into the van. But his strength waned, and pretty soon, she didn't feel pressure on her legs anymore.

She realized then that the carjacker had told her

the truth, that he was only messing with her. That meant that he had no intention of killing her or even incapacitating her. The carjacker could have located his handgun that Kelsey had shot out of his hand, but he hadn't shot at her while she was dangling there in the window, like a target at the gun range.

Had Roxanne really given him instructions to keep Kelsey alive? Then again, Roxanne was an enigma. Kelsey believed that she had no problem hurting Kelsey and making her pay for being one of the women that her sleazy husband had bedded.

Just not today.

God, thank You for having forgiven me of my past. If I die now, I know I die forgiven.

The carjacker's grip on her legs was subsiding. Kelsey guessed that his bleeding shoulder was causing him problems.

Her arms flailed in the air as she dangled in the van window, her stomach as the fulcrum with her shoulders and arms on one side and her legs and hips inside the van.

All around her, the night was dark on this rural road, save for the vehicle coming toward her, two front headlights drawing closer and larger.

She squinted in the glare.

Pain seared through her palms as she waved frantically in the air. "Help me!"

Maybe she should've just killed the carjacker instead of trying to escape through the back window that she had barely fitted through. Too late for regrets.

She closed her eyes, bowed her head, and prayed, trying very hard to think of what to say to God.

Oh Heavenly Father...

Before she could form the words, she heard a gunshot. It sounded like it was coming from inside the van. Or maybe her brain was imagining things. After all, she hadn't slept in two days.

She slumped over the window, still stuck. She kept her eyes closed tightly.

Lift me up to heaven, Lord.

She heard tires screech to a stop and vehicle doors slam.

"Kelsey!"

Hear that? The angels are calling my name...

She heard a click, and felt the back door open—like someone was opening it—with her hanging there, still stuck in the window, swinging slowly. Swinging...

Swing low, sweet chariot...

"Kelsey!" It was a male voice in her ear.

She felt strong hands on her arms.

"Kelsey, it's me!"

~

Never a Fugitive (Defender Sweethearts Book 3)
JanThompson.com/traitor

Defender Sweethearts
JanThompson.com/defender

For Book News from Jan Thompson:
JanThompson.com/newsletter

ACKNOWLEDGMENTS

Many thanks to my Georgia Press publishing team for keeping up with my writing schedule.

Thank you to editor extraordinaire Kim Kemery for editing and proofreading this novel. And special thanks to two of my early readers, Christie and Zanese, for their feedback.

Thank you to these first responders for answering my questions about real life scenarios.

• Police detective and author Dony Jay, about police and SWAT procedures.

• Emergency medicine physician and author Dr. John Galt Robinson, about trauma and medical treatments.

• Retired firefighter captain and author Ken Shoemaker, about fire and rescue.

A special thank you to my husband for our chats about outdoor life. Even though I hiked and camped as a Girl Scout (and I was a company leader at that), he has hiked and camped more than I ever did. It was fun to go down memory lane and compare notes.

As per usual, not all of my extensive research materials make it into my books, but I feel that it is necessary to thank everyone for their time and kindness in answering my many questions. And yes, all mistakes and creative licenses are mine.

I am grateful to God for my husband and son for their support and encouragement. I also thank God for my parents and my three brothers for my happy and memorable childhood. I'll always remember my beloved mother and my late father for having instilled in me the love of reading and writing from a very early age. I miss my father here on earth, but I will see him again in heaven someday.

Most of all, I am eternally thankful to my Lord and Savior, Jesus Christ, who died on the cross to save me from my sins and rose again from the grave to give me eternal life. Without Him, I can write nothing (John 15:5).

Joyfully in Jesus,
Jan Thompson
John 3:16

BOOKS BY JAN THOMPSON

Contemporary Christian City, Coastal, and Beach Romance

Seaside Chapel (7 Books)
JanThompson.com/seaside
Savannah Sweethearts (12 Books)
JanThompson.com/savannah
Vacation Sweethearts (8 Books)
JanThompson.com/vacation
Midtown Christmas (4 Books)
JanThompson.com/christmas
Christmas Sweethearts (3 Books)
JanThompson.com/christmastown

Christian Romantic Suspense and Near-Future Technothrillers

Protector Sweethearts (6 Books)
JanThompson.com/protector
Defender Sweethearts (6 Books)
JanThompson.com/defender
Guardian Sweethearts (2 Books)
JanThompson.com/guardian
Binary Hackers (4 Books)
JanThompson.com/binary

Subscribe to Jan Thompson's mailing list:
JanThompson.com/newsletter

PROTECTOR SWEETHEARTS

Private investigator Helen Hu and her associates specialize in searching for missing persons and hunting for lost treasures. Join them in their adventure suspense around the world in *USA Today* bestselling author Jan Thompson's Protector Sweethearts, a series of Christian Romantic Suspense with a side of mystery.

Protector Sweethearts is a spin-off of Savannah Sweethearts and Vacation Sweethearts.

JanThompson.com/protector

- Book 1: *Once a Thief*
- Book 2: *Once a Hero*
- Book 3: *Once a Spy*
- Book 4: *Twice a Fighter*

- Book 5: *Twice a Convict*
- Book 6: *Twice a Soldier*

DEFENDER SWEETHEARTS

Defender Sweethearts is a sister series to the Protector Sweethearts Christian romantic suspense collection. While the heroes in Protector Sweethearts search for lost treasures and lost people, the Defender Sweethearts novels focus on protecting the helpless and hopeless. The main characters in Defender Sweethearts come from the supporting cast in Protector Sweethearts.

JanThompson.com/defender

- Book 1: *Never a Traitor*
- Book 2: *Never a Hostage*
- Book 3: *Never a Fugitive*
- Book 4: *Always a Maverick*
- Book 5: *Always a Champion*
- Book 6: *Always a Guardian*

BINARY HACKERS

Like more suspense with your Christian romance? Like to read suspense thrillers? If you're looking for clean near-future romantic suspense without compromising the Christian faith, these books are for you.

From *USA Today* bestselling author Jan Thompson come these inspirational near-future cyberthrillers combining technothriller and romance, starting with Binary Hackers that feature computer specialists living at the edge of cyberspace, where they have to juggle being law-abiding truth-telling Christians while carrying out their assignments by any and all means possible.

The Binary Hackers series is set in the same story world as Jan's other books, and characters from the other series may make cameo appearances in this series and vice versa.

JanThompson.com/binary

- Book 1: *Zero Sum*
- Book 2: *Zero Day*
- Book 3: *Zero Out*
- Book 4: *Zero Trust*

SEASIDE CHAPEL

Welcome to *USA Today* bestselling author Jan Thompson's Seaside Chapel Christian beach romance series. These novels are set on real-life St. Simon's Island, Georgia—a beach town where history is all around and the future is a moment away—and the neighboring fictitious Seaside Island, where the rich and famous live.

Savor the small-town atmosphere and the warm southern beaches of St. Simon's Island and the idyllic Golden Isles along the Atlantic Ocean. Enjoy the music of the orchestra and hymns of the church, and hang out with our Christian friends who attend Seaside Chapel, a little church by the sea known for its beach weddings and fair share of love and life.

As these Christians grow in their knowledge and understanding of God, they are tested in their spiritual maturity, their love lives, and their relationships with others. Share their heartaches and healing, and cheer them on as they celebrate faith, family, and friends.

~

JanThompson.com/seaside

- Book 0 (Prequel): *His Surprise Proposal*
- Book 1: *His Longing Heart*
- Book 2: *His Wake-Up Call*
- Book 3: *His Morning Kiss*
- Book 4: *His Quiet Serenade*
- Book 5: *His Waiting Love*
- Book 6: *His Beach Retreat*

SAVANNAH SWEETHEARTS

Welcome to the new south! From *USA Today* bestselling author Jan Thompson come these clean and wholesome, sweet and inspirational Christian romances set on the romantic beaches of Tybee Island and in the coastal town of Savannah, Georgia. Meet a group of multiracial and multiethnic churchgoing Christians who love the Lord, work hard in their careers, and seek God's will for their love lives. Against a backdrop of ocean, sand, and sun, these inspirational romances showcase aspects of the human need for God and for one another. Have some tea, settle in a comfortable reading chair, and enjoy these sweet celebrations of faith, hope, and love in Jesus Christ.

JanThompson.com/savannah

- Book 1: *Ask You Later* (Artist Romance)

- Book 2: *Know You More* (Multiracial Romance)
- Book 3: *Tell You Soon* (Asian-American Romance with Suspense)
- Book 4: *Draw You Near* (International Romance)
- Book 5: *Cherish You So* (Wheelchair Billionaire Romance)
- Book 6: *Walk You There* (Old-Meets-New Tour Guide Romance)
- Book 7: *Love You Always* (Romance with Suspense)
- Book 8: *Kiss You Now* (Multiracial Romance)
- Book 9: *Find You Again* (Multiracial Romance)
- Book 10: *Wish You Joy* (Christmas-Themed Romance)
- Book 11: *Call You Home* (Deaf Chef Romance)
- Book 12: *Let You Go* (Asian-American Romance with Suspense)

Read *Ask You Later* (Book 1) for free:
JanThompson.com/ask-free

VACATION SWEETHEARTS

Travel with our friends from Savannah, Georgia, to the coast and to the mountains. Cheer them on as they celebrate the immeasurable grace and undeserved mercy of God through Jesus Christ.

The Vacation Sweethearts novels are a spin-off of Jan's Savannah Sweethearts series, and fans will recognize familiar faces from Riverside Chapel, a church in the coastal city of Savannah, Georgia. In fact, we might even visit the beach town of Tybee Island from time to time to visit old friends and beloved families...

JanThompson.com/vacation

- Book 0 (Prequel): *Time for Me*
- Book 1: *Smile for Me* (International Romance)

- Book 2: *Reach for Me* (Romance with Suspense)
- Book 3: *Wait for Me* (Romance with Suspense)
- Book 4: *Look for Me* (Romance with Suspense)
- Book 5: *Pray for Me* (International Romance)
- Book 6: *Care for Me* (Small Mountain Town Romance)
- Book 7: *Cheer for Me* (Destination Wedding)
- Book 8: *Stay for Me* (Romance with Suspense)

Read *Time for Me* (A Vacation Sweethearts Prequel) for free:

JanThompson.com/time-free

MIDTOWN CHRISTMAS

Big city romance, small town feel. Four Christian couples minister at Midtown Chapel in metro Atlanta, and Midtown Village, the community of tiny homes for needy families. From November to January every year, this place turns into a Christmas Village for a small-town feel right there in the metropolis of Atlanta, Georgia.

- Book 1: *Let Me Hold You* (Levi Theroux and Maggie Jacobs from *Pray for Me*)
- Book 2: *Let Me Want You* (Erika Song from *Look for Me* and Hiroki Yamada from *Walk You There*)
- Book 3: *Let Me Need You* (Forsythia McDevitt from *Call You Home* and Owen Grayson from *Find You Again*)
- Book 4: *Let Me Love You* (Leila Patel from *Find You Again*)

ABOUT JAN THOMPSON

USA Today bestselling author Jan Thompson writes clean and wholesome contemporary Christian romance with elements of women's fiction, Christian romantic suspense with an air of mystery, and inspirational international thrillers with threads of sweet Christian romance. Jan's books are for readers who love inspiring stories of faith, hope, and love in Jesus Christ.

Raised on a tropical island in the eastern hemisphere, Jan now lives and writes in the western hemisphere. Her international background gives her a unique multicultural and multiracial perspective to her novels and books. The island has never left her, and she reminisces about beach life in her beach romance novels.

When Jan is not busy writing small-town stories, she writes big-city romantic suspense and international technothrillers, a nod to her previous career in computer science. She weaves technology with human interests, reflecting the current and future digital world. And romance. There's always romance.

Beyond the printed page, Jan is a wife, mother, family scribe, avid reader, occasional artist, erstwhile pianist, and chief of staff to the family cat.

Find out more about Jan Thompson:
JanThompson.com

Subscribe to Jan's book news mailing list:
JanThompson.com/newsletter

For God so loved the world,
that He gave His only begotten Son,
that whosoever believeth in Him should not perish,
but have everlasting life.
—John 3:16

www.ingramcontent.com/pod-product-compliance
Lightning Source LLC
Chambersburg PA
CBHW030248270626
47156CB00021B/198